BELUGA

ALSO BY RICK GAVIN

Ranchero

BELUGA

Rick Gavin

Minotaur Books ✿ New York

This is a work of fiction. All of the characters, organizations, and events portrayed in this novel are either products of the author's imagination or are used fictitiously.

www.minotaurbooks.com

Library of Congress Cataloging-in-Publication Data

Gavin, Rick.
    Beluga / Rick Gavin.—1st ed.
      p. cm.
    ISBN 978-1-250-01522-8 (hardcover)
    ISBN 978-1-250-01599-0 (e-book)
    1. Money laundering—Fiction.   2. Delta (Miss.: Region)—Fiction.
I. Title.
    PS3607.A9848B45 2012
    813'.6—dc23

                            2012030068

First Edition: November 2012

10 9 8 7 6 5 4 3 2 1

For Slyvie and Jill with gratitude

ONE

It seemed like a good idea even if it came from Shawnica's brother, who was a lowlife and a chiseler but could be inspired sometimes. Me and Desmond had been casting around for investment opportunities, and Shawnica knew we had a little money we were willing to let out. We'd taken it off a crazy Acadian meth lord the year before and didn't mind turning some loose now and then for a rate.

Shawnica's brother had done time in Parchman Prison for robbery and grand theft. Larry had stuck up a pharmacy and stolen a tricked-out Mercury Monterey that he'd insisted straight through to conviction his cousin had told him he could drive. He ended up doing a three-year bit, and all he got up to inside was filing the papers to legally change his name. While the rest of the cons were studying law books and writing their appeals, Larry petitioned the state to let him become

Mr. Beluga S. LaMonte. It was his way, I guess, of starting fresh without doing anything constructive.

Larry was staying with Shawnica, and we drove over to hear his scheme. Shawnica's house set Desmond off. It was the one he'd been thrown out of once Shawnica had wearied of him. He'd ended up back at his mom's place in the room he'd grown up in, and Desmond hadn't been twin-bed size in a decade and a half by then. He was decent enough to still be helping Shawnica with the mortgage and repairs. Desmond was the one who cut the grass and kept the porch screen mended. He fixed the leaks and painted the walls, paid for Shawnica's cable TV, and he did it all with typical Desmond grace and fortitude while Shawnica barked at him and worked her way through a string of sleazy boyfriends.

I took it as my job to keep Desmond calm and focused no matter what we met with once we'd stepped inside. But then Larry was stretched out on the sofa with his feet against the wall. He was eating microwave popcorn and rubbing grease all over the afghan that Desmond's aunt had knitted Shawnica as a wedding gift. Desmond claimed to cherish it, but it was yellow and green and brown and so badly made it looked like it belonged under a saddle.

By the time Desmond had said, "Larry, dammit," there was nothing I could do. Once Desmond had decided a boy needed scuffing up, you couldn't really hope to stop him.

Desmond chuffed like a bear, crossed the room in two strides, and snatched Larry off the sofa. Popcorn went all over the place, along with all of Shawnica's remotes.

Larry said, "Hey!" or something, the way people will with

Desmond. It's hard to know what to tell a man when he's turned you upside down.

Shawnica came scurrying out of the kitchen. She shrieked and slapped at Desmond. She was done up like usual with glittery stick-on nails and a couple of dozen metal bracelets, so there was the outside chance that Desmond would get sliced or brained outright. He ignored her for as long as he could while he lifted Larry over his head.

"Put. Him. Down," Shawnica told Desmond. I would have gone another way, since putting people down tended to be a key feature of Desmond's brand of scuffing.

He deposited Larry on the coffee table. It was made like a wagon seat, built out of knotty pine that went to splinters when Larry hit it. The whole house shook. The lights flickered. Larry landed on a couple of remote controls and busted them to pieces. It wasn't like we could keep from lending him money after that.

Shawnica blamed me. She always blamed me. She came storming over to wag a finger directly under my nose. So I got a full dose of her gardenia scent and the music of her jangly bracelet clatter.

"Uh-huh," she told me. I took it to mean that me and Desmond were living down to her expectations.

Larry had decided he'd best stay on the floor. He laid there checking for injuries. Larry was fine, of course. He was always fine. Larry was as indestructible as a cockroach and far luckier than he had any need to be. A fellow chasing him with a rifle once had been felled by his own ricochet, and some Little Rock Mafia hard-ass who Larry had sorely offended found Jesus for no good reason and let Larry off the hook.

Larry had grown to think, the way people will, that that was how the world worked. So he'd get all shirty when he'd meet with minor upsets, like getting pitched around his sister's front room by her former husband.

"What the hell!" Larry said.

Desmond objected to his tone and kicked Larry in the sternum, which caused Shawnica to slap me since I was handy for it.

"Hey," I said to Desmond. I knew better than to touch him. Once he'd started, Desmond would scuff up anyone who came to hand. *"Hey!"*

Desmond finally drew a deep breath and deflated a little. "All right." That was all he ever said to let me know the fever was broken.

"Damn," Larry told us all and rubbed his chest as Desmond helped him up.

Larry plucked up his empty popcorn bag and shook it at his sister. Instead of crawling up his sphincter, the way she would have done with us, Shawnica stepped into the kitchen to make a fresh sack for him.

Larry flung himself onto the sofa and tried three busted remotes before I leaned over and switched the TV off. Desmond parked in his skirted Barcalounger—Shawnica's Barcalounger now—and I perched on a hassock alongside him so he could only get at Larry if he crawled straight over me.

"Okay now," Desmond said. "Let's hear it, Larry."

Larry just looked at us. Wouldn't speak. He finally crossed his arms.

Desmond snorted. "Beluga," he said at last.

Even then, Larry passed a good half minute eating what popcorn he could forage off the couch. He finally told us, "Boy I know up in Collierville got a line on this thing."

It was going to be one of those conversations. I said to Larry, "What thing?"

"Tires," Larry told us. "Michelins. Tractor-trailer load."

"What boy?" Desmond asked him.

"Skeeter," he told us. "From the yard."

I didn't like either end of that. So this was some con he knew from Parchman with a name like a waterbug.

"Skeeter who?" I wanted to know.

Larry waved me off. "Don't matter."

If Larry hadn't been an in-law, we would have already tossed him onto the porch. A trailer full of tires and a couple of Parchman grads?

"Tell it," Desmond said to Larry.

Shawnica came in with his popcorn and half a roll of paper towels that Larry tossed directly onto the floor. He explained himself by informing Desmond, "You went and broke the damn table."

Desmond shifted. "Sorry about that . . . Beluga."

"Skeeter knows tires," Larry told us. "These ain't no re-treads or nothing. Straight out of the factory in Kansas or somewhere. Got the stickers and everything. Just like you'd buy them in the store. But that ain't even the beauty part."

Larry dug a fistful of popcorn out of his sack and shoved it in his mouth. About a third of it ended up on his lap until he'd brushed it onto the floor. He waited. We waited. We were going to have to request the beauty part.

"So?" Desmond said. "What's the beauty part?"

Larry laughed. "Them tires is stole already."

"Who by?" I asked him.

He waved a hand dismissively. "Some shitbag in West Memphis."

"Which shitbag?"

Larry pointed at me and grinned at Desmond as if to say, "Who the fuck is this?"

Ordinarily, I wouldn't have cared, but West Memphis is a hellhole. It's across the river on the Arkansas side and makes actual Memphis seem, by comparison, the seat of enlightenment and grace. The place is the Arkansas version of Tijuana without the college kids. Just ample drink and petty crime and the occasional beheading.

A West Memphian stealing tires by the truckful might be somebody we shouldn't know. That's all I was thinking, but the power of in-lawdom seemed to trump even that.

"What's the play?" Desmond asked Beluga LaMonte.

"Skeeter knows this guy, got a truck and shit. Said we could hire him out. Trailer's parked right down on East Monroe, back behind a church."

"You seen it?" I asked him.

Larry nodded. Larry told me, "Skeeter swung round there. He seen it, tires and all."

Desmond still wouldn't look at me.

"How much you need?" he asked Larry.

"Hold on. Let's hear the whole thing."

Desmond turned and studied me now. He gave me a look to let me know this was no time to get particular.

"I just want to know what they've got in mind," I told him. "Somebody's probably watching that trailer. Don't you think?"

Larry proved pleased for the chance to lay it all out. "We'll go in like . . . three in the A.M. and haul it out of there. Got a buddy in Belzoni with a big tractor shed. We'll drop it in there and let the shit all calm down."

"What shit?" I couldn't help myself.

"Somebody bound to be mad."

"Who exactly?"

Larry pointed at me again in his *Who the fuck is this guy?* way.

"How much?" Desmond asked him.

Larry shoved more popcorn in. He gave us a number we couldn't make out. It was just as well, because once he'd swallowed and told us again, it turned out that he'd said, "Fifty."

"Thousand?" I tried to make it sound like a point of clarification, but getting up off the hassock as I said it didn't help.

"Seems like a lot," Desmond told Larry. He turned around to find Shawnica in the kitchen doorway. "Seems like a lot," he told her, too.

She nodded and said to Larry, "Tell them what you need it for."

"Expenses and shit," Larry informed us.

I glared at the side of Desmond's head.

"Got plans for the tires?" Desmond asked Shawnica's brother.

Larry pressed his lips together and nodded like him and Skeeter had given that some deep thought.

"Going to find out what kind of sizes we have." Then he looked at me. "Tires come in like a hundred different sizes."

"I've heard."

"So we figure what we got"—he was back on Desmond now—"and we work from here like down to Vicksburg maybe and let them go for a price. Stop at the garages and shit, take orders like people do." Meaning people who hadn't passed three years in Parchman changing their names.

"How many tires are we talking?" I asked him.

"Full load. Skeeter seen them. I don't know. Four or five hundred maybe."

"What are you going to ask?"

Larry reached down beside the sofa and plucked a catalog off the floor. It was from the Walmart in Indianola and had a page devoted to tires. Mostly tires from Bangladesh or Borneo or somewhere, but there were a few Michelins in the mix. They started at two and a quarter.

"We're thinking a hundred."

"Think seventy-five and get puckered to take fifty," I told him.

Larry pointed at me again.

"A hundred's steep," Desmond informed him, and then he informed Shawnica too.

"Might go eighty," Larry allowed.

"The shit's hot, genius. The trick is to move it."

This time he only looked at me, couldn't be bothered to point.

"I don't know," Desmond said. "Sounds all right to me."

"For fifty thousand?" I'm sure my tone had more of an edge to it than I'd intended. We'd taken three hundred grand off our Acadian fuck stick, so we had fifty to spare, but I just couldn't see the sense of giving it to Larry.

Desmond grunted. "I might can see about forty from here."

"Where the hell you looking?"

"Maybe," Desmond said and paused to swallow, "Beluga . . . you ought to tell us about your expenses."

"Got to pay the truck guy. Got to grease a couple of boys in West Memphis, the ones that put us onto this shit in the first place. Need to pay some rent to the boy in Belzoni with the tractor shed. Then me and Skeeter'll be needing to get around all over the place. Ain't got no car between us. Got to have some money for that."

"What do you figure on driving?" Desmond asked him.

Larry described a Jaguar or something. He'd seen it on a lot over in Jackson. He veered into something close to raptures about the faceted chrome wheels.

I let him finish before I told Desmond, "I can see maybe fifteen from here."

"Hold on now," Larry told us both. "I'm going to double your damn money. You want that magic on fifteen or you wanting it on fifty?"

"Five hundred tires?"

Larry nodded at me.

"Fifty apiece?"

"Says you."

"That's two hundred and twenty-five thousand. You double our fifty and give it back, that's a big bite out of that. Ought to whittle the expenses down. Bare bone it."

"Might listen to the man," Shawnica told him. I hadn't expected that.

"Forty, then," Larry suggested.

"I might can see twenty," I told him.

Desmond slapped his massive thighs with both his massive hands. "Thirty," he told us all and got up out of his Barca-lounger, which was kind of a process given how much of Desmond there was to lift.

"Six months to turn it?" I asked Desmond once he was fully upright. He nodded.

"I hear you," Larry told us. He reached for the afghan to wipe his popcorn grease away and then offered his hand to Desmond, who swallowed hard and took it. He shook it once and grunted. He let Beluga have it back.

TWO

In Desmond's Escalade on the way to my place, I laid out my misgivings. Larry was preeminent among them, but I would like to have known who he was stealing from as well.

Desmond was in a grunting mood. Family will do that to you, so it was me talking mostly, with Desmond content to grumble behind the wheel.

"If Larry's right and this guy stole a load straight from the Michelin factory and has the stones to park it downtown, even in West Memphis, you got to figure he's connected somehow. One end or the other. Got people at the factory. Got people in West Memphis. Might be hooked up at both ends. You hearing me?"

Desmond turned onto my street off the main Indianola drag. It was a beautiful April evening with the rich Delta scent of flowers in the air.

"Yeah," he said. "Larry's problem. I'm sure we won't be messing with them."

"That's optimistic," I told him, and Desmond gave me a Desmond look that let me know we were finished talking about it.

"I'm taking it all out of your box," I told him as he wheeled into the drive.

Desmond grunted. Desmond said, "I would."

My landlady, Pearl, was out in the driveway looking for a cat. She had one of her late husband Gil's old flashlights with batteries he'd probably put in it. She would have been just as well off with a couple of birthday candles.

"Fergus!" She shouted it toward the neighbor's house, toward the back of her lot, toward me and Desmond rolling to a stop in her driveway.

Desmond looked at me.

"Cat," I told him. "Been AWOL for a week."

"Didn't know Pearl had a cat."

I flung my door open. "Doesn't."

That was about as near to a spat as me and Desmond ever got. I went in for door flinging. Desmond preferred neck noises. He made one and climbed on out.

"What are you looking for, Miss Pearl?"

Pearl was a proper Delta belle through and through. She might have been a fading flower and more down at heel than she'd ever imagined she'd get, but she still had that Delta debutante way of talking down to the coloreds. It wasn't a choice with people like Pearl. It was like being blond or having teeth.

"Aw, honey," she said and laid her tiny white hand on Desmond's shoulder. "My cat's run off. Told a friend I'd keep him for her. Don't know what I'm going to do."

That was typical Pearl. She couldn't keep anything straight in her head anymore. One of Pearl's friends had passed away. Not a Presbyterian friend but a canasta friend. Pearl had once explained the difference. It had nothing to do with the Lord. Canasta friends, as I understood it, were casual and fair-weather. If one of them got sick or had trouble in her life, she'd just get set aside and somebody else would take her seat. Presbyterian friends were different. You had to pretend to care about them.

So a canasta friend had passed away, a woman named Ailene. I'd actually been kind of fond of Ailene. She carried a pint of apple brandy in her handbag and was loud and vulgar, chain-smoked Salems, and played cards like a pirate. I could always hear Ailene laughing when Pearl had the game at her house.

She'd died a couple of weeks back in the beauty shop under the dryer. The girls thought she'd just dropped off to sleep and had a heroically high threshold for heat. Pearl ended up over at Ailene's house picking through her closets since Ailene didn't have any children, just second cousins down in Destin. When Pearl and her other canasta friends came away with what they wanted, Ailene's cat must have sensed that the jig was up and slipped into Pearl's car.

I remember the afternoon she came home from Ailene's because of all the screaming. I was changing my oil in the car shed and came out to check on Pearl. She was sitting in her Buick with the driver's door open. She was quivering and close to tears.

"You all right?"

She shook her head. "Went right across my lap."

I looked around. I didn't see anything. "What?"

"Possum, I think."

"Coming in? Going out?"

She pointed toward the side yard, more specifically to-ward a Nuttall oak that her Gil had planted and nursed. It came with a story like most everything around Pearl's house, and she launched into it automatically. That was the way with Pearl and her stories. Of course, I'd heard about Gil's Nuttall oak by then. How he'd dug it up down by Yazoo in a spur of the national forest and had brought it home wrapped in a towel and little more than a twig. Then he'd fenced it in to keep the squirrels away, had raised it to a sapling, had very nearly lost it in the '77 drought. But he'd watered it every night in direct op-position to city ordinance, and there it was—a glorious Nuttall oak right in Pearl's side yard.

It was south of glorious, truth be told, because the power company tree trimmer had been through a few years back while Pearl was off in Birmingham. He'd butchered the thing quite thoroughly. Those boys have a talent for that. So it was a glori-ous Nuttall oak up to where it turned to power line topiary.

Pearl was carrying on about that tree, the way she seemed obliged to, while I looked for the possum that had run across her lap. I checked under the car. I checked in the backseat where Pearl had laid a pile of Ailene's Salem-stinking clothes. Then I walked over to Gil's Nuttall oak and looked up in the stunted canopy. There was a tuxedo cat on a limb up there about the size of a beagle.

"Where have you been?" I asked Pearl.

"Ailene's."

"She have a cat?"

Pearl nodded. "Fergus."

"Black and white?"

Pearl nodded.

I pointed him out, and Pearl said, "Oh."

She'd tried to feed and tame him during the time that had passed since then, but Fergus was on the feral side and wouldn't be domesticated.

With Desmond out on the driveway, Pearl could give him both the Fergus story and the saga of Gil's transplanted Nuttall oak. He was a trapped man and knew it. For my part, I veered off toward the basement.

"Checking on something," I called to them both once I was halfway across the yard.

Pearl never locked her basement, so we were taking a chance keeping money down there, but the place was such a cluttered mess—almost everything in it was broken—that you could look inside and see there wasn't anything to take. Since there weren't any stairs up into the house, it was just its own junky thing and didn't even lead to a place that might be better. A fellow would have to be sorry and industrious both to wade into that thicket, and those are traits you rarely find paired together in a man.

Our cash was all in a big plastic toolbox on a low shelf in a back spidery corner. There were lawn chairs leaned up against the cabinet in case the spiders weren't enough. Even Desmond wouldn't mess with the thing. He'd linger in the basement stairwell and have me go get money out whenever he needed some.

I moved the chairs. I opened the box. We had maybe two hundred and forty thousand left from the three and change we'd started with. As I counted out Larry's money, I was already writing it off.

I might even have dwelled a bit on Larry and grown sullen in the basement if Fergus hadn't scared me half to death. He didn't leap out or anything. He had too much bulk for that. Fergus was just sitting on a patio table, an old wooden one with a couple of splintered slats. He was watching me with his yellow eyes until he got a sudden urge to bathe. When he went to lick a paw, I vaulted and nearly hit a rafter.

"How'd you get down here?"

Fergus yawned.

"She's looking for you," I told him.

Fergus got an urge to lick his belly, indulged it, and then studied me the way cats will. If he could have talked, he probably would have said, "You still here, asswipe?"

I'd been around cats enough to know how to pick a strange one up, but I couldn't be sure that Fergus's neck scruff would support Fergus's tonnage. He burbled some when I hoisted him. For my part, I swore quite a lot and then went running up the steps and across the yard, desperate to set him back down.

"Look here," I shouted, and Pearl turned her wan light beam upon us.

"Oh, baby!" Pearl made me give him to her against my better judgement, and he stayed in her arms for a nanosecond before clearing out for Gil's oak. Fergus scrabbled up the trunk and perched on a limb. Pearl turned her flashlight on him.

"Kind of big for a cat," Desmond said.

"Kind of big for a pony," I told him.

I let Desmond handle Beluga. I'd done my bit by showing up and listening to Larry's spiel. It seemed certain somebody would make some money. I just wasn't convinced it was us.

"You going to give it to him all at once?" was the only thing I asked Desmond.

"To her," he told me, and that was about the best thing he could do.

Then four or five weeks went by. I didn't think much about it except for when the twinges hit. I'd imagine Larry in new sneakers we'd underwritten. Larry in Gucci glasses. Larry riding around in a Range Rover with a gold-plated Rolls-Royce grille. I kept it all to myself since I knew that Desmond was just doing for an in-law, by which I mean I didn't come right out and complain, but me and Desmond did chafe for a bit.

We work together. That's how we met. For a couple of months there, after we'd taken all that meth kingpin's money, me and Desmond were men of leisure, up to nothing in the middle of the day. It was all right for the first few weeks, but it wore poorly after a while. We were like kids out of school for the summer, hating the classroom but bored half to death.

So we started showing up back at the shop where we'd worked and getting in the way. Kalil, who runs the place, tolerated us for a bit. It's a rent-to-own store, and he let me and Desmond hang around the showroom and harass all the guys who were actually working until a call came in one day, probably about a year ago now. Kalil had sent Ferris out to repo a stove, just him alone with his ratty Ford Ranger and a hand truck. We didn't like Ferris. Nobody liked Ferris. His girlfriend would even come by to belittle him two or three times a week. He was a bony, tattooed fellow with his eyeteeth missing and no experience with a bathtub or a comb.

Every time he introduced himself he said, "Like the wheel, goddammit." It didn't matter the circumstances. He would have said it to the pope.

"Got him in a closet," Kalil told us and handed Desmond a scrap of paper with an address scribbled on it.

"Who's got him?" I asked.

Desmond studied the address. "Down below Moorhead?"

Kalil nodded. "Lawtons."

"Which Lawtons?" I asked him, and Kalil just flattened his lips and shook his head.

"They'll feed him to their pigs," Desmond said.

It was a real possibility with those Lawtons. The good side of the family wasn't prosperous exactly, but they were decent and reliable. When they got behind on payments, you knew there was nothing else they could do. The bad Lawtons were mean and sorry and didn't care who found it out. They were all cousins or something—the good and the bad—and spent holidays together. There would reliably be a picnic ham and most usually an assault.

Desmond waved the scrap of notepaper. "Who?"

Kalil hated to tell us. "Oscar."

"Give it back to him" was my suggestion.

"Send one of them," Desmond suggested to Kalil.

We all looked at Kalil's staff on hand. They were sitting on the homely sofa Kalil could never sell. With the tufts and the skirts and the Chesterfield buttons. They weren't, as a group, inspiring. I knew the boys on either end. They'd get put in a closet, too. The ones in the middle were entirely new to me, but Desmond was acquainted with one of them.

"What about him?" Desmond asked and pointed at the boy he knew.

"Some fool went after him with a Garden Weasel. He's still a little gun-shy."

"We don't even work for you anymore." I knew that was a last resort when I said it.

"Maybe you miss it," Kalil suggested. "Or maybe you ought to find out."

"It's a stove?" Desmond asked him.

And there we were, right back in it again.

We drove over in my Ranchero and parked it back beyond a hedgerow, well out of gunplay range. The good Lawtons lived in a Lawton compound that backed onto a rice field. They had dirt instead of grass and a couple of cannibalized sedans, but their place overall was a shade more neat than not. The bad Lawtons lived in a domesticated landfill. They just went to the doors, both front and back, and pitched out whatever they'd decided didn't belong under the roof anymore. That might be last night's pizza boxes or a dinette chair.

When we peeked around the trees, we spied a county cruiser parked in the Lawtons' yard. Parked, anyway, behind a harrow and some sort of busted seeder. The driver's door was open, and Kendell was sitting under the wheel.

He saw us, too.

"Can't leave it alone," he shouted out our way.

We went over to him crouching low since you couldn't be

sure a Lawton might not squeeze off the odd recreational round.

Kendell was Desmond's cousin somehow. He was a ferocious Baptist and had disapproved of how me and Desmond hadn't been up to much for a while. He had suspicions about what we were living on and everything we'd gotten up to, but I guess he decided to pray for us both instead of haul us in. I liked Kendell. He was what I had instead of a stout, unwavering conscience.

"Kalil snared us," I told him.

Kendell nodded. "Bound to in the end."

"What are you here for?" Desmond asked him.

"They took a shot at the meter reader."

"What the hell for?" I knew when it came out the sort of looks I'd get. Desmond and Kendell eyed me the way Delta people often did when I tried to apply some regular standard of cause and effect to the place.

The bad Lawtons were essentially sovereign citizens without the impeccable philosophical underpinnings and the patriotic good humor of constitutional crackpots most everywhere else. They'd shoot at you, if you were a meter man, because they had bullets and a gun.

"What brings you?" Kendell asked us.

Desmond sort of pointed at the house. "Boy in the closet. One of Kalil's."

"Who?"

"Ferris," I said. "Know him?"

Kendell nodded. "Like the wheel."

"You waiting on backup?" Desmond asked him.

Kendell climbed out of his cruiser. "Guess you'll have to do."

They didn't believe in SWAT in the Delta. There was never a shortage of hulking rednecks wearing a county badge, the sorts of eager brawlers you could pitch into trouble like a terrier down a rathole. I could tell by the way Kendell glanced at me, I was his cracker for the moment.

"Me and him," he said and pointed at Desmond, "we'll work our way around back. You get them talking. See what they want this time."

"Want to keep their stove, I'm guessing."

"Why don't you talk them out of that."

"Already shot at the meter reader," I reminded Kendell.

"Make yourself little," he told me. Beyond that he only winked.

Kendell and Desmond went the long away around, through the corn instead of the rice field, and I saw them take cover in the back of the lot behind what had once been an outhouse. It was vine-choked and tumbledown but big enough to crouch behind.

"Hey, Oscar," I shouted.

A couple of dogs barked from under the porch. They'd been Lawton dogs long enough to have the good sense to stay just where they were. People who'd shoot at a meter man wouldn't think twice about a mongrel.

After maybe half a minute, Oscar shouted back, "He's not here."

"It's Nick Reid, Oscar. I know it's you."

"Ain't me."

"You got a fellow in the closet?"

"Maybe."

"Think I can have him back?"

"Well," Oscar told me, "I don't know about that."

So we'd finished with the preamble and had arrived at the terms.

"What'll it take?"

I could hear racket from inside and Lawtons shifting around. It wasn't much of a house. The windows were all flung open, and the nasty curtains were hanging over the sills.

"Says he wants our stove," Oscar finally shouted. "Can't have it."

"All right."

"And we want some Fritos."

"Fine."

"The big bag. And a twelve-pack of Busch." There was some muttering in the wake of that. "Hell, a case."

Kendell eased out from behind the viney outhouse far enough to look my way. I just shook my head and shrugged. A Lawton would want what a Lawton would want.

"All right," I said. "I can do all that."

I let the Lawtons enjoy their moment of triumph before I shouted out, "Hey, Oscar."

"What?"

"You'll need to send that boy out first."

"The hell I will."

"That's the only way it'll work."

There was discussion about that inside.

"And some cigarettes," Oscar called out. "Three whole damn cartons. Winstons."

"All right," I said and waited.

The front door opened, and Ferris came out. He was blinking and in his stocking feet. I motioned for him to come over to me, but he turned instead toward the doorway to piss and moan about his shoes. Then he changed his mind the way that people often do at gunpoint. He crossed the yard to join me at a trot.

"Shit, man," Ferris told me. "I ain't had them boots a week."

"You're welcome."

"Quitting this damn job." Ferris went stalking toward the road in his filthy socks.

"So?" Oscar called out.

"Going in a minute. I'll pick up all your stuff," I told them. "Got to get this guy you shot at straightened out first."

"What guy?"

"Meter reader."

"Ain't done it!" Oscar had a gift for righteous indignation.

"Somebody did."

I could hear from inside the sound of a Lawton huddle. That was how they always decided who exactly would get blamed for what. It was like what people do with their Visa cards, trying to pick out the one to use that's got a little more room on it than the others. If a Lawton in there had no charges pending, he was going to get the blame.

They must have all been in trouble, because Oscar soon told me, "That boy of yours, he did it."

"Ferris shot the meter man?"

By now Kendell and Desmond had slipped up through the side yard and were pressed against the house, easing toward the front.

"Tried to stop him. Wouldn't pay me no mind."

"So you put him in the closet?"

"Couldn't figure what else to do. Got a bad streak or something. Ought to tell somebody about it."

I glanced toward Ferris out in the road. He was having an animated conversation with himself.

"Well, all right, then. I'm sorry for all the upset."

I waited until Kendell had slipped up just alongside the front door. He nodded.

"Fritos and what now?" I said, and that was enough to bring Oscar out. He hated to have to repeat a thing. Everybody in the Delta knew you didn't ask Oscar Lawton to say something twice.

Oscar jerked open the door and came onto the stoop. He looked half determined to shoot me, but Kendell grabbed Oscar's rifle barrel and snatched his gun away before Oscar could react.

Like usual, he was wearing a pajama top and a pair of undershorts. What hair he had left was standing straight up. I had to think Oscar was pushing eighty.

He told Kendell, "Aw," which was Oscar's standard version of "I guess I'm just giving the hell up."

Kendell supplied him with the usual instructions, and Oscar invited his household out into the yard. His two boys carried their mother out on what looked like a toilet chair and set her down hard enough to prompt her to bark at them a little. One of those boys was sixty if he was a day. I think the other one was about seventeen.

"Who's going in?" Kendell asked them.

They all pointed at the teenager. He shoved his hands together to make it easy for Kendell to cuff him up.

"How much?" I shouted at Ferris.

He stopped raging in the road and looked at me.

"What do they owe on the stove?"

Ferris scratched his head. He fished a sheet out of his pocket and studied it briefly. "Thirty-two dollars," he said.

"I ain't got it," Oscar told me. That's what he always told us.

Me and Desmond went inside and found two twenties in the Bible. We left change and came back out. Even if it was only thirty-two dollars from bad Lawtons, it felt good to be up to something after nearly a year of swanning around and living on our swag.

Kendell was having a word with Oscar. The Baptist in him made him tireless.

"You can't just shove folks in your closet."

Oscar nodded. "Tell me about it." He pointed at his son, the older one. He had on a pajama top, too. "Weren't no room until he took his golf clubs out."

THREE

So we went back to work, but me and Desmond were like the special forces. Kalil called us in on the thorny jobs, and as the economy sank in the Delta and the available work ebbed away, Kalil would have me and Desmond go in and sort his business out.

He stayed firmly unsympathetic. You couldn't bend him with a story. People would try all sorts of calamities on him. They couldn't pay for their dinette, their sofa, their TV because of the flood or the *E.coli* or their momma's emergency surgery or some Social Security snafu or the radiation in their basement or a boss (for no damn reason) holding up their check. A few of them would even come right in the store and try to be persuasive. They'd drag children with them and have them rehearsed so they would cry when the time was ripe.

Frequently, Kalil would hold his fire until they'd finished.

Then he'd tell them, "Thirty dollars," or whatever sum they owed and assure them me and Desmond would come haul away their stuff.

That's when the crumpled bills would come out from handbags and trouser pockets. I even saw a boy once pull (I figured) his last twenty from a tiny pouch on his daughter's tennis shoe. Kalil would do the math on his clipboard. The thing was always right at hand. He'd produce a receipt and offer it like he was conducting regular commerce.

There was never so much as a hint of compassion from him. I guess that's why Kalil drank. Armagnac mostly with a splash of Tab. Once he had two in him, he'd sing.

So me and Desmond, if you can believe it, were the human face on the operation. We'd agreed to take the "troubled cases." That's what Kalil liked to call them. He knew if we came back empty-handed, there wasn't a thing to be done. He paid us a retainer—cash on the first of the month with no taxes drawn from it. It all went straight into our big plastic toolbox down in Pearl's basement.

I don't know why we hadn't thought to work a little before we went back to Kalil. If you roll around all day doing nothing, people get suspicious. People who wouldn't pay you any attention otherwise. So not just Kendell but Kendell's colleagues, and not just Pearl but Pearl's friends, too. Everybody suddenly wonders how you get by doing nothing, where the profit might be in spending your afternoons detailing your car.

I'd even lost a girlfriend over it. I'd sort of been seeing Pearl's niece, Angie. She worked at a hospital up in Memphis, all but ran the place really, and she sort of knew where me and

Desmond had come by our pile of cash. Only because I'd gotten full of wine one night and had essentially told her.

She was okay with it until she'd decided she was less okay than she'd thought. So we drifted off the way people will, her one way and me another, and I didn't want that to happen in the general course of things. I didn't want me and Desmond to fall out of favor with everybody. Or just have people like Larry and his buddy Skeeter left for friends.

Once we could say we were back with Kalil—he let us call ourselves supervisors—it was a handle folks could hold to, and that's exactly what they did. The trouble was that as the economy in the country soured, opportunity dried up in the Delta to the point of desiccation. So the ordinary cases got special at a pretty alarming rate.

Kalil wanted to be paid. He had the right to be paid or get his merchandise back, but his clients as a rule were only barely slipping by, so every hiccup turned into a problem. They'd get furloughed from the catfish works for a week or two, and there me and Desmond would be at the door to repossess their bedstead or relieve them somehow of cash they didn't have. It was a sorry state of affairs to be caught between Kalil and decent, luckless people. And me and Desmond without much appetite for Armagnac and Tab.

We weren't three months into supervising when it all came to a head. Kalil had sent me and Desmond out after a washer-dryer. The people only had a couple of payments left, but they couldn't come up with the cash, and the boy Kalil sent out first had only brought back washer hoses.

So me and Desmond rode out. They lived on Black Bayou halfway between Leland and Greenville. Their house wasn't much, but the grass was cut, and there was hardly any junk in the yard. They were out where we could see them, the whole family, I guess. The mother and father, a couple of kids. They were all gathered around a swing set, a brand-new one the man of the house was finishing tightening up with a wrench.

When he gave them the high sign, the kids swarmed the thing. Two girls. One tall and slender, the other half her size and chubby. They parked on the swing seats, and their father pushed them. Their mother, pregnant, sat on an upturned joint compound bucket and watched.

"Probably sold the washer," I told Desmond.

He'd decided the same himself.

The girls laughed. The skinny one jumped out at the height of her arc and rolled through the grass.

"What do they owe?" Desmond asked me.

I checked the invoice. "Forty-seven ten."

Desmond fished out his cash. He counted out fifty. This was something we'd promised each other we'd never do. Or never do again, anyway. We'd let a woman sway us with a pitiful story about her stomach tumor, and we'd pitched in together on her overdue payment, pretended it had come straight from her.

I remember the three of us standing there, me and Desmond and Kalil. Kalil checked the invoice. He looked at the money. He eyed me and then Desmond and me again. He smiled that way he sometimes does.

"Show you her scar?" he asked us.

It was all he ever said about it. It was all he ever needed to say.

This was different, we told ourselves. Then we told it to

each other. We had plenty of money and a better sense of who exactly the shitheads were, so if we wanted to bail out a guy who'd sold off his washer to buy his girls a swing set for the yard, then that's exactly what we'd do.

Kalil knew somehow. He always knew. He studied Desmond's money.

"Well, all right" was all he told us and dropped the cash in his money drawer.

We redeemed ourselves not a full week later by scuffing up four Lynches at once. Desmond started with the one who'd shouted though his locked door, "Fuck all y'all. Go on."

Then a trio of cousins had come rolling into the yard to get all mouthy with us, so we ended up with a full quartet of Lynches in a battered pile. They were still making threats against us, even semiconscious, which we felt gave us license to keep on kicking them until they shut the hell up.

The initial Lynch owed on a TV. He owed on a PlayStation. He owed on a laptop. He owed on a side table. We hauled it all back into the shop and set it down in the middle of the sales floor.

"Renting to a Lynch?" I asked Kalil.

Kalil gave us both his gassy smile.

"Well, all right," Desmond told him, and we were even after that.

So me and Desmond could stop saying, "Taking time off," when people asked us what we were up to. We got to be regular again. We got to go around unnoticed. We had somewhere to be on the way to. We had somewhere to be coming from.

In fact, I was cutting across from a job when I met Tula Raintree's cruiser. People in the Delta drive like fools, dead fast and all over the road. I was in my lane when I passed her, both hands firmly on the wheel, and if I was going over eighty it was only by a click or two.

When I looked in my mirror and saw that cruiser whipping around in the road, I thought it was probably Kendell wanting to fill me in on something. So I pulled off and waited. I was leaning against the hood when that Grand Marquis pulled in behind me and stopped.

We were alongside a massive soybean field down around Hollandale. The pivot irrigator had just started up, a monstrous, mechanized thing. It was hooked at one end to a wellhead in the field and rolled slowly in a circle watering scores of acres at once. The tires on it would fit a tractor. It was hundreds of yards long and probably thirty or forty feet high. The water shot out in majestic arcs and rained down iridescent on the beans.

The sheer scale of agriculture in the Delta was a thing you could become blind to. The huge combines, and the crop dusters, and the satellite-guided tractors. The robust emerald green of the fields, the rich blackness of the earth. It was good to get out and just look at it sometimes instead of racing by with the radio loud and your head full of other stuff.

I had a question for Kendell about the wells they'd bored all over the place. What they drew. How deep they were. It was something I could stand to know, but before I could shout out to him (I heard him on the cindered shoulder), somebody else entirely told me, "Sir, let's see your hands."

It was a woman's voice. I swung my head around, and

there she was. Her uniform crisp. Her hair drawn back. She had a hand resting on her Glock.

"Let's see them," she said.

I uncrossed my arms and showed her both my palms.

"License and registration."

I was going to say, "You're kidding," but she clearly wasn't kidding. Everything about her told me that. I checked the tag above her pocket flap. T. Raintree.

"What's the problem?" I asked her.

"License," she told me. "Registration."

I fished out my wallet. I was still driving on a Virginia license that hadn't yet expired. I'd been in the Delta maybe eight or nine months by then. My tags were Mississippi, though, which was kind of a contradiction.

She studied my license. She asked me of my Ranchero, "This thing yours?"

I nodded and stepped around to the passenger door, reached into the glove box. I brought out the registration and gave her that as well.

"Is this a current address?"

My license had a central Virginia P.O. box number on it.

I shook my head. "Been down here a little while now."

She gave me a little nod. I watched her. I couldn't help but watch her. She'd gone to some effort to look stern and pinched and tough, but that couldn't really hide the fact that she was exotic and lovely. Choctaw, I had to figure. Dark eyes. Raven hair. A café au lait burnish to her. I tried to look without her knowing I was looking.

"You staying?"

I shrugged like we were there just making small talk. I can't say I knew exactly what she meant.

"Do you intend to stay here," she said, enunciating each word crisply.

"Oh," I told her. "Yeah. Maybe. I guess."

"Go to the DMV and get relicensed."

"Been meaning to."

"Do it."

"Right. First thing."

I figured that essentially wrapped up our business, so I moved on to the personal.

"You know Kendell?" I asked her. "Kendell Fairley. He's a sergeant or something."

She nodded. Not a dent otherwise. She still had my license and registration both.

"I've got you at eighty-two in a fifty-five."

I'd been in the Delta long enough to know that the proper response was "So?" Instead I pressed my lips together and managed not to say it.

"Any reason I shouldn't write you up?" She glanced at my license. "Mr. Reid?"

It wasn't the sort of place where locals got tickets for eighty-two in a fifty-five, so that meant I had to go to the DMV to make myself a local. Until then, I was just some guy from Virginia who got cited for all grades of shit.

"No, ma'am," I told her. "Guess I've got it coming."

"Right," she said and turned and headed back to her cruiser. I watched her all the way. If I was going to get a ticket, that was the least I could do for myself. Then I leaned back against the Ranchero hood and waited while a breeze worked through the soybean field and a bank of clouds closed off the sun.

"T. Raintree," I told myself and grunted like Desmond would.

I heard her door slam, her shoes on the cinders. She gave me my license and my registration wrapped in my speeding ticket. She didn't bother with any warnings and cautions about how I ought to drive.

"You can pay it at the courthouse in Greenville or mail a check."

"Convenient."

"We aim to please." She didn't smile exactly, but something changed in her eyes.

"Looks like rain," I said and glanced toward the clouds to the west.

She glanced, too, and told me, "Not really."

Then she was on her way back to her cruiser, and I was standing there watching her go.

"Tula," Kendell said.

Desmond asked him, "Buddy's girl?"

He nodded, looked my way. "How do you know her?"

I had the ticket in my pocket. I unfolded it and offered it to Kendell. He wiped the biscuit grease off his fingers and looked it over. "Probably ought to slow down."

"Middle of no damn where."

"She's kind of a stickler," Kendell told me.

Arnette came by with the coffeepot, but Kendell covered up his cup. He sugared and creamed his coffee with the pre-

cision of a chemist. He was not the sort of gentleman to tolerate a splash, and there he was calling somebody else a stickler.

We got together for breakfast a couple of times a week at a
place in Indianola that was either called Hank's or the Chit
Chat, depending on how old you were. Hank had passed
away in '78 when the "new" people had taken over, a guy they
called Suet and his bride with big hair, but that was three
wives and a string of girlfriends ago. Now the place was run
by Suet and his various children mostly, but women he'd been
involved with would often drop by for a quarrel.

Suet's specialty was an omelet with every damn thing in it
and biscuits made with just enough flour to keep the lard in
place. Kendell always went for the Cream of Wheat. He was
disciplined that way. Desmond was partial to the fried bologna, which came for some reason with sausage *and* bacon. The
coffee always tasted like they'd drained it through a tube sock
the previous week. But the place was convenient, and we had
a regular table where people knew not to sit.

I let Kendell get his Cream of Wheat ready, butter his biscuit, adjust his flatware, sip his water. When he looked settled,
I said to him, "Tell me about her."

"Why?"

I shrugged like I was curious but in an indifferent sort of
way, just equipped with an innocent eagerness to know about
my neighbors.

"Bony," Desmond volunteered. That was hard talk coming
from him. Shawnica was bony, and look what she'd gotten
up to.

"Choctaw?" I asked Kendell.

"Daddy was. Mother's blacker than me. Buddy had a

welding shop out by Metcalfe. Went up to Memphis for some kind of operation. Five, six years ago. Didn't ever come back."

"And her?"

"What about her?" Kendell asked me. He spooned Cream of Wheat on half a biscuit and smiled.

"She's a pretty girl, all right? It's not like this place is infested with them."

"Got a kid," Desmond offered. "Boy?"

Kendell nodded.

"Husband?" I asked them.

"Marine," Kendell said. "Killed over in Iraq."

"When?"

"A while ago," Kendell told me. "Long enough, if that's what you're asking."

"You hire her?"

"Would have. Captain brought her in. She was down in Baton Rouge or somewhere. Wanted to come home."

"You like her?" That was for both of them.

"Hate to see her end up with you," Kendell told me. He sipped his coffee. Somehow, he neglected to smile.

Desmond thought for a second. He took his time nodding his approval. "But bony," he said and went back to his bologna. "Bony," he muttered at his plate.

We were on our way to call on the Duponts when Desmond rode me by her house. He didn't tell me that's what he was doing until we were well back off the highway. I thought he knew some shortcut that I wasn't acquainted with. She was north of Leland, off of Clear Creek at a place called Nepanee. Or it had been a place once, anyway, given the half block of tumbledown ruins. Now it was mostly plowed under with some civic wreckage and a sign.

"Right there," Desmond said as he slowed before a small frame house in a pecan grove.

"What?"

"Tula," he said and stepped on the gas. "Just saved you half a day."

The Duponts we visited lived up in Shaw. They liked to claim kinship to the Delaware DuPonts, but their brand of raging shiftlessness sort of gave the lie to that. We'd all at one time or another begged Kalil to put them on his no-go list. He kept a separate book for people he simply wouldn't do business with, and you can imagine how far beyond the pale those customers had to be.

More than a few of them were fugitives. They were gambling addicts and alcoholics. People so filthy you'd rather rent furniture to an incontinent cat. Even then, they needed to have offended Kalil's sense of proper commerce usually three or four times before he'd finally put them in the book.

The Duponts were on their way there. They were sorry as far as it went. Got behind on payments. Tore up stuff. They'd even sold off a TV or two. Once they spent the money on a tractor mower even though none of them had a lawn. They were dirt and thicket people, long-term composters—trash piled up everywhere. They'd have all the garden soil they'd need right around Judgment Day.

Even all that wouldn't have been enough to turn Kalil against them. Tidy, upstanding citizens rarely rent a couch. The trouble with the Duponts was that the whole pack of them smelled like feet. I don't know if it had to do with their diet or general hygienic neglect, but every one of them (even the Dupont children) had a penetrating reek about them. It got all over everything they came around or touched, so you couldn't really repossess from a Dupont to any decent effect.

They knew they smelled. They knew you'd have to toss out what you took. So what the rest of us might have thought of as a liability, the Duponts took for leverage.

"I went in last time," I told Desmond as he pulled up in front of the Duponts' house. Their dogs boiled out from under the place to menace us and bark. They all smelled like feet as well, and carrion a little.

"Uh-uh," Desmond informed me. He tapped his chest. "Refrigerator."

"When?"

"Me and Ronnie. Year ago maybe. You were over in Jackson or somewhere."

"Like hell."

Desmond grunted. Desmond nodded and shoved open his door.

We argued up to the front porch steps, as if it even mattered by then. What with the dogs and the general proximity to Dupont goods and Dupont holdings, we were already so far along toward smelly that staying out or going in wasn't worth quibbling about.

"What are we after?" I asked Desmond.

He pulled a tissuey, yellow invoice from his front shirt pocket and checked the details. "Dinette table. Four chairs. K-Lo thinks he can fumigate them."

"K-Lo thinks professional wrestling is real."

A Dupont cracked the front door to see what all the fuss was about. It didn't matter that he shut it again after only a couple of seconds. We got wafted at enough to give us pause.

"Why didn't we stay retired?" I asked Desmond.

"Appearances," Desmond told me. "They owe sixty-eight dollars."

I turned back toward the road. "Not anymore," I said.

Desmond was right there with me. "This going back to work might get a little expensive."

We kept coveralls in the back of Desmond's Escalade. We stripped down to our underwear right there at the tailgate, shoved our clothes in a sack and tied the neck shut, and headed for the laundry on Highway 1 just south of Greenville where they still claimed to Martinize in an hour and usually even meant it.

There was a car wash next door, and who should pull in while we were sitting there waiting but Beluga S. LaMonte and a buddy of his in an unduly tricked-out Tercel. With the Rolls-Royce grille and the shiny chrome spinners, a spoiler with flame decals on the trunk.

"Don't say it," Desmond told me as we were walking over. Larry had probably had our thirty thousand dollars for six weeks.

Larry was pumping quarters into the washer. His buddy was holding the wand. Larry glanced at us. Except for hockey masks, we looked like that guy in the slasher movies. So first he was frightened and then just squirrelly in the usually Larry way.

He looked like he had some line of Beluga bullshit to visit

on us, but me and Desmond happened to be upwind. So Larry's buddy covered up his nose with his forearm while Larry told us the only thing that human nature would allow.

He grimaced and said to me and Desmond, "Shew!"

FOUR

Larry was all for squirting us down with the power washer. Or he was all for his buddy squirting us down until Desmond assured him we'd kill them both. Instead we got directed downwind, to the far end of the stall where Larry and the guy who turned out to be Skeeter guessed they could tolerate us.

"What you been into?" Larry asked us.

"About to ask you the same thing."

Larry smiled and pointed at me. I'd grown to hate it when he did that.

"So?" Desmond asked.

"Look here," Larry told him and pointed at the front left tire of his Toyota. It was a brand-new Michelin. They were all new Michelins. They still had the factory chalk marks on them and ratty residue from the tags.

"You did the job?" Desmond asked.

Larry and his buddy nodded.

"So how did it go?" I asked Larry.

He started to smile and point again.

"I'll rip that arm off and beat you to death with it."

Larry glanced at Skeeter. "Told you."

Skeeter nodded like I'd lived down to everything that Larry had assured him I'd live down to.

"Answer the man," Desmond said.

"Went all right," Larry allowed.

Larry's only virtue was that he couldn't help but be transparent. He could tell glorious lies, but you always knew they were entirely manufactured. Larry routinely got this look in his eyes when the truth was something else. It hadn't gone all right. I knew it straightaway. Desmond knew it, too. Skeeter was standing there with the power washer wand, just wincing and waiting for the reckoning.

"What happened?" Desmond asked them.

Larry showed us both his palms. "He's okay. They fixed him up."

"Who?"

"What was that boy's name?" Larry said to Skeeter.

"Bugle's all I ever heard."

"Bugle?" I said. "Who the hell's that?"

Larry pointed with his thumb what he took for West Memphis way. "Boy up there," he told us. "Got under the truck some way."

So me and Desmond stood there stinking at the downwind side of the car wash stall while Larry and Skeeter piddled out scraps of their calamity at us. The great tire caper—we finally pieced together—had not gone according to plan.

Larry, as it turned out, had been late to the rendezvous. He was supposed to meet Skeeter and the man with the truck—they didn't seem to know his name at all—at one in the morning at the interstate truck stop on the Arkansas side of the river. Larry was "tardy," to hear it from Larry. That turned out to mean four hours late.

"I got busy," Larry told us. "Doing shit and stuff."

Skeeter did a bit more wincing. Me and Desmond watched Larry squirm.

"Casbah?" Desmond asked him.

It was a club up by Clarksdale, the sort of place a guy like Larry would think the picture of class. They had a bandstand and beer glasses, professionally installed urinals.

Larry told us, "Hell no!" in a fashion that we both knew actually meant yes.

"Told you." I couldn't help myself.

Desmond hardly needed me piling on, but people like Larry were exactly the reason we avoided people like Larry. There he'd organized a job and couldn't show up on time to do it.

"So what happened?" I asked him. "Just lay it all out. It'll go better for you in the end."

"Little late getting started," Larry told us.

Skeeter couldn't help but snort.

"Sun up?"

Larry couldn't decide, but Skeeter nodded my way.

"And you went through with it anyway?" I asked Larry.

"We was all there." Larry smirked at me like I was some kind of meticulous dope. Yet another stickler plaguing the world.

I was too disgusted to take much part in things after that.

Desmond walked them through it. The guy whose name they didn't know backed his Peterbilt into the alley where the trailer full of tires was parked. Larry and Skeeter were moving the chocks from the wheels when Bugle came out to make trouble.

"The lookout, right? The guy watching the tires?" Desmond asked them.

They both nodded.

"Thought you bought him off or something. Wasn't that the plan?"

Larry's mouth said, "I did," but his eyes said, *I sure wished I had*.

I got reinvolved to the extent of pointing at Larry's new snakeskin sneakers.

Desmond grunted. Desmond showed me his massive open hand by way of inviting me to shut up.

"Boy went crazy. Didn't he?" Larry glanced at Skeeter.

Skeeter nodded. "Kept coming at us." He shook his head. "Little white kid. Kind of dopey."

"Little?"

"Twenty maybe," Larry said, "but puny and tweaked or something."

Again he glanced at Skeeter, and Skeeter nodded. "Not acting right."

"So he gets run over," Desmond said.

Larry nodded, shrugged, managed an exasperated smile.

"And you just left him?"

"Kind of in the middle of something." Larry was all indignant now, like Desmond needed the ins and outs of trailer hijacking explained.

I was attempting to squash my agitation by wandering around the lot, but it was a small lot, and I kept circling back where I'd just been and picking up my own Dupont stink in baleful concentrations.

"I checked on him," Skeeter told Desmond. "Know a boy who's an EMT. He tracked him down. Leg broke in two places, but he's going to be okay."

"And the tires?" Desmond asked them.

"Down where I told you," Larry said, all smug now like he was some sort of mastermind.

I wanted to hit him a couple of times hard.

"Did you pay that guy? With the shed?" I shouted.

Larry pointed and grinned at me again. I'm a sensible man and, by every practical measure, Larry seemed to be needing to get beat the fuck up. So I decided that was just the business I ought to be up to at the moment. Even Desmond couldn't stop me. He appeared to understand my needs.

He said, "Nick," as I stormed past him.

Larry told me, "Come on now."

Beluga LaMonte wasn't the sort to take a punch. Larry collapsed before I'd even hit him. He went all invertebrate on me, just laid there on the cement in a pile, so I kicked him a couple of times since we were both there already. Then I picked him up and hung him on the bracket the car wash people had thoughtfully supplied for cleaning floor mats with the pressure washer.

I told Skeeter, "Give me that," and reached out for the wand.

It was set on power wash already, and I gave Larry the once-over. A woman came in from the stall next door to see what all the howling was about.

That woman went back next door and finished washing her Riviera. She must have called the law as well, because a deputy showed up. White guy, the short, thick one I didn't really know. He'd come from Atlanta or somewhere and made out like Delta crime was small-time and provincial compared to what he'd seen back east and everything evil he'd known.

Desmond knew him a little through Kendell. We were all just standing there by the time he arrived. Larry was wet and was missing a layer of skin in a couple of places, but he was quick to tell the deputy that he was doing fine.

"Dropped the damn thing," he explained and pointed at the wand, which I'd handed over to Skeeter while I took Larry off the wall.

"Well," he told us. "All right." He pointed vaguely. "Scared that lady."

"What lady?" Desmond asked him.

She'd parked her Riviera over by the vacuum cleaner island. She was glaring at us through the driver's window until we all glanced her way, when she dropped that sedan into gear and lurched off.

The deputy made a show of sniffing the air. He considered me and Desmond. "Duponts?" was all he said.

We made them show us the tires. We followed the two of them all the way to Belzoni. They had some trouble finding the farm where they'd stashed the trailer, didn't own a map between them, couldn't dredge up their boy's number. He was running a catfish operation for some conglomerate out of Nashville, and that was about all Larry and Skeeter knew.

They stopped about every human they came across and asked after that boy, so soon enough there was nobody much around who didn't know we were there and who we were hoping to find.

"Don't say it," Desmond instructed me, probably a half-dozen times.

Sometimes I held my fire. Sometimes I said, "All right, but . . ." and laid out my encyclopedic claims against Beluga anyway.

We finally found the tires. I think we were just driving around by then. You could see the damn trailer from the road. I don't quite know how that counted for hidden. It was parked up under a tractor shed alongside a string of catfish ponds. The trailer had slatted sides, so you could see the tires right through them. It didn't help that the word MICHELIN was painted on the slats as well.

Larry was all cocky again climbing out of the car. "See?" he said. "Right here."

"You couldn't buy a tarp?" I asked him.

He very nearly pointed at me and grinned.

"Nick," Desmond cautioned me. He needn't have worried. I could see that Beluga LaMonte was entirely uncorrectable by then.

The boy they'd entrusted the tires to was aerating the pond with an old Ford tractor. He had what looked like a giant screw gear attached straight into the drive joint, and he'd backed up and dropped it into a pond and was churning the water with it.

"What the hell's he doing?" Larry asked just generally. Larry clearly knew next to nothing about anything.

Skeeter told him, "Oxygen's low."

Larry said, "Oh," like a man who wasn't better informed but had just moved on already.

Larry gave us a tour of the tractor shed, which took about half a minute. Then we all climbed up and looked in the trailer.

"That's not six hundred tires."

"You can't know that," Larry told me. "I had a guy figure it for me."

"Wasn't Rain Man." I tallied up a couple of rows and multiplied them out. "Two fifty, maybe. Two seventy-five."

Larry just told me back, "Naw."

"Unload them at fifty apiece and get out," I told him and then said to Desmond, "Let's just get our thirty back. They can keep the rest."

"Fifty apiece?" Larry shouted at us. "They Michelins, man."

"You ran over a guy with a trailer full of tires that anybody who comes by here can see." I pointed toward the road to head off rebuttal from Larry. "That brings in the police. They've surely got a BOLO out by now. Description of the truck. Description of the trailer, and here the damn thing sits. And we don't even know yet who you stole it from. It seems pretty unlikely he'll just stay up there in West Memphis and take it."

"Don't worry about him. Half in the grave." Larry looked to Skeeter for confirmation, and Skeeter nodded.

"What do you mean?" Desmond asked him.

"Sick," Larry said and shrugged. "Got other shit on his mind. He won't be worried about no tires."

"Who?" I asked him.

Larry grinned and pointed at me. "Some white guy." Larry shrugged.

I told Desmond, "I'll check on it. You just get him to cover this up."

Desmond nodded and laid out how life would work for Larry in the coming few days. "Put ten or twelve in a pickup and sell them down south of here. Yazoo City. Vicksburg. Go to Jackson if you have to."

"Ain't got no truck," Larry said.

I couldn't help myself. I pointed at Larry's tricked-out Toyota. "You bought that with our money?"

Larry admired the car. He nodded.

"Tried to tell him," Skeeter mumbled my way.

"Title in it?"

Larry got cagey. "Maybe."

"Give me the keys."

"You ain't got no right to . . ."

I drew back a fist, and Larry dropped like a fainting goat.

"Key's in it," Skeeter told me.

I said to Desmond, "I'll take care of the truck."

The catfish pond boy shut down his tractor, climbed off, and came our way. He was a white guy, a farmer by the looks of him. He had a scraggly beard and a gut and jeans with the outline of a snuff tin on the left back pocket.

"Hey here," he told us. Then him and Larry engaged in some sort of Masonic Def Jam handshake that ended in a hug. They had to have met in Parchman. There was no explaining it otherwise.

"Got a tarp in there?" I asked him.

"Probably scare something up," he said.

I told Desmond, "You do that, and I'll get these boys a truck."

"Don't be coming back here with no goddamn Chevy." Larry had gone all bold now that his prison buddy was at hand.

I hit him anyway, a straight shot to the stomach. When it came to Larry, that was my Masonic Def Jam thing.

I had to think Larry was the one who'd crapped up that Tercel already. He'd spilled Crown Royal or something all over the console, and there were corn chip crumbs and tiny scraps of paper littering the floorboard like he was thinking of building a nest and had started gathering the goods.

So I first had to find the car wash in Belzoni, vacuum that Tercel out, and buy some wipes to tidy it up. Then I drove to a car lot just up 49, near a place called Bellewood. They had a couple of Dodge trucks. I tested both of them. One quit after a half mile. The other had a transmission that sounded like it was made from ball peen hammers. It clanged and rattled every time it even thought about shifting gears.

When I told that fellow, "Nope," he tried to sell me a Galaxy station wagon. It didn't have the suspension to haul around tires, was almost sitting on the ground as it was, but I surely would have loved to have seen Beluga LaMonte rattling around the countryside in it.

So I kept heading north, stopping at car lots. I was a day late for a Ranger up around Isola, and then I struck out east toward Tibbet, where I knew a body man. He'd done a little work on my Ranchero and sometimes had a truck or a car or something for sale.

I was tearing through the countryside, fuming about Larry. I was having a conversation with Desmond in my head, trying to persuade him to my view of in-laws. I had an ex-wife, too, and she had a brother I felt no obligation to help. I sort of glossed over—even alone in Larry's Tercel—the part about him being a Lutheran minister and a narcotic in human form.

I was too busy, consequently, to notice the flashing lights at first. In fact, I didn't see them at all until I'd heard the siren. A couple of short yips snagged my attention, and I told Desmond and me together, "Aw, shit."

I pulled over onto the shoulder. I went digging through the glove box. There was nearly an ounce of pot and a .22 derringer. I finally located the registration shoved behind the passenger's visor.

Officer Tula Raintree bent to peer in at me. "Well now" was all she said.

FIVE

My license was in my wallet. My wallet was in the cup holder of Desmond's car. While Larry's Tercel wasn't stolen outright, the claims of ownership were murky, and civilians were generally discouraged from carrying loaded guns and sacks of weed.

Tula Raintree explained all this to me in patient, officious detail.

When she asked if I had any questions, I showed her my cuffed wrists and just said, "Really?"

"Could have hooked them behind."

True enough. "Yeah, well. Thanks for that," I said.

As cop cars go, her backseat was clean. Either she hadn't picked up any vomiting drunks or seepy meth heads lately or she was a stickler about her county cruiser along with every other thing. I figured the latter, since she seemed to have an eye for criminals in the landscape, so I had to guess she hauled in plenty of riffraff.

"What happened to your truck thing?" she asked me.

That was what most people called it. Ford should have gone with that instead of Ranchero.

"Been riding with a buddy."

"And the Toyota?"

"In-law's car. That stuff's all his. I didn't know what was in it."

I could just see her eyes in the mirror through the Plexiglas divider. Her black hair was braided and coiled in the back with only a wisp or two hanging loose.

"Right," she told me.

"Ask Kendell. He knows me. I used to be a cop."

"Oh yeah?"

"Just taking a break."

She gave me a look. "Right," she said again. The dirty cops were often the ones who ended up taking breaks.

"Can you put this window up a little?" She had them both down all the way in the back, and my eardrums were fairly thumping.

She eyed me in the mirror. "Duponts?"

"This morning." There's only so much Martinizing can do.

The windows stayed where they were.

Given the circumstances, I thought we got on pretty well. That's what I told Kendell, anyway, when he came by to see me on the holding bench. It was an old church pew out in the Greenville precinct hallway. They'd drilled holes in the seat that cuffs would fit through.

"I would have introduced you, you know," Kendell told me. "You didn't need to go to all this trouble."

"Wasn't like that. Beluga." That was all I needed to say.

Kendell groaned and shook his head. He had vast personal experience with Beluga LaMonte. "What's he into now?"

Kendell was about as straight as straight arrows come, so our heart-to-heart out in the hallway couldn't really amount to much. I couldn't let him know that me and Desmond had bankrolled Beluga's heist.

"Laying around. Borrowing money from Shawnica, who's getting it from Desmond. Says he needs it for clothes, for interviews and shit, but it's mostly going for reefer and all the usual Larry crap."

"Like that car?"

I nodded. "Bought it from some fool on time. I was trying to take it back."

Tula stepped out into the hall. She saw me and Kendell in conversation and went back into the squad room.

"What are we going to do?" Kendell asked me.

"I don't want to send Larry back up. Think of what that'd do to Shawnica and what Shawnica would do to Desmond." Mostly I didn't want Kendell getting any sort of whiff of Larry and Skeeter's truckload of tires.

"So the reefer's on you?"

"Can't I just have the gun and maybe the ticket instead?"

"Reefer's got to go somewhere."

"Commode's all right with me."

Kendell just smiled and shook his head.

"How much weight?" I asked him.

"Under a quarter. Hardly more than dust."

That's not what I'd seen in the glove box. That much I knew for certain. If Kendell had dumped the bulk of it out, he sure didn't give anything away. That wasn't his style, though. He was a committed Lord's will sort of guy.

"Just going to fine me, right?"

"Got any warrants out on you?" Kendell was kidding, but hell, you never know.

I shook my head. "Can I beat the shit out of Larry?"

"Let Desmond. You can watch, though."

"He won't do it. Shawnica'll keep him from it. She's a witch or something. I haven't quite figured it out."

"Well." Kendell stood up. "Go on, but don't kill him."

"He just falls down when you hit him. He's even shiftless in a fight."

Kendell made his usual going-about-my-business noises.

I was going to ask him to put in a good word for me with officer Tula Raintree—let her know I wasn't some nutty low-life she'd be pulling and citing in a regular way—but I got the feeling, given the reefer she'd dumped, she might have figured that out already. That's what I'd decided to believe, anyway, by the time she joined me on the bench.

There was just one other guy, a scrawny oldster at the far end who was coming out of his shoes at the soles and smelled almost as bad as a Dupont.

"You all right, Teddy?" she asked him.

Teddy said something back. A few more teeth and a little less fortified wine would have helped.

"Throws rocks," she told me of Teddy. "Usually at the Methodist church."

Teddy, as if on cue, broke monumental wind. He told us, "Ha!"

Officer Raintree gave me my paperwork. I looked it over. The pot was down to a trace, and the derringer was written up "unloaded." I was still going a solid thirty over the posted speed.

"Kendell tells me you're a stickler," I said to her as I signed the charge sheet.

"I pick my spots."

I raised my cuffed hand as far as I could and rattled the chain. "I'm not this guy. You know that, right?"

She sort of nodded, almost smiled. "Kendell tells me stuff, too."

It was sort of like a first date, and I thought we were only halfway through it when she walked with me out to the street. We stopped in the shade of an ancient live oak. The precinct house in Greenville was on a formerly grand boulevard in a formerly sizable city that was dying with precious little grace. The air was hot and stank of fertilizer. A sedan rolled by and bottomed out in a pothole. Aside from me and Officer Raintree, there wasn't anybody else around.

I was going to offer to buy her lunch or something, but I was a touch too slow to talk.

"See ya," she told me. "Slow it down a little."

"You're not taking me back?" I was a good twenty miles from Larry's Tercel on the shoulder.

She stood there eyeing the middle distance like she was weighing her options. She finally told me, "Nope." She smiled. She climbed the stairs and went inside.

When I couldn't reach Desmond, I called Pearl instead.

She happened to be in Greenville already with one of her ladies groups. Cards or garden society or maybe even Presbyterians. She told me when I climbed in, but there was so much attendant prattle that the bare facts got swamped, undone, and washed away.

Pearl was wearing enough knockoff Chanel to keep her from smelling the Dupont on me, and she never even asked what I was doing in Greenville or why she'd picked me up in front of the police station. She pointed out empty storefronts all the way out of town and told me who'd occupied them through the years and what they'd sold.

Pearl was an appalling driver, a two-footer, a drifter, an incoherent speeder. She'd race to stop signs and dawdle on open straightaways. I didn't ride with her much. A trip with Pearl always had a curative effect. This day, I found myself doing probably a little more steering than Pearl. She'd get off on a story and veer from her lane. I'd reach over and pull us back. Our trip was a series of avoided head-on collisions and near sideswipes.

With every calamity we dodged, Pearl would giggle and say, "Oh my."

It was the Delta belle in her that made her try to be girlish, even in her seventies. She and her friends all dressed young in flouncy blouses. They wore their hair in elaborate upswept dos, and they were more flirty and off-color with their chatter than the vast run of Presbyterians care to be. It was a Delta thing, I had to figure. They had cotillions in their pasts and had spent their early, glamorous years as princesses of the place. Now they held fast to the memories to the point of strangulation.

Pearl laid a hand to my thigh and finally asked me, "What

in the world are you doing out here?" She didn't mean a thing by it. That was just the way that Pearl and her girlfriends were.

"Helping Desmond out," I told her.

"Just saw his girlfriend," she said and pointed.

"Shawnica?"

"The skinny, loud one?"

I nodded.

Pearl shook her head. "Not her."

"What girlfriend?"

"Works at Zelda's."

I must have looked baffled.

"Back by the levee. You'd never go in there. All shoes and handbags and underthings."

"What's her name?"

Pearl shook her head. She very nearly clipped a combine that was taking up the majority of the road. It was my fault chiefly. I'd been distracted and a little hurt by the notion that Desmond had kept a romance from me. Especially considering that we were currently all tied up with his ex-wife.

"Pretty girl," Pearl said. "Might drop a few pounds." Pearl said that about most everybody because she was naturally emaciated. She thought that was a look most everybody would be best advised to aim for. "You don't know her?"

I shook my head.

"Funny."

"Yeah." I pointed out Larry's Tercel on the shoulder. "Funny."

Pearl rolled up behind Larry's Toyota and banged it with her bumper. That was business as usual for Pearl. She was a contact parker.

She let me out and asked me the shortest way back to Indianola.

I pointed. "Straight to 49 and then left."

She wiggled her fingers and told me, "Toodles."

She pulled out in front of a bread truck and turned right about a half mile down the road.

I found a car lot on the truck route on the river side of Leland. The guy had pennants strung and a sort of picnic tent set up by the road. He had a bright yellow helium blimp tethered over his lot. It was bucking in the breeze. He was sitting in the tent shade sweating and waving at passing traffic. When I got there, his promotion consisted of him, his rat terrier, and me.

He offered me a go-cup full of iced tea, and I took it. The cups were embossed with crossed checkered flags and the words SPEEDY'S MOTORS.

"You Speedy?" I asked him.

He shook his head and swabbed his neck. "Weren't never no Speedy."

"Then why not just Speedy Motors?"

He said something to his dog I couldn't quite make out. Then he turned back to me. "You want a car or something?"

He wasn't thrilled to hear I'd come for a swap. He groused about it as he circled Larry's Tercel and soaked it in. He lifted the hood, then stuck his head through the passenger window and surveyed the interior.

"Title clean?"

I nodded.

He eyed the shiny Rolls-Royce grille. "I don't know. Guess the niggers'll buy it. Key in it?"

I nodded again. The guy who wasn't Speedy climbed in, started Larry's car up, and tore out onto the truck route. I could still hear him winding the gears when he was probably a half mile away.

His terrier came over and sniffed me. Duponts. He backed off with a growl.

The guy who wasn't Speedy traded straight up for a Chevy pickup. He was willing to go for a Ford, but I knew Larry would like a Chevy less. It was their pint-sized model and was a little rusted out from hauling fertilizer. The radio didn't work and the compressor was dead, so Larry and Skeeter wouldn't have any air-conditioning or music. All in all, it was a fitting vehicle for a worthless layabout.

The guy who wasn't Speedy wanted fifty dollars from me. When I asked him why, he said, "Got to get something out of the deal."

"You're getting that," I told him and pointed at Larry's Tercel.

"You know what I mean." He rubbed his fingertips together in the universal sign for lucre. "Got to feed Homer." The terrier barked. We settled on twenty-five.

Rats or something had built a nest back under that Chevy's dashboard. They'd gotten insulation from somewhere, and it kept boiling out as I drove. I was coughing like a miner by the time I got to Indianola.

Desmond was just where I expected to find him, in his spot at the Sonic. Larry was riding shotgun. Skeeter was pitched up between the seats watching Desmond demonstrate how to dress a Coney Island. Like Kendell and like Tula Raintree, Desmond was a stickler, too, but he concentrated the bulk of his stickling on his hot dogs. He couldn't do much about the rest of the world, but he could control his ketchup and relish.

I pulled in beside them and blew the horn. They all glared at me at first. Particularly Desmond. Horn blowing wasn't acceptable Sonic etiquette. Then they saw who it was, and only Larry continued to have a fit.

"Shit, man," he told me.

He came out of Desmond's Escalade to survey what he knew must be his Chevy.

Beluga LaMonte shook his head and groaned. "What did I tell you? What did I tell him?"

Skeeter said, "No Chevy."

I shrugged and tossed Larry the keys. "Best I could do."

"Shit," Larry told me. He eyed his new wheels. "Shit," Larry told me again.

"We're going to check on that trailer in two days' time, and it'd better be half empty," I said.

Larry huffed and looked exasperated. He glanced at Desmond, who nodded.

"What's your damn hurry?"

"Day after tomorrow. Got it?" Larry just looked at me. "Got it?" Skeeter nodded. "Go on," I told them.

With a show of distaste, Larry climbed into the Chevy. Skeeter gathered their lunch and joined him as Larry fired the engine up. That Chevy smoked a little. It chugged. It was hitting on most of its cylinders but in no useful sequence.

"Ain't no tunes," Larry told me. "And what's this shit?" He showed me a tuft of insulation.

"See you Thursday," I said.

Larry found reverse, and they went sputtering out of the place.

"What took you?" Desmond asked me. He had a mouthful of hot dog by then.

"Took a while to find a truck. Got arrested." Desmond stopped chewing. "Kendell didn't call you?"

He shook his head. "Arrested for what?"

"The shit in Larry's car."

Desmond chewed some more and squinted at me.

"Sack of pot. A gun."

Desmond managed a nod. "He kind of remembered after you'd left."

"Kendell says I can't kill him."

"Kendell's like that."

"Why didn't you tell me about your girlfriend? The one in Greenville. I've got to be hearing this shit from Pearl?"

That caught Desmond by surprise. He studied his Coney Island. He took a huge, deliberate bite. He chewed for a quarter minute before he asked me, "What girlfriend's that?"

"The one at the shoe store. Pearl knows all about her, and here I'm doing shit still for Shawnica."

This was about as close as me and Desmond ever came to arguing. He ate a curly fry and weighed his options.

"Ain't my girlfriend. I just see her sometimes. Church friend," Desmond told me. He went to a Pentecostal place up the road in Moorhead when he was feeling especially sinful or his mother was too much of a trial. He'd go off and pray or just sit for three hours in the sanctuary where the bishop who ran the place would tell his flock what appalling sinners they were.

I'd gone to a service once with Desmond. He was having some sort of crisis, a blend of blood pressure trouble and Shawnica. He'd parked on a pew and dropped off to sleep. I'd stayed awake for the music and the testimony. The sermon wore me out a little, a fractured bit of business about end times and homosexuals. I came away believing there'd be no mincing when the final trumpet blew.

"Why didn't you tell me about her?"

Desmond shrugged. "Sorry," he said. "Probably should have."

"Don't want to hear stuff like that from Pearl."

"How does she know?"

"Given that her ears are ornamental, I can't say, but she knows, all right."

"My momma probably."

"She knows, too?"

Desmond nodded.

"Tell me this means you're putting Shawnica behind you. And that goddamn Larry."

"Trying," Desmond told me.

"They get these tires all sold, we're done? Right?"

Desmond nodded. That took the sting out of the secret girlfriend a little.

"Want to give me a bite? I'm starving."

Desmond was spreading relish on his second Coney Island. He looked from me to the dog and back again. He finally told me, "No."

SIX

Skeeter and Larry had both been pals in Parchman with a guy called Izzy. He was nervous and scrawny and got along by being agreeable. He was the sort of inmate who'd get you what you needed or find somebody who could.

Izzy was from Oklahoma or somewhere, not the Delta, anyway. He was a meth cooker when he first got arrested. Then he was a burglar. Then he was an arsonist. Then he was a vagrant and a meth cooker again. Kendell had considerable experience with him, didn't put much stock in Izzy. Izzy was one of those guys you were better off doubting because he couldn't tell anything straight.

So when Kendell called me a couple of days after I'd traded in Larry's Tercel and told me, "Got something from Izzy you might want to hear," I got a bad feeling because Izzy usually trafficked in stuff nobody anywhere would want to know about.

It was our day to catch up with Skeeter and Larry. I was due to pick up Desmond at Kalil's. He was checking on repo jobs between Indianola and Belzoni. Desmond was efficient that way. As long as we were driving by, we might as well scuff up whoever had gotten behind and needed scuffing.

Desmond had a couple of possibles by the time I found him at the counter with Kalil.

"Did you tell him we're through with Duponts?"

Desmond nodded.

I said to Kalil, "I had to throw my clothes away."

Kalil shook his head and threw up his hands in his usual show of exasperation.

I nudged Desmond. "Wrinkle," I told him. "Take what you've got and let's go."

On the way to Greenville in my Ranchero I told Desmond everything Kendell had told me.

"Little guy with the twitch?"

I nodded.

"What do you figure?"

"Must be some kind of Skeeter and Larry shit. Otherwise, Kendell wouldn't have bothered."

"Think Izzy gave it up to Kendell? The whole damn thing?"

"If he did, me and you don't know shit. Larry needed money, and we made a loan. Shawnica's brother and all that. We didn't ask him any questions."

"He won't buy it," Desmond told me.

"Might if it's all we give him."

We eased our way into Greenville proper practicing what we'd say. It had been the grandest of Delta towns back when the cotton went out on the river and the steamboats called in a regular sort of way. It was still beautiful with its wide boulevards and massive live oak canopies if you squinted and managed to close off the rot and the barrenness of the place. The churches were still operating. The storefronts were half empty. What had once been sprawling hotels by the levee were more plywood than glass these days.

I was hoping I might run into Officer Raintree and let her get a look at me uncited and unarrested. When I'd rolled out of bed, I'd put on better clothes just on the outside chance that I'd be racing along somewhere and she'd come up behind me. She wasn't around, though. The culprits pew was empty in the hallway. We found Kendell at the desk he kept in the squad room. He didn't use it much, preferring to be in his cruiser out on the prowl. He wasn't looking to hit his twenty and retire. Kendell was keen to make earthly improvements, while me and Desmond, in this instance, were doing what we could to nudge things the other way.

"What's up?" I asked him.

He shook his head. "Not here."

There were only a couple of clerks around and one tubby lieutenant I saw sometimes at the tamale hut in Greenwood. Kendell stood up and motioned for us to follow him. We went not just into the hallway but out of the building and back to the street.

"What's Larry into?" That was for either of us to take.

I gave Kendell my best blank shrug.

Desmond said, "Shawnica's Larry?"

Kendell applied to Desmond a hard once-over before he nodded sharply once.

Then Desmond shrugged and looked at me.

I said to Kendell, "Best ask Larry."

We were poor thespians. Kendell exhaled and said, "All right." He stepped to his cruiser and opened the driver's door. "Follow me over," he said.

"We're fucking awful," I told Desmond once we'd climbed in my Ranchero. "You especially. *Shawnica's Larry?*"

"Ain't like there's only one Larry around."

Kendell headed out Washington toward the truck route.

"Where the hell's he going," I said.

Desmond just shook his head. We followed Kendell east on the truck route and then north on 61 all the way up to the town of Cleveland, about thirty miles altogether. Then Kendell turned back east on Route 8 and whipped in at the Bolivar County Medical Center, where we parked alongside him in the lot.

I climbed out from behind the wheel, pointed at the building, and said to Kendell, "Izzy?"

He nodded. "Got beat half to death."

"You thinking Larry did it?" Desmond asked him.

Kendell shook his head. "I'm thinking Larry's next."

Kendell talked us onto the proper floor, not ICU exactly but close enough. The nurse at the desk, a brittle woman in a sky blue cardigan, gave Kendell the stink eye. She didn't appear to have any use for cops.

"Washington County," she said and looked us over like we'd come from Lapland and were dressed in reindeer fur. "Stay here."

She went down the hall and ducked into a room, came back shortly and told us, "Five minutes." She walked us down to the door she'd just come out of and tapped her wrist to make us mindful of the time as we walked in.

It was a double room. There was a greenish guy in the bed nearer the door. He had drips going in and oxygen, and he was about as dusty sage as a human can get. He looked at us as we crossed toward Izzy's bed over by the window. He said something, I had to think, by the way he clouded up his oxygen mask.

My first impression of Izzy was that he was cleaner than I'd ever seen him. They'd shaved off all his hair just to stitch up his head. He had a cast on one leg, and it was up in traction. His left wrist was broken. His right wrist, too, and a bunch of fingers judging from the plaster and the splints. Both of his eyes were black. He had stitches along his jawline and some kind of drainage tube coming out of a hole in his chest.

"Sweet Lord," Desmond said at the sight of him. It was about the only thing fitting to say.

Izzy grinned at us, revealing a couple of broken teeth.

"Who did this?" I asked. I directed the question at Kendell, but Izzy volunteered an answer that I couldn't begin to make out. Part toothlessness and part Percocet. He laughed and drooled in closing. Then he tried to scratch his nose and about clubbed himself unconscious. Izzy's twitchy nervousness didn't blend well with narcotics.

"They found him like this in the road."

"Where?" Desmond asked.

"Out by Laughlin," Kendell told us. "Mile or two from his place."

"Somebody toss him out of a car?" I wanted to know.

"Eventually," Kendell said.

He pulled a notepad out of his back pocket. He flipped it open and read out injuries like they were menu specials. "Sixty-seven stitches. Eight broken fingers. Two broken wrists. One fractured forearm. A leg busted in two places. One broken foot." Kendell reached over and uncovered what I'd taken for Izzy's good leg. "A bunch of busted teeth. Collapsed lung or something. Cop I was talking to couldn't say."

"What's this got to do with Larry?" Desmond asked.

"Getting to that," Kendell told him. That was the stickler in Kendell. You couldn't hope to hurry him up. He did things in the order he saw fit. "The cop that found him asked Izzy to describe who did it. The boy can draw a little, so he took down the details and went ahead and made a sketch, too."

Kendell pulled a lone folded sheet of paper from his front shirt pocket and handed it to Desmond. He opened it up, looked at it, handed it to me. It was a girl of some sort in what looked to me like a prep school uniform, right down to the socks and shiny patent leather shoes. She had short black hair. Nose studs. Eyebrow rings. A tattoo on her neck. The drawing made her look petite.

I held up the sketch so Izzy could see it. "She did this?"

Izzy nodded. Izzy told me, "Eeahh."

"Who'd she have with her?"

Izzy shook his head.

"Just her," Kendell told us. "She chatted Izzy up at the

grocery store. Asked him for a ride. Checkout girl remembered her, said that was pretty close."

"Still don't see what this got to do with Larry," Desmond said.

Kendell was ready now. "That's all she wanted from Izzy. Wanted to know where Larry was."

"Izzy wouldn't tell her?" I asked Kendell, eyeing Izzy's battered body up and down. "Or Izzy didn't know?"

"Told her what he could. Must have sent her over where Shawnica used to live."

"Place in Sunflower?" Desmond asked.

Kendell nodded. Shawnica had moved out six months back. Fight with the landlord. Fight with the neighbors. She was a bad one for quarrels and hard feelings.

"What happened over there?" I asked Kendell.

He consulted his pad. "Mrs. Ruth Marie Messick. She's in the ICU in Ruleville."

"Same shit?"

"Same shit," he told me.

Me and Desmond eyed each other. Kendell saw us do it. He just stood by and waited. Kendell was awfully gifted at that sort of thing.

"Think Ruth Marie Messick knows where Shawnica went?" I asked Desmond.

"Doubt it."

"Fifty-three-year-old white woman," Kendell said. "Not even conscious yet."

"What the hell's that girl want with Larry?" Desmond asked like he couldn't imagine the answer.

"That's kind of what I was hoping to know," Kendell told us both.

He stood there waiting, giving us time to break. I don't know why we didn't.

"This girl have a car?" I asked Kendell.

"Does now. Ruth Messick's Dodge."

"We'd better find Larry," Desmond said. "No telling what he's up to."

Desmond sold it a little too hard. Kendell told us both, "Yeah, right."

The nurse in the sky blue sweater came back and jabbed her thumb toward the hallway.

Back in the lot, Kendell said to us both, "I don't care much about Larry. He gets what he gets. It's plain to me he's mightily pissed somebody off. But this kicking the shit out of folks between here and him, that's going to stop one way or another."

What could we do but nod and mumble?

"Bring him in," Kendell told us. "You hear me?"

We did. We nodded.

Me and Desmond were leaning against the Ranchero tailgate as Kendell drove away.

"Don't say it," Desmond told me.

"We need a shiftless ex-con in-law policy. Don't you think?"

Desmond grunted.

"We probably ought to start with Shawnica."

"And tell her what?" Desmond asked me.

"Ninja schoolgirl assassin on the loose. It's something she ought to know."

"I'd almost like to see those two go at it."

"Yeah," I said. "Almost."

The clinic where Shawnica worked was just south of Indianola. If I'd had a dog, I wouldn't have taken him into the place on a bet. A fellow who thought Shawnica was a good choice for reception wasn't likely to know the first thing about veterinary medicine.

I parked in the shade and stayed in the car, sent Desmond in alone. He was gone for a good ten minutes before they both came out together. Shawnica was wearing a lab coat covered in, I guess, cat hair, and she was in something far more incendiary than her usual rage, which made it an apocalyptic, endtimes sort of thing.

"What's this *SHIT*?" she was yelling at me as she stalked toward my car.

I climbed out. There wasn't a thing to do but stand before her and take it. You had to hand it to Shawnica. She knew how to pitch a fit.

She waved her arms and sniped at me in that sassy voice of hers. She told me back everything Desmond had just finished telling her in the clinic. Somehow the whole bloody business was our fault.

"We've got to sit Larry down," I told her, "and figure out exactly who he pissed off."

"Who is this bitch?" Shawnica asked me. "She don't want to be finding me."

"Got a gun?" I asked.

Shawnica told me, "Ha!" She pulled a knife out of her

pocket. Springloaded. A mother-of-pearl handle. It opened with a wicked metallic click. She whipped it around so close to my chin I could feel the air of the blade.

"All right" seemed appropriate, so that's what I said. "How about Larry?"

"He's got one of those little guns," she told me.

"A derringer?'

Shawnica nodded. He didn't even have that anymore.

"Did they go to Belzoni this morning?"

"Hell," she told me, "I don't know."

"You don't want to stay somewhere else until we figure out what's what?"

Shawnica gave me one of her primal sneers, folded her knife shut, and went back inside.

Me and Desmond just stood there and watched her go.

"Fiery," Desmond told me like it was something he admired.

"Your church girlfriend got any of that?"

Desmond thought for a moment. "No."

SEVEN

We rode all the way to Belzoni, found the trailer still untarped. There were tires gone from it. That was obvious to us, so we figured Larry and Skeeter were down Delta making sales calls.

"That ought to be enough," I suggested to Desmond, "to keep them out of harm's way for now."

"Who do you figure she is, a girl like that?"

We'd been chewing on the matter in the car. Desmond couldn't wrap his mind around that brand of sadistic violence from a woman. He was old-fashioned that way, I guess, and believed women were better than men. More honorable and decent, less likely to go off. Maybe even squeamish and retiring.

"Might have been some guy in a wig," he suggested.

"And a skirt and knee socks?"

"Why the hell not. It'd be throwing us off. Here we are all looking for a girl."

We went riding around that catfish farm in search of Larry and Skeeter's buddy, but there wasn't any sign of him either, so we headed back toward home.

"I'm just wondering who sent her," I said to Desmond once we were back on 49. "Or *him*."

"It's not like we can say what kind of shit Beluga's been up to," Desmond allowed. "Maybe he pissed somebody off before we ever heard of those tires."

"Maybe. Why don't you try him again?"

Desmond had been dialing Larry all along and just getting the "mobile caller is unavailable" message.

"Ringing," he told me. "Larry?"

I could hear the squeak of a voice on the phone.

"Where are you?"

More squeaky chatter.

"You're breaking up."

No squeak.

"Larry?" Desmond shook his head.

"Where is he?"

"In a fucking Chevy," Desmond told me. "That's all he got out before I lost him."

I dropped Desmond back at Kalil's place so he could pick up his car. It was about quitting time by then, so Kalil was into the Armagnac.

It never seemed to relax him much. His anger just got more scattershot and appreciably less coherent. He'd go from vilifying deadbeats to pitching a fit about crows in his yard. Then he'd complain about the dodgy components in Korean televisions. It was all bilious and hotheaded but didn't really amount to much.

This evening he came out into the lot to yammer at us. He was mad already before Desmond said we'd get to his invoices tomorrow. Desmond told him we'd been tied up with a buddy at the hospital and tried to leave it at that, but Kalil got off on the cost of insurance for him and his employees and something he'd read about a woman who'd gone in for a nose job and ended up getting a kidney taken out.

"Well, all right," I told him and tried to climb into my car, but Kalil had another insurance horror story to share with us. Unfortunately, he couldn't quite remember what it was.

He kept sipping at his go cup and making the odd agitated comment. He was talking to us. He was talking to himself. He didn't seem to notice that me and Desmond were having a side conversation.

"I'm going to go arm up," I said. "Meet you at Shawnica's in about an hour."

"Bring one for me. Momma's got the PPK. Lent the Steyr to a cousin."

"So you've got nothing?"

"Nothing I'd want to depend on."

Kalil had started singing. He was wailing out "Lullaby of Broadway" as we pulled into the street.

Pearl had a serving of casserole for me. She came out to the driveway when she heard me pull in. She'd found that casserole in her freezer, back behind the sherbet and underneath a pie crust.

"Didn't even know it was there," she said.

It wasn't in a proper container, one with a lid, anyway. The plastic wrap was just laying there. The casserole had ice all over it. There was something green in it and something brown in it. Something yellow in it, too.

"Just zap it," Pearl suggested.

I gave her my usual "All right" and threw the stuff into the sink as soon as I'd walked in my apartment.

The more defrosted that casserole got, the less like food it looked. You had to figure the woman in my life who was always giving me dinner would have to be the woman in my life who couldn't cook a lick.

My apartment above Pearl's car shed was just a big room with a full bath off the back. I had a bed and a sofa and a twenty-inch TV, plus a drop-leaf dinette table I could make into something grander if I ever felt the itch to throw a dinner party. Mostly I just piled mail on it. I tended to eat over the sink.

There was an attic space behind a knee wall on the south end of the building, and I kept most of my weapons back there in a big canvas duffel. I crawled in and pulled that duffel out so I could sort through what I had. I couldn't quite say how much firepower might be needed for a ninja schoolgirl. The evidence was she liked her instruments blunt. She'd not plugged anybody yet.

I set aside a couple of pistols and an air-cooled M-4A1 that I'd traded a spanking-new Fryolator for. I had a little Bersa .308 I carried sometimes in an ankle holster, and that seemed like a sensible option given who we were dealing with. It was small caliber but still more firepower than a tattooed girl with a club. By the time I'd packed up what I needed and loaded all the clips I could find, I was beginning to smell Pearl's casserole. Raccoon, I figured. Or maybe goat.

Desmond was already parked outside Shawnica's house when I got there. The front door was shut. The lights were low. There didn't appear to be anybody home. It was late spring twilight, and the mosquitoes were swarming, so we sat in Desmond's Escalade with the windows rolled up and the air conditioner running.

That was one of the leading troubles of the Delta, as far as I could tell. When it was hot, it was too damn hot. When it was cold, it was windy and bitter. When the temperature was tolerable, the bugs made for misery. Lovebugs and mosquitoes mostly, biting flies every now and again, and in such concentrations there wasn't enough DEET on the globe to keep them away.

I got in complaining about the mosquitoes. Desmond had heard it all before. He let me talk. He even watched me like he was listening to me. I finished. He gave a little nod and said, "Heard from Kendell."

"They catch her?"

He shook his head. "But they found that woman's car. Lady beat up over in Sunflower. It was parked at the IGA on Highway 1, over there by Greenville."

"Isn't that where she picked up Izzy?"

Desmond nodded. "Kendell figures she drove in from somewhere. Parked in the lot. Picked up Izzy, rode with him, tore him all to pieces. Took his car to Sunflower and beat up that woman there. Drove her car back out to Greenville to get the one she'd come in."

"Prints or anything?"

"Working on it. Kendell didn't sound too hopeful."

"Why? Did she wipe it down or something?"

"Other way. He said the car was a nasty mess. Woman has dogs or kids or both. He said he wouldn't keep pigs in it."

We both heard the backfire together and turned to see Larry's Chevy truck chugging down the road.

Larry whipped into the yard. The bed was empty. I took that as a good sign. The truck lurched to a stop, and the suspension creaked. Larry piled out and slammed the door. He made a show of brushing the insulation off himself. He hawked and spat. Skeeter climbed out and just leaned on the bed rail and watched him.

"This ain't no way to go," Larry shouted my way and stormed toward his sister's house.

"Pray to Jesus for patience," Desmond told me as he threw open his door.

"How did it go?" I asked Skeeter.

He nodded. "Everybody wants them."

We made for the house with Skeeter just behind us. Larry had already turned on the television and flopped down onto the couch.

"Where's Shawnica?" he asked Desmond.

"Don't know."

"You didn't bring no beer?"

I switched off the TV, and Larry very nearly got up off the couch. He pitched and whined, uncorked an additional Chevy complaint.

Once he'd stopped to draw breath, I told him, "We've got a problem."

Larry nodded. "I ain't got no supper."

Desmond said, "Somebody's looking for you."

"Who?"

Desmond described the creature, right down to the eye rings and the nose studs and the elaborate neck tattoo. I watched Larry, glanced at Skeeter. The girl wasn't ringing any bells.

"What the hell she want?" Larry asked us.

"You in the ground, sounds like," I told him. "She found your buddy Izzy. Broke him all to pieces."

"A girl," Larry said.

Desmond nodded. "Busted him up pretty bad." Desmond described the sack of fractured bones we'd seen at the hospital. "You're just lucky he didn't have anything to give up."

"A girl?" Larry muttered. "She don't want no piece of me."

"The woman in the house where Shawnica used to live? Sent her to the hospital, too," I told Larry.

"Whose tires did you steal?" Desmond asked him.

"What did you do with my gun?" Larry wanted to know of me.

"Who'd you take them off of?" That was Desmond again.

"Little silver thing in the glove box."

"Gone," I told him. "Weed, too."

Larry had just enough of a fit to let him stay on the sofa to do it. Something on the order of a shiftless seizure.

"Who's after you?" I asked Skeeter this time.

"I don't know them West Memphis boys," he told me.

"Who?" I asked Larry.

Larry picked the one unbroken TV remote and pointed it at the set.

"I'll put that in your colon," I told him.

Larry said to Skeeter, "Shit." He told us, "Bugle's people. Way I figure it, anyhow."

"The kid you ran over," Desmond said.

Larry nodded.

"Bugle what?" I asked Larry.

"Shambrough," Larry said. Desmond and Skeeter knew enough to groan.

"Shambrough?" I said. "Who's that?"

Desmond, who'd been all over me to take it easy on Larry, stepped over to the sofa, picked Larry up, and tossed him into the kitchen.

"Shambrough?" I said to Skeeter.

He shook his head. He looked deflated and more than a little unnerved. "Don't want to be messing with them."

"Well, we're kind of in the middle of messing with them, aren't we?"

Skeeter showed me both of his palms at once. "Didn't know nothing about it."

Larry yelled at Desmond, gathered himself, and came back into the front room. Desmond snatched him up and pitched him straight back into the kitchen again.

"Who are these people?" I asked Desmond.

Even he didn't want to say.

"Some kind of Arkansas mob?"

Larry was stirring. Desmond told him, "I'd stay in there."

"Business people, right? Let's just square it with them."

"They're not business people," Desmond told me. "They're Shambroughs."

"What the hell does that even mean?"

"You can't square shit with those people, and you sure as

hell don't fuck with them," Desmond shouted into the kitchen.

Desmond charged into the kitchen and pitched Larry into the living room. Another hour or two of that, and I'd probably have to intercede.

"Bunch of cons?" I asked.

"Worse," Desmond told me. "Been around here forever. They own a big spread. Pass for decent people. Got enough money to make us all disappear."

I didn't like the sound of that. At least you knew where you stood with cons. Vicious bastards all dolled up and walking on their hind legs presented another problem altogether.

I was about to quiz Desmond and Larry and Skeeter further about the Shambroughs when the door spring twanged and the door jerked open. I pulled my Ruger out of my waistband. Desmond did the same with the Glock I'd lent him, and we brought both barrels to bear on Shawnica. She was standing in the doorway with a number-ten can full of tamales, a sack of saltines, and a bottle of Russian dressing—the traditional Delta accompaniment.

She looked from Desmond to me and back to Desmond. She told us both, "Uh-huh."

EIGHT

Frightened wasn't one of Shawnica's emotions. She was partial to incensed. She informed us there wasn't a white girl on the planet who could drive her out of her house. To his credit, Larry knew to stay wherever Shawnica was, and Skeeter decided he'd stick by as well. Shawnica had a shotgun in the kitchen closet. We cleaned it up, loaded it, and put it out where they could get it. Then me and Desmond left them for the night.

"Why didn't you tell her who was behind it?" I asked Desmond out in the yard.

"She'd kill Larry," he told me, "and we don't need him dead just yet."

"Where do they live?" I asked him. "The Shambroughs."

"Come on."

I followed Desmond back into Indianola, west through

town on the truck route and then south just shy of Leland on the Tribbett road to a place called Geneill. They had a sign, anyway, and an old commissary building overgrown with creepers and collapsed on one end. There was a cinder shoulder just beyond it where we could both pull off. I eased in behind Desmond and followed him on foot back up the road.

"They call it Eponia, or something like that." He pointed across what looked like a wheat field. I couldn't really tell my crops apart in the dark. There was enough moonlight to illuminate the white clapboards. It was a sprawling plantation house set well back across the field in what looked like an oak grove. The windows were lit. We heard a hound bark. A screen door slapped against the jamb. Even in the dark and well away across the field, it looked like a grand old pile.

"Homeplace?" I asked Desmond.

"Uh-huh. Shambroughs built it probably a hundred and fifty years ago now. They owned everything around here for miles. But this new batch, they don't farm. Sold off big chunks. Leased out the rest."

"What are they into mostly?"

"Big on stealing shit, the way I hear it."

"You mean like . . . tires?"

Desmond grunted. He appeared to be nodding. "Started with barge loads of fertilizer. That's the story, anyway. Coal. Fuel oil. Got to where they'd take any damn thing."

"Take it where?" I asked Desmond.

"I don't know. Had crews and stuff to move it, and then the shipping folks started paying them to leave them alone."

"Protection?"

Desmond nodded.

"So now they're down to stealing whatever they don't get paid not to steal?"

"Something like that. Guess the tire people got behind."

"How many of them are there?"

We could occasionally hear voices drifting our way from the big house on the breeze.

"Mr. Lucas runs the show. He's got a brother in New Orleans or somewhere who's into shit down there and a couple of boys, I think, around here somewhere. Maybe down by Yazoo City. He's got crews of locals. Hoyts and Tuttles mostly. They've been working for Shambroughs since back when they used to farm."

"Anybody up in West Memphis?"

"Must have. Don't know for sure. That Bugle must be one of his."

"Think the ninja schoolgirl's contract work?"

Desmond nodded. "They're proper people as far as it goes. The studs and the tats and every damn thing pierced—that ain't Shambroughs at all."

"Think we ought to fill Kendell in?"

Even in the dark I could tell Desmond was looking at me like he'd decided I was daft. "He'd lock Larry up. Skeeter, too. Maybe even you and me."

"We might all be safer in jail. No ninja schoolgirl. No Shawnica."

Desmond gave it a moment's placid thought before he told me, "Naw."

We'd been standing outside in the open air a good ten

minutes by then, and I hadn't swatted a single mosquito. They just weren't anywhere around.

"How come I'm not getting chewed up?"

"Overspray," Desmond told me. "They've killed everything to the road."

The Delta could be so alive in spots—so snaky and bug-ridden and verdant—that I forgot sometimes it was a poisoned place at heart. The sky was full of crop dusters for three-quarters of the year. I spent more time than I cared to think about washing overspray off my Ranchero. The tang of fertilizer, pesticide, and defoliant in the air was the constant perfume of the Delta.

"So what do we do?" I asked Desmond.

"Get rid of those tires. Dump that trailer. Get Skeeter and Larry some damn place else."

We parted company out there on Geneill Road. Desmond headed back toward Indianola, but I went another way and got on the route that would take me past Officer T. Raintree's house. I rode by going one way, turned around, and came back. Then I pulled up and parked just across the street.

Her small house was lit up throughout. It made quite the contrast with the Shambroughs' sprawling pile of a place in its grove. I could see the shifting light from the TV and the top of Tula's son's head as he ran back and forth across the front room before the picture window.

Then Tula showed up to give him what looked, from where I was, like a talking-to. She was wearing a T-shirt and jeans, had unclipped her hair and let it fall. All that womanliness she kept bottled up to make life possible on the job was on display through her picture window as she told her son a thing or two. About being a little man, I had to guess. About going to bed when she said so.

I sat there and watched until I felt a little creepy at it. Then I started up the engine and eased off, turned my lights on down the road. I tried to pretend as I drove toward home that I didn't know what I'd do in the morning. That I'd not settled on my usual way of dealing with upset in my life. But I knew. I only had a couple of gears, and I was partial to the one that involved blundering dead ahead.

With my mind made up, I slept well enough. I strapped on my Bersa when I got dressed, and I called Desmond to get a read on what he thought we ought to be up to. He wanted us helping Skeeter and Larry to hurry up and dump those tires. He figured we could make Kalil's collections going down and coming back.

"Sounds good," I told him. "I'll meet you in Belzoni. I promised Pearl I'd carry her to her doctor this morning."

"She okay?" Desmond asked me.

"Female thing," I said, knowing that was sure to shut Desmond up.

Desmond's mother had passed the previous year through a regular female-thing minefield, and Desmond had gotten to where he'd sooner stick his hand in a bucket of moccasins than have to even think about a gynecologist again.

I drove straight over to Geneill Road and parked where me and Desmond had parked. I walked down past the commissary for a look at the Shambrough place in the daylight. I could see where the roof was patched and the paint was coming off the siding. The yard looked a little ragged, and they had dead limbs in their trees. So they weren't superhuman after all but just as half-cocked and neglectful as everybody else.

I went back to my Ranchero, started it up, and made my way straight over to the Shambroughs' gravel driveway. They had a sign out by the end of it, a few yards off the road, a raw cypress plank suspended by chains with the name of the plantation burned into it. Not anything like Eponia. The place was called Elysium.

There was no gate. I drove straight down to the house. There were the usual trucks and 4×4s parked in front of the place. A two-car garage off the north end off a sunroom had both of its doors raised to reveal two bays full of packaged merchandise, no room at all for cars. I saw what looked like about fifty food processors, twice as many dehumidifiers, a few dozen window air-conditioning units, and several of what appeared to be boxed up sewing machines.

A hound came over from the side yard, crept up to me like it was used to getting kicked. It blinked that way battered dogs do, rolled over and showed me its belly. The creature was hanging with plump tics. I guess there are some things even crop dusters can't kill. I gave it a rub anyway, and it wriggled in gratitude.

The front porch wrapped around and was thick with ferns. There was a stack of yellowed newspapers on the glider. I knocked on the door screen but couldn't raise much racket and so pulled it open and banged the big bronze knocker a few times.

A small black woman with sleepy eyes and a lavender maid's uniform finally unbolted the door and drew it open.

She just stood there looking at me like I'd made some horrendous mistake. Either nobody ever used the front door or no one was fool enough to just come knocking.

"I'm here to see Mr. Shambrough," I said.

"Mr. Lucas?" The pitch and rasp of her voice was surprising. She sounded just like Miles Davis.

"Right," I told her.

She looked me over one time further and shut the door.

I could hear the floorboards creak as she exited the hallway. Then there was nothing for a while but the occasional whimper of the Shambrough hound. The dog knew enough to stay down in the yard and not venture onto the porch. I parked on the glider. I waited. I read a week-old *Clarion-Ledger*. Finally I heard the floorboards pop and squeak and the front door swing open again.

I got up off the glider and went back over. The maid told me, "Come on."

I stepped inside and followed her. That house was built on a scale you just don't see much anymore. A staircase swept up out of the foyer to a grand mezzanine. The ceiling was probably forty feet away. The walls were hung with taxidermy and formal portraits of long-dead Shambroughs. Grandma on one side and the business end of a black bear on the other. There was a sideboard along the south wall with a stuffed albino raccoon parked on it.

I followed that maid to the parlor doorway. She pointed inside and looked at me with all the warm humanity she probably mustered for a chicken before she shoved it in the oven.

"Thanks," I told her and stepped into the parlor.

She snorted at me by way of reply.

The room was decorated like a Tennessee Williams fever dream. More taxidermy. More portraiture. Bronzes all over the place—horses and wolves and Indian chiefs and noble-looking hounds. Every tabletop, every shelf. There were even a few on the floor. I could readily see that the maid, aside from doing a splendid Miles Davis impression, didn't waste too terribly much of her time with the feather duster. But then the blinds kept the room in half light, so it probably looked cleaner than it was.

I heard a toilet flush, the sound of water running. A door on the far wall swung open, and out came Lucas Shambrough (I had to figure) in pajamas and a bathrobe. A silk bathrobe that he was cinching shut as he stepped into the parlor.

I don't know what I'd expected, but I'd not quite expected him. He was wearing a Texas Rangers ball cap. He had stringy gray hair and chin stubble. He looked about sixty to me.

He reached up and shoved at one of his bicuspids with his thumb. "Goddamn tooth's killing me" was the first thing that he said.

He stopped behind a massive oak desk in the far corner of the room.

"Do I know you?"

I told him, "No sir."

He sat down and shouted, "Flora!"

The maid from before showed up in the doorway. "Toast or something," he told her. She turned and went back out.

The Shambrough place felt like one of those houses where nobody bothered to stir before noon.

"Do I want to know you?"

"Probably not."

"Figures." He was piddling around with the clutter on his desk, opening drawers and shutting them. I half expected him to pull out a pistol, shoot me twice, and have me stuffed.

He just yelled again, "Flora!"

The maid showed up.

"Where's my damn . . ." He plucked up a pair of spectacles and waved them at her. "Go on."

She went.

"So?" he said.

"Here about some tires."

He put on his glasses, well down his nose, and studied me over top of them.

"Service station's up the road."

"Michelins," I told him. "Whole trailer full. A couple of fellows I know drove the thing off by mistake."

"Mistake?"

"That's what I'm hearing."

"I just might want to talk to those boys."

"They'd be nervous about that. That's why I'm here."

"You don't get nervous?" he asked me.

"No cause. I didn't take anything."

"But you know the wrong people."

"Have a knack for that."

Only once he'd glanced past me did I realize we weren't alone. She was in a bathrobe, too. It wasn't a wig. She wasn't a guy. Her jet-black pageboy was a little out of whack. He must have called her somehow—a button on his desk or something—because she looked like she'd been summoned out of bed and wasn't happy about it.

"Friend of mine," Lucas Shambrough told me.

I gave her my best oblivious smile and said, "Hello."

She shoved a hand in her bathrobe pocket and closed on me slowly across the parlor like she was just wandering my way and had no intentions about me at all.

"This is Mako," Lucas Shambrough told me.

I gave her a smile and a nod.

"Used to be Aurora or something."

She said, "Isis."

Lucas Shambrough chuckled and shook his head. "These damn kids."

She wasn't a kid, though. She had the tats and the studs and the row of bling pierced into her eyebrow, but she looked well into her thirties once you got past the hair and the stuff. She was hard like a gym rat or a meth head, all veins and sinews. I could see it in her forearms, in her calves below her robe. She was taller than I expected, about 5'10" I had to guess. She had weird blue eyes. Too blue. When I glanced her way, she opened her mouth, and I could see the stud in her tongue.

She was attractive in an exotic and dangerous sort of way, but you'd probably be safer having sex with a bobcat. She was far too tightly coiled for affection.

I tried not to pay much attention to her, tried to let on to seem comfortable with her in the room. Lucas Shambrough, however, couldn't help himself. He felt like he knew just what was coming. He smiled at me. He smiled at her. It was about to be a far better day than he'd even dared hope.

"Now about those tires," he said to me, I guess by way of distraction.

She was close enough for me to smell her. Last night's bourbon. Bedclothes. A little talc maybe off the robe. I'd singled out the bronze I wanted. It was a setter at full point. Maybe eight inches long, and I counted on gripping that dog right at the haunches. I let her get within arm's reach. I grabbed that setter and wheeled. She was pulling her hand out of her robe pocket. I didn't wait to see what she had. I cracked her across the side of the head with the front end of that setter. She staggered back, pitched over a coffee table, and landed face-down on the floor.

I bent low and pulled my .308 out of my ankle holster before Lucas Shambrough could reach for anything. I stepped over and had the barrel in his ear while he was still groping around in his desk drawer.

He went all cool-under-fire on me. I hate that sort of thing.

"Think I haven't had a gun pointed at me before?"

I didn't bother to answer beyond drawing back and hitting him with the pistol. It knocked his Rangers hat off his head and caused him to tell me, "Ow!"

I hit him again, mostly for dramatic effect. Then I jerked him up by his bathrobe collar and hauled him across the room. The girl was stirring by then. We stopped alongside her.

"Kick her," I told him.

He looked at me and laughed. I swatted him another time with my pistol hand. He laid a foot into her, shoulder height.

"Lower," I said.

He caught her midsection. This was just the sort of sadistic pastime that Shambrough could get interested in. Then he kicked her again without my asking him to, and she rolled over and groaned.

I reached into her bathrobe pocket and came away with a compact Taser. It was heavy and black and looked like something a proper spook would carry.

"Plans for me?" I asked Lucas Shambrough.

He grinned. I hit him again.

Flora was coming with toast when we reached the foyer. She didn't seem terribly surprised that I was manhandling her boss toward the door at gunpoint. Shambrough reached for a slice of toast as we passed her, so I clubbed him another time.

We went out the door and down the steps. When he tried to kick his hound, I walloped him a good one. That broke the shell a little.

"You fucking piece of . . ." he managed to get out before I smacked him one more time.

He went down in Larry fashion, just piled up in the yard. I booted him toward the driveway.

"Now that's how you kick somebody."

He managed to start informing me how goddamn dead I was.

"Cuts both ways," I told him. "Forget those tires and move on while you can."

He started gurgling at me, telling me how it was going to be. I didn't stick around to hear it all. There was a fair bit of mucus to it, but I had the drift by the time I'd climbed into my Ranchero and aimed it up the drive.

Out on the blacktop, I called Desmond to find out where he was.

"Jake Town," he told me. "Plasma TV, but the whole damn trailer's gone."

"That's one way to do it," I said.

"Pearl all right?"

"What if I told you I didn't take Pearl to the doctor? What if I told you I drove out to Shambrough's instead?"

Desmond got real quiet.

"Ask me how it went."

He asked me.

"What's worse than sideways? Upside down?"

Desmond did that thing he gets up to in extremis where he groans and grunts together all at once.

NINE

We rendezvoused at some sort of Sonic knockoff near Belzoni on the Yazoo City Road. They didn't even have a Coney Island. Desmond had opted for the corn dog, which, to judge by his expression, he was not enjoying at all. Since there was no curb service—another disappointment—I found him sitting at a picnic table under a ratty umbrella around back. It was conveniently located next to a sweltering Dumpster that was leaking iridescent juice into the lot.

"What the hell's wrong with you." Desmond said by way of hello.

I shrugged. Didn't know what else to do. "It seemed easier than messing with Larry."

"Did you go in the house?"

I nodded.

"People say he's got a rhino or a camel in there or some-thing."

"White raccoon. Half a bear. Lot of shit nobody dusts."

"What happened?"

I laid it out for Desmond, described the place, the parlor, the conversation. My hopes and dreams going in. Eventually, I got around to the girl.

"Mako?"

I laid her Taser on the table. "Tried to use that on me."

Desmond picked the thing up, examined it. "Where do you even get one of these?"

"Cute, isn't it. Must be how she managed Izzy. Lady in Sunflower, too."

"How did you get away?"

I described the bronze setter.

"Think she'll live?"

I nodded. "She was coming around before he kicked her."

"Why did *he* kick her?"

"I might have asked him to."

Desmond glared at me. He sniffed his corn dog. "How did you leave it with him?"

"He said I was a dead man. Shit like that. You know how they go on."

"They'll be all over this place looking for you." He pointed at my Ranchero. "Drove that over?"

I nodded. Desmond groaned.

"Wasn't a crew around or anything. Just him and her."

"Shambrough hires them as he needs them. Every Delta shithead with a trigger finger'll do whatever he asks."

Desmond tossed his corn dog into the Dumpster without even getting up. "You always do this. You know that, don't you? Go off trying to straighten shit out and make everything that much worse. Remember that guy with the alligator?"

I'd never live that down. When a Mississippi swamp rat tells you he's got an alligator in his bathtub, you'd probably better take him at his word. You don't need to go marching in to see for yourself.

"Technically," I told Desmond like I bothered to tell him sometimes, "that gator wasn't in the tub, and that's how he came out like he did."

Desmond rolled up his trouser leg the way he always rolled it up to show me the scar that gator's tail had left. "You just had to stick your nose in. Shambroughs. Gators. What's the fucking difference?"

"I like to think I'm inquisitive."

I got the grunty groan again.

"Larry and Skeeter still on it?" I asked him.

Desmond nodded. "Headed down toward Vicksburg with a load. At this rate, it'll take us a week to empty that trailer."

"Why don't you and me move a load or two."

"Might as well," Desmond told me. "Glad you got the orange one," he said of my Ranchero. "That'll make us easy to spot."

I followed Desmond out to the catfish pond where the tire trailer was parked. The tarp that friend of Larry's had promised had gotten closer to the trailer. I could see it laying on the ground behind the back tandem wheels.

I looked around the place. Twenty ponds. A bunch of light

boxes and paddles for aerating. No scraggly bearded friend of Larry's as far as I could tell.

"Seen that boy?" I asked Desmond.

Desmond nodded. "Went off after a tractor part or something."

"Do we want to tell him to watch himself or just figure he'll be all right?"

Desmond got that look like he was about to explain how I was four kinds of stupid when an Ag Cat went screaming overhead, probably fifty feet off the ground. They were a common sight in the Delta but could still be a little unnerving when you weren't expecting a plane and one came racing low and fast.

"Shambrough flies," Desmond told me. "You know that, don't you?"

I shook my head. I wasn't up on Shambrough's details.

"Used to be a duster for the hell of it. Story goes he'd load up with Roundup and drop it on people he didn't like. Wipe out their fields to send them a message."

"Worked, I'd bet."

"Ruined a few folks."

"Better than getting shot in the head."

We managed to fit a good dozen tires in the bed of my Ranchero.

"Who gets them?" I asked Desmond.

He had a guy down by Rolling Fork he knew from *inside* (Desmond called it).

"You missed an alimony payment. Spent one night in jail."

"A cell's a cell."

Desmond gave my Ranchero a hard once-over. "I don't even want to ride with you."

"Get in. Shambrough's still picking up his teeth."

Desmond vented more racket as he slipped into the cab. We kind of made up on the way down south. I asked him about his jailhouse buddy. He'd been *inside* on account of a roadhouse fight. Desmond recounted for me the night they'd spent being under the thumb of the Man. All I had to do was drive and take it.

"Welded some tailpipe hangers on for me."

"Touching."

"You got no friends like that."

"You," I told him, "but you can't weld."

Desmond nodded. He said, "Right."

His name was Ricky, and he was a greasy white guy with a shop back behind his house where he installed tires and mufflers and tailpipes. Did brake jobs in a pinch. It looked like he'd blundered into a spot of transmission work that he regretted. As we pulled in, him and a buddy were either dropping a tranny out of an old Ford Bronco or maybe trying to shove a rebuilt one in.

I couldn't really tell because they were mostly just screaming at each other.

"Push it."

"I am."

"No. Push it that way."

"Won't go that way."

Then there'd be some clanging and banging. A hammer is generally a poor choice in transmission tools.

Then there'd be a "Fuck it!" or something in a similar vein and one or both of them would light a cigarette.

It took Desmond a couple of minutes to get his buddy Ricky's attention because the tinny radio was playing country music at full volume. Somebody's hound had died or his wife had gone off in his buddy's truck. Maybe with his hound. Or maybe even the hound was driving. I couldn't make it out for all the fiddle and twangy harmonizing.

Desmond finally went over and kicked the bottom of one of Ricky's shoes. The Bronco was on jack stands, and those boys were both on creepers beneath it. Ricky, of course, lurched up in surprise and banged his head on something dead solid that rang. The catalytic converter, I guessed.

He came out bleeding and furious but calmed down when he saw Desmond.

"Hey here!" he shouted and tried to stanch the blood flow with his sleeve.

Him and Desmond wandered around the shop looking for a clean rag or a paper towel while they caught up on what they'd both been up to since they'd seen each other last. Ricky's buddy rolled out from under the Bronco and looked up at me from his creeper.

"Buddy ever asks you to help him with a damn thing, for the love of Sweet Jesus, don't."

"All right," I told him.

He took a contemplative puff on his cigarette and then rolled back under that Ford.

Desmond's buddy Ricky had found some toilet paper, and him and Desmond were over by Ricky's nasty sink on the far wall. Ricky had a mirror he could almost see himself in, and he was dabbing at his cut. I stayed where I was until Desmond waved me over.

"Tell him," he said to Ricky.

"Heard about your tires."

"Heard what?" I asked him.

"Might run across some Michelins on the cheap." Ricky dabbed. Dirty, bloody tap water ran down to his nose.

"Who told you that?" I asked him.

"Think it was the Snap-on guy."

"Did he say anything else?"

"Tell him," Desmond said.

"He said if you see those Michelins coming, head the other way."

Me and Desmond exchanged sour glances.

"Did he say why?" I asked.

Ricky shook his head. He drew his wet toilet paper away from his cut and had a good look at it.

"Nothing?"

"Just head the other way. I figured the tires were bad or hot or something, and now here you are with a load of them, right?"

Desmond said, "Yeah," and nodded.

"So why don't you tell me."

With a glance, Desmond let me know that would be my job.

"You ever been married, Ricky?" I asked him.

"Married right now," he told me.

"Wife of yours got any brothers?"

He nodded.

"Has she got one that's maybe not worth a happy damn?"

Ricky didn't have to think about that. "Oh yeah," he told us both.

I pointed at Desmond. "He's got one of those."

"These his tires?"

Desmond nodded.

"Stole them?"

Desmond nodded again.

"Who from?"

If a shrug can be a lie, then Desmond told one to his cellmate.

"How much you asking?"

"Fifty for you," Desmond said. I was entirely with him by then, anything to get those Michelins gone.

"How many you got in there?"

"A dozen," I said.

"Check okay?"

Before I could offer that cash would be better, Desmond said, "Oh hell yeah."

We even had to unload them and pack them onto Ricky's tire rack. Ricky examined them as we worked.

"Yeah, I can get these right out of here."

"If you want some more . . ." Desmond started, but Ricky waved a hand and told him, "Naw."

Then Ricky's buddy under the Bronco started putting up a fuss. "We doing this or what?" he wanted to know.

That's just when Dolly Parton came on the radio and drove me entirely out of the shop.

For the first few miles back north, Desmond unfreighted himself of various fond anecdotes about Ricky. Evenings they'd

had, particularly the ones that had failed to land them both
in jail. I let him go on and didn't bring up the nut of our troubles until we'd reached the junction at Hollandale where we
could both see the road sign for Belzoni.

"Why don't we just dump those tires," I suggested to Desmond. "Bury them. Burn them. Whatever the hell it takes."

Desmond was equipped with a natural resistance to that
sort of thing. He liked to go around saying he didn't care to
be wasteful, but the trouble was that Desmond was tight. His
mother was tight. His sister was, too. His father might have
been dead, but he was still legendary for the corners he'd cut
and dollars he'd stretched and retail prices he'd avoided. When
Desmond's mother was looking to buy stuff, she'd tell Desmond, "I wish your daddy was here." She didn't seem to pine
for him much the rest of the time.

Desmond was a lot less skinflint proactive than his father
must have been, but he'd balk instinctively whenever I'd make
to bid to cut our losses.

I'd always weigh the trouble before us against the money
we'd let out and do the math without affection for any part
of the equation. Desmond's natural ardor for money always
seemed to get in his way. He'd come around eventually. He
always did. But bringing Desmond to a cash write-off was a
little like herding a goat. You could do it, but never easily and
certainly not at first.

"If the Snap-on guy is warning people off . . ."

"No sir," Desmond told me. "Might as well sell them. Now
that you've scuffed up Shambrough, he isn't going let us off."

I drove back to the catfish farm, but there was no sign of

Larry or Skeeter. Their buddy, though, was in the tractor shed fooling with his power lift.

"Seen them?" Desmond asked him.

He spat a stream of snuff juice and shook his head.

"Got a number for Skeeter? I think Larry's phone's dead or something."

He shook his head. He spat.

"If they come back through here," I told him, "make sure Larry gets up with Desmond."

The buddy nodded. He pointed at disassembled tractor parts spread out on a square of Visqueen. "Ever had one of these apart?"

It was a bunch of gears and hydraulic fittings with springs and gaskets and such.

I shook my head. "I'd rather buy a new tractor."

Since Larry and Skeeter weren't going to, me and Desmond put the tarp on the trailer. We got the thing covered just as Larry's buddy managed to get a toe under his Visqueen and spill his disassembled power lift all over the dirt shed floor. I've got to hand it to him. He was a man of snuff and moderation in all things.

He spat a stream. He told us both, "Well, shit."

TEN

For a few minutes there, I was even actually planning on going home. Then I reached the turnoff up around Isola and found myself working west with Greenville in my sights. I decided I was going to have a word with Kendell face-to-face. Get a read on him, a feel for his personal opinion of Lucas Shambrough.

You couldn't tell much about Kendell on the phone. He was short with everybody. A face-to-face, I told myself, that'd be worth driving for. Then there was the Officer Raintree factor that I thought about a little, too.

So I both drove and rationalized. I even took the chance of swinging north up by Geneill on the way. I found a spot where I could get a good look at the Lucas Shambrough homeplace without running the danger of anybody glancing out the window, seeing my Ranchero, and deciding, "There's that fucking guy."

There were more cars parked in front of the house now, most of them trucks and 4 × 4s. I had to figure Shambrough was holding some sort of powwow in my honor, guessed if I rolled on down the driveway, I'd get turned right into soup. Instead I continued out to Hollyknowe, hit the truck route, and went west. I was in downtown Greenville in twenty minutes, just me and the half-dozen crows perched on the meters and the trash cans out in front of the Greenville precinct house.

Kendell was working a split shift. That's what the sergeant at the front desk told me. I recognized him. I'd watched him beat up a guy at the hotel bar over in Greenwood once. A loud, drunk guy from Madison, a suburb north of Jackson that attracts the sort of people who get loud and drunk in hotel bars. They usually wear loafers doing it, and they almost never wear socks.

I saw the whole thing by accident. The sergeant, a Mc-Carty who was off duty, followed the loud drunk guy into the men's room, where I happened to already be. I was washing my hands and probably would have been gone, but the drunk guy started talking to me. He parked himself in front of a urinal, groaned once, and then said, "Hey, sport . . ."

Since it was just me and him, I had to guess I was the sport he meant. He burped before he bothered to even try to tell me something, and that's just when McCarty came in. He approached the vacant urinal like he meant to use it, but instead he punched the drunk guy in the kidneys one time hard.

That gentleman went down and stayed down. Whimpered a little. Started talking about his lawyer.

The sergeant relieved himself and flushed. He told the drunk guy, "Go somewhere else."

I don't know what he'd done or how bad a day the sergeant had been having, but I couldn't even muster the barest twinge of sympathy for the guy. He was one of those fellows who'd be improved by a kidney punch three or four times a day.

I yielded the sink, finished drying my hands, and said to the sergeant, "What are you drinking?"

So we had kind of a relationship after that—I stood him for a couple Jack and Gingers—which meant I could pry and meddle a little.

"When does Kendell come back on?" I asked him.

"Around eight," he told me.

"How about Officer Raintree?"

"Right," he said. He had eyes just like me. He knew what I was up to and why. "How about Officer Raintree?"

"Still here?"

He nodded and pointed at the ceiling.

"You mind?"

He didn't and let me go on up. Teddy was shackled to the bench again. He must have been Greenville's only vagrant, or at least the only ill-mannered and lawless one, or maybe just the easiest to catch. He would need to have been up to some powerful crime before I would have hauled him in since he served to perfume the place to a fare-thee-well. Urine and feet stink and human clothes grease.

I told him, "Hey," as I walked past, and he asked me for a

dollar. He didn't even have a southern accent. Teddy had come here to be poor.

I gave him five dollars. "Where do you sleep, Teddy?"

Teddy pointed nowhere much. "Back in there somewhere."

I gave him ten dollars more. "Did you eat today?"

Teddy broke savage wind and said something phlegmy.

"What did they pick you up for?"

"I ain't done it."

I gave him twenty and nodded. "I hear you, brother."

I turned around to find Officer T. Raintree standing in the squad room doorway. She was half out in the hall, watching me and Teddy.

I pointed at Teddy and told her, "He ain't done it."

I think she smiled. I couldn't quite tell. She went back in the squad room. I found her at her desk.

"Kendell's working splits," she told me.

"Back at eight, right?"

She nodded.

"You?"

"I'm done." She closed her warrant book.

"Anywhere to eat around here?" I was laying the usual groundwork. I was expecting the usual result, which would be me finding out where to eat and then going there all alone.

She'd been tidying her desk, but she stopped. There was only one other officer in the room, well away from us and over against the far wall and on the phone. Officer T. Raintree named a couple of local restaurants, and then she waited.

"You think maybe you want to get some dinner or something?" I had to hope it was only half as painful to hear as it was to string together. I tried to say it while looking pleasant and hopeful and ready for rejection, which I was prepared to tolerate with a jolly shrug.

Officer T. Raintree didn't help me much. She just let it sit there for a bit. When she finally spoke, it was just to ask me, "Why?"

"Why . . . dinner?"

She nodded.

"With you?"

Kept nodding.

I hadn't worked up a why. I knew I found her beautiful and exotic and was hoping to get a chance to see her outside of her official duties where I could try to be at least a little winning on my own. That kind of thing's tough in handcuffs.

"Well," I said. "I thought we could talk."

"About what?"

"Just, you know, get to know each other."

"I know a lot about you already." With that she opened her middle drawer and drew out a manila folder. It had a few typed pages in it. "Kendell gave me this." She ran her finger down the top sheet. "Born in March of 1975. Roanoke, Virginia. Four years in the marines. Six different police jobs in twelve years. One ex-wife. One daughter. Deceased. Independently wealthy somehow. Kendell had thoughts on that."

"'No thanks' would have worked just fine," I told her and stood up like I'd be leaving.

"Sit down."

I did.

"June 1980. Clarksdale, Mississippi. Two years in the marines. Two different police jobs—Baton Rouge and here. One husband. Deceased. One son. He eats, too."

I was upset with the woman for not just saying no. So it took me a quarter minute to figure out what was going on.

"That's a yes?"

"Let me change. Pick up CJ. Shotgun House all right? He'll eat about anything there."

"Yeah. Great. Am I meeting you there?"

She nodded. "When you hit the levee, turn left."

She shut my folder, dropped it into her drawer, and closed it.

"What else did Kendell tell you?"

"Told me you'd ask me that."

I headed for the squad room door.

"Hey," she said.

I turned around.

"Keep your money. Teddy eats it."

Damned if he wasn't chewing my twenty when I passed him in the hall.

The Shotgun House turned out to be a joint—barbecue and burgers and even alligator, battered and fried. There was a bar crowd drinking Bud Lights and eating crawfish straight off tin trays and then a room to the side with tables where there were a few kids eating already.

"One, hon?" The waitress was the hostess as well. She had a couple of pencils stuck in her hair and a basket of fritters in hand.

"Three," I told her with, I guess, comical manly pride.

She winked and said, "All right."

I read the menu about fourteen times and drank two huge

iced teas. I'd already switched tables once and then switched back again.

"You okay?" the waitress swung by to ask me. I knew by now her name was Holly.

I nodded, but I must not have looked it. She lingered. I said, "A little edgy." That's when Officer Tula Raintree and her son came in.

Tula had changed, but not the way most people change. Your dentist out of his crisp white tunic still looks like your dentist in his tailored suit. The Tula in the restaurant hardly resembled the Tula at the station. She was what she had to be on duty. Downtime, she was something entirely else.

Holly knew them. She picked up CJ, and when Tula pointed my way, Holly said, "Him?" with what, to my ear, sounded a touch more incredulous than I'd have liked.

I was standing with my napkin in hand when they finally made it to me.

"CJ," Tula said. "This is Mr. Reid."

"Nick," I told him. He had a firm shake for a kid.

Then CJ said, "I'm going," and he went scampering off toward the toilet.

"I'll go with him," I said.

I like kids. I think I like kids. CJ made it easy on me. It was all I could do to keep up with him. He knew right where the men's room was. The door was locked, and he banged on it until the guy inside shouted, "Give me a damn minute."

CJ looked up and told me, "Oooohhh."

The guy came out angry but softened straightaway. "Go on, then," he told CJ and held the door for him.

I couldn't say much but "Sorry" and followed the kid inside.

He had no need of me beyond escort. He wiped the seat. He got undone. He perched on the toilet and told me, "Peeing." More a point of information than anything else. He finished. He flushed. He fixed his trousers. He went to the sink and soaped and washed while I went over to do my business.

He just stared at me until I said, "Peeing."

CJ was a happy, well-behaved boy. That made itself plain right away. He went back to the table in decent order, no running through the place. The black woman who cooked in the tiny kitchen came out to give him a hug and a corn dodger fresh from the fryer. His mother had fixed a chair for him with a booster seat, to my left and to her right so I'd be looking at her right across the table.

She was something to see out of uniform and not trying to look all mannish. I was trying not to stare at her, but the transformation was pretty stunning. In her uniform, she wouldn't let herself project much beyond handsome. No makeup to speak of. Tight hair. Only the occasional, hard-won smile. She was all undone in the restaurant. Beautiful black hair sweeping across her face. A little eye shadow or something that brought out the girlishness in her. Her dark skin against a white blouse. She was wearing a locket or something. She sipped her tea, glanced at the menu. It was a pleasure to see her up to something other than writing me a ticket.

"So," I said. "Glad you guys are here." I turned toward CJ. "What's good, buddy?'

"Burger."

"He's kind of a specialist," Tula told me.

CJ was singing to himself and playing with his fork. Officer T. Raintree leaned my way. "Got a whiff of something on the radio this morning. Kendell thought maybe you could clear it up."

"I'll give it a shot."

"EMTs got called to a house out by Geneill. Elysium. Know it?"

I gave her my best blank stare and casual shake of the head.

"Shambrough plantation. Ringing a bell?"

I went with my sad smile. "Can't say it is."

"They treated a girl on-site. Stitches in her head. She wouldn't let them take her in. Said she fell down. The techs said Shambrough looked like he fell down with her. For some reason or another—he wasn't exactly clear on this—Kendell thought of you."

"Huh," I told her. "Can't see why."

"I couldn't either until he filled me in. Kendell thinks you and Desmond have been up to all kinds of no good."

"That's just the Baptist in him talking."

"And he's still fond of you. That's what I don't get. You might start by explaining that to me."

I sipped my tea and thought about it. "Kendell knows I'm one of the good guys," I said.

CJ had been saying for a quarter minute there, "Momma, momma, momma." Tula had ignored him, boring in on me instead. She gave me a final hard once-over. "You'd better be," she told me. Then she turned to her son and asked him, "What is it, sweetie?"

The rest of dinner was given over to small talk and general chatter. With CJ. With Holly, the waitress. With some whiskery old bar rat who came in and knew Tula one way or another. It was easy enough as first dates go. That's how I thought of it, anyway.

I saw her out to her car, an impeccable little Honda. I helped strap CJ in. She was half under the wheel before I could get around to her side of the car. I ended up laying a hand on her shoulder like I was her priest or something.

"See ya," she told me.

I think I said, "Yeah."

And that was pretty much that.

ELEVEN

I drove past Officer T. Raintree's house to make sure she'd gotten home all right. Then I headed straight home and watched the Braves play a meaningless late-season game against a team a little deeper in the basement than they were.

Desmond woke me with a phone call. It was going on eight in the morning by then. I figured he had some K-Lo work he was waiting on me to show up for.

I told him, "I'm coming," instead of "Hello."

"We've got a problem," Desmond said.

Our lives at that moment were little more than a tapestry of problems. So having *a* problem sounded to me like a noticeable improvement.

"Larry?" I asked him.

"Belzoni," Desmond told me. "Kendell wants you down here in half an hour. Out at the catfish ponds."

"That's not even his county."

"Just get in the damn car and come on."

So I drove out to that catfish farm. I needn't have worried about the tires. The trailer was gone. The blue tarp we'd covered it with was piled on the ground. There was a fire truck parked by the tractor shed, a trio of county cruisers, a couple of rescue squad trucks, what looked like a state sedan, and a 4×4 with its back hatch open. I'd seen that vehicle before. It belonged to the gentleman who served as crime scene coroner for four contiguous counties. I'd met him over breakfast once. Kendell had introduced him. He'd told two lame jokes right in a row and then had hit us with a pun.

"Gallows humor," Kendell had said by way of apology.

"Hell, man," I told him, "don't blame the dead for that."

Kendell and Desmond were standing with a guy in a necktie up past the tractor shed. Kendell whistled and waved me over. Somebody was sure to be killed.

He was wet. They'd fished him out of a pond. I realized I didn't even know his name. He was just Larry's con friend with the snuff box and the honest wage. He was laid out faceup on a scarlet blanket from one of the EMT trucks, and he clearly hadn't needed to drown because he'd probably died from the beating he'd had.

"Know him?" Kendell asked me.

"Friend of Larry's."

"Yeah, but do you *know* him?"

"Just to say hey. Couldn't even tell you his name."

Kendell consulted his notepad. "Jonathan Randolph Simms."

"What the hell happened to him?"

Kendell turned to the guy in the necktie. "Show him," he said.

The gentleman handed me a digital camera and showed me what button to hit. I got a parade of images. They'd stuck him in the nearest pond headfirst. There were a couple of shots of just his boots poking out of the water, his pale shins exposed. Then photographs of a couple of EMT techs hauling him up and placing him on the blanket they'd spread out for that purpose.

As I was handing the camera back, the guy in the necktie told me, "Fish went at him a little. Something else went at him a lot."

"Who are you?"

He dug out his state police badge. An Arkansas state police detective.

"What's Little Rock want with shit like this?"

"Tell him," that guy said to Kendell.

"Izzy's girl," Kendell said. "They've been onto her for a while." He pulled a mug shot out of his notebook. It was her, all right, but with peroxided hair. She was wearing a jailhouse jumpsuit unzipped to reveal her neck tattoo.

"Who is she?" I asked.

"Gloria Marie Johansson," the Arkansas cop told me.

I glanced at the girl in the mug shot and then handed it back to Kendell. "This the girl that did the number on Izzy?"

Kendell nodded.

"Ever seen her?" the guy from Arkansas asked me.

I'd become awfully glib at lying. I shook my head and told him, "Not sure I'd want to."

I can't say why exactly I didn't tell them what I'd gotten up to out at Shambrough's. Now that we were all agreed they were treacherous lowlifes and possibly homicidal, there probably wouldn't have been much harm in me confessing what I'd done. I suppose it was habit by this point. I'd learned to hold everything close.

Desmond hadn't uttered a word. I was waiting for him to chime in so I could get a read on how much he'd let out of the bag. If anybody was going to give up Larry and Skeeter, it had to be Desmond.

I just waited. There was plenty to look at. The coroner was kneeling beside the body. He had his liver probe in hand and showed it to us. "Water'll throw everything off." He plunged the thermometer probe straight through the skin before I could turn away.

"What do you figure they wanted?" Kendell asked me.

"They who?"

"That girl and . . . whoever."

"I thought Izzy said it was just her."

Kendell nodded. "Guess he did."

Kendell motioned for us to follow him into the tractor shed. Once he'd turned his back to me, I gave Desmond as inquiring a look as I could manage. He just shook his head a little, and I couldn't at all be sure what that meant.

There were tools all over the place. The dirt floor of the shed was churned up. A length of sack rope was tied to the tractor's steering wheel. Another to its exhaust stack.

"He's got marks on his wrists," Kendell told us. "Looks like he got tied up." Kendell leaned back against the tractor with his arms extended—farmyard crucifixion. "Something like this," he told us. "I wouldn't call that much of a fight."

Kendell pointed to where the trailer had been. "Looks like they took something out of here."

Desmond nodded and finally chimed in. "Looks like."

Then nothing got said for longer than me and Desmond were comfortable with. Kendell let us soak in the carnage, even pointed out some of it to us. That old tractor was blood spattered and gored up pretty good. There were drying puddles of blood and stray human giblets on the ground.

"Anybody you want to call? Tell him to look over his shoulder?" Kendell pointed toward the road. "Best go on and do it. If it was me, I might just bring him in before he gets dead, too."

Desmond managed a groany grunt.

"We'll get back to you," I told Kendell.

The Arkansas guy looked like he wanted to keep us around for a while, but Kendell did some explaining to him, and he let us walk away. Down the gravel track and past all the vehicles to where we'd both parked, hard by the blacktop.

"What did you tell him?" I asked Desmond.

"Told him I'd tell him shit in a while."

"You giving up Larry?"

"I don't know. Got to do some thinking."

With Desmond, that meant he had to eat, so I followed him to the knockoff Sonic.

Since we were sitting at the same table as the day before, Desmond hit the Dumpster without even bothering to aim. He just bundled up his sack and made a blind, forlorn toss.

"I don't want to defend Larry," I told Desmond, "but he might go up for good this time. It's not just tires anymore."

"He didn't have nothing to do with that."

"The law might see it another way. But for Larry and Skeeter and the shit they got up to, none of this would have happened."

"If we hadn't put the money up, it wouldn't have happened either."

Desmond had a point, and I acknowledged it by letting it just sit there unchallenged.

"What am I going to tell Shawnica?"

I had to figure that was coming.

"You might start with 'Your brother's a shithead' and go from there."

"How much you figure the catfish guy knew?"

"Ever seen him up in Indianola?"

"Never seen him anywhere before last week."

"Beat up like that, he would have told them what he knew. Must not have known anything. Not enough, anyway."

"Maybe," Desmond said and then added a little hotly—hotly anyway for Desmond—"Just had to go and poke them, didn't you?"

"Did you forget Izzy and that woman in Sunflower? Some people come prepoked. Primed for shit like this."

"What are we going to do?" he asked me.

"First thing, we've got to figure how we want this to play out. Do we want to give it all over to Kendell and the Arkansas state police? Just let them have Larry and Skeeter, and whatever happens happens? Or do we want to clean up this damn mess ourselves?"

Desmond tapped his chest with his beefy index finger.

"I'm guessing these guys are all in from here on out. Nobody goes to the hospital. Everybody goes to the morgue."

"So what do we do?" Desmond asked me.

"We go after *them*."

We started with Kendell. Desmond called him and told him we wanted to have a word. Just him and us. No necktie guy. Desmond set it up for some bow lake on the far side of Panther Burn. It was back in a wildlife refuge, a scrubby patch of fallow ground.

These spots go in and out of cultivation as the crop prices fluctuate. This one had been wild for three or four years and was a glorified eighty-acre thicket with a sandy road going in to what I guess you could call a pond. If you'd never seen a pond and had a high opinion of puddles. It was a mud hole really, overrun with snapping turtles and blue herons, and I'm sure it was the buggiest spot for many miles around.

When Kendell finally found us, he pulled up in his cruiser and even climbed out of it and left it for half a minute. The gnats and mosquitoes went for him with such relish that he hopped back in his car and called Desmond on the phone.

"Follow me," he said. So Desmond did, and I followed the pair of them out of that wildlife thicket, west a few miles, and onto the levee road. If there was a breeze to be caught in the Delta, you were sure to catch it up there. The road runs along the crown of the levee. I had a clear view of the Mississippi to my left and a swampy wooded island called Kentucky Bend. There was even a small herd of cattle up there to keep the levee grass down.

Kendell found a grove of sycamore trees and parked in the shade beneath them. There was enough breeze stirring—

maybe the river current kicked it up—to drive most of the bugs away. The rushing water provided a sort of constant background tremor.

"You know what I think?" Kendell asked us both straightaway. He didn't wait for an answer. "I think I'm not going to like any of this."

"It's nothing we're into," Desmond said. "We just let out some money."

"To Larry?"

Desmond managed a reluctant grimace.

"What did he get into?"

"The problem is . . ." I said to Kendell.

He pointed a finger at me. "Shut up."

He looked back at Desmond.

"Tires," Desmond told him. "Must have been Shambrough's or something."

"Are you the one that kicked him around?" Kendell asked Desmond.

Desmond shook his head. "Uh-uh."

"You, then," Kendell told me.

"What's a Shambrough?" I said.

"Sounds like you. Went over to see if you could straighten everything out. Probably started out regular and friendly. Ended up in a fight. You saw her, didn't you? Had her right there."

"Don't know what you mean."

Kendell exhaled. Chuffed really, like a black bear might. He looked out over the great river. Big brown ropy strands of current racing south.

"Dead guy's a jailbird," Kendell said. "Figures to be one of Larry's friends."

When me and Desmond didn't say anything, Kendell looked at us and shook his head. "I can help you," he said. "I'm not hoping to see any of you locked up or dead."

"Desmond's in kind of a delicate spot," I told him.

"Shawnica'll kill me," Desmond said. "Might just kill you and him, too."

"Didn't you put Larry in Parchman the last time he was up there?" Kendell asked him. "That was you, right?"

"He stole Momma's car. They caught him in Jackson. We didn't know it was him when we called it in."

"You're shitting me," I said to Desmond. I'd never heard that one before. "Why are you worried about his sorry ass now?"

"That's the question, isn't it," Kendell said.

But we all knew the answer.

"She won't like this," Desmond told us, more in downtrodden, pathetic sorrow than anything else.

"Let me talk to Shawnica," Kendell suggested.

"She's got a knife," I told him. "And a bad attitude. And no volume control. And those stick-on nails are sharp."

"She's my wife's cousin," Kendell told me. "I think I can handle Shawnica." Spoken like a man sure to be getting sewn up later on.

"What are you going to tell her exactly?" Desmond wanted to know.

Kendell was almost chipper now. "I'll just ask her how she wants her brother—planted in the churchyard or locked up?"

TWELVE

I called Officer T. Raintree because I thought I should. It seemed the polite thing to do, and I wanted to talk to her anyway. I wanted to see if Kendell had phoned in to update my bio, adding the beat-up boy in the catfish pond I might have helped get killed.

She didn't quite say what I'd hoped she'd say when she answered.

"How did you get this number?" she wanted to know.

"Didn't you give it to me?"

"No."

"I don't know. Kendell maybe. You heard from him today?"

"Saw him at roll call. What's the problem?"

"No problem. Just got a thing I need to talk to him about."

"You got his number?"

"Must somewhere," I told her. "Enjoyed last night," I said.

"Right. Yeah." I heard some clanking and a dull roar in the background. Tula shouted at somebody, "Hey!" Then she said to me, "Got to do this," and she hung up on me.

I didn't feel any better for having dialed her. I was pretty certain I felt considerably worse.

Since Kendell was heading over to talk to Shawnica, me and Desmond stopped in at Kalil's to see if he had the sort of job that might make us both feel better. We'd worked plenty of repos where the customer was just low on luck. He'd lost his job or the last of his cash had gone to a bill he couldn't not pay, so he'd gotten behind on whatever creature comfort he'd contracted for with Kalil.

There he'd be with his head in his hands sitting on his rented sofa, and me and Desmond or some fool like Ronnie would show up at his door to take it.

We didn't want one of those, and we sure didn't want to mess with any Duponts, but we were hoping for a loudmouth, wrongheaded redneck. He'd threaten us with a bat or a length of rebar, ready to lay down his life for his TiVo, so me and Desmond wouldn't have much choice except to go on ahead and scuff him the hell up.

It was sure to be therapeutic for us and probably good practice for Desmond. I'd had a little workout with Lucas Shambrough and his schoolgirl assassin. Aside from Larry, I couldn't remember the last time Desmond had wailed on anybody hard.

Out in Kalil's parking lot, I asked him to name his last victim.

Desmond thought. He told me, "Hmmm." Then he thought some more. "That Ketner, I guess. The one with the hat."

I could just about picture him. The hat had been a fedora. He'd fancied himself some sort of backcountry hipster. I believe he'd quoted Bukowski at us. Hard to know. He was short a few teeth, so everything came out sounding about the same.

"Table saw, right?"

Desmond nodded.

That Ketner had been building an addition onto his trailer. He'd been going at it, I have to think, the way backcountry hipsters all over would. He'd collected some lumber and a roll of Tyvek. He'd bought a saw on time from Kalil, and then he'd left it all to sit out in the weather for going on three months.

He got offended when I asked him, "What's all this shit?"

That's when he quoted the poetry, I think, and reached back inside for his shotgun. It was nearly as rusty as the saw. He'd whacked the barrel off for convenience's sake.

Desmond has a talent for dealing with people who've decided to point a gun at him. It's a gift really, and I lack it entirely, so my first move—I can't help myself—was to show my palms to that Ketner and tell him with the best smile I could muster, "Let's just hold on here, buddy."

Desmond does something else entirely. He always goes toward the gun. Desmond is massive. There must be a Samoan somewhere in the woodpile. Desmond is just a huge heap of a guy, so he's got to really know what he's up to to make himself seem unthreatening.

When the guns come out, he just starts talking in a low and humble way. He has this story he likes to tell about a cousin on his daddy's side who met every kind of upset with a weapon until one of them finally went off. He either killed somebody or didn't, depending on whatever Desmond happens to think will serve his purposes best.

With that Ketner, Desmond's cousin inadvertently gunned down a simple man collecting a wage, just hired to do a job. A man like Desmond. A man like me. A man just like that Ketner. Except, of course, for the fedora. I felt certain that was setting Desmond off.

Desmond hates poseurs in a deep-seated and instinctive sort of way. Hipsters especially, who dress like they're living in 1928 but are twenty-first-century stupid in the regular, modern way. So that Ketner had to be working on him. The fedora was bad enough, but he was wearing a vest and pleated trousers and two-tone wingtips as well.

All of it out in a swampy wasteland down past Itta Bena. His trailer was shoved back into a hedgerow. His garbage was piled up in sacks. He'd bought all the wrong wood to build his addition that he wasn't even building, and he had two car seats by way of lawn furniture—another of Desmond's dislikes.

Desmond fought through all of that and gave that Ketner the cousin story with all the usual blandishments and dramatic grace notes and the sorts of touches that always saw Desmond safely into what he called *Oh, fuck!* range.

He'd ease forward as he spoke, making a friend along the way of whoever had a firearm pointed at him. The theme of Desmond's story was felonious regret. His cousin had known a full dose of it. Desmond had taken that lesson to heart and was prepared these days to talk almost anything out.

He was close by then. I'd about made it to a cypress tree that I could put between myself and that Ketner if he decided to pull the trigger.

We got more poetry (I think) as Desmond arrived in *Oh, fuck!* range. He was saying something soothing when he snatched at that Ketner's shotgun, racked it around, and plucked it out of his hands. Desmond had hinged the barrel open, ejected the loads, and broken that Ketner's nose with the butt within about seven seconds. Then Desmond proceeded to truly scuff that boy up. He reserved some hard treatment for the fedora as well.

Then that Ketner helped us load his table saw into my Ranchero. By "helped" I mean we watched him, and he did it all himself. Desmond bent his sawed-offed barrel for him between two saplings, handed the gun back to that Ketner, who was covered in nose blood by then.

Desmond supplied him a bit of counsel as well. "Straighten the fuck up," he told him.

That was back in March, and I remember how good we'd felt driving away from that Ketner with the saw he'd probably ruined and both of us unshot. We probably felt like soldiers feel when they come out of a firefight unscathed. We were elated, giddy even, and more than a little revived.

After seeing Larry's buddy all beat to pieces and drowned, me and Desmond both knew that we could do with some reviving. Kalil, God bless him, had a morsel for us. He was standing by the counter and waving the tissuey invoice as we came in.

"Dale," he said. "I sent Paco this morning." Kalil pressed his lips together and shook his head. That meant Paco was probably visiting the critical care clinic by now.

Paco was from Alabama. He wasn't Mexican. He just ate burritos morning, noon, and night and was about as slow-witted as a man can be and still boast of a fifth-grade education. I think Kalil kept him on because, somehow, Paco had a current driver's license. It had to be some kind of DMV oversight.

We hated Dale. He'd been a state policeman, and he'd been married to Patty, who used to work for Kalil. We'd hated Patty, too, but mostly because she was fond of Dale. Once they'd divorced and she'd grown to despise him, we'd softened on her a little.

Dale had skimmed. He'd chiseled. He'd taken bribes outright. He'd moonlighted for a meth kingpin and worked as muscle for a while. He finally beat up some girl he was seeing, a hot mess over in Grenada who'd threatened to bring him up on charges and then even actually did.

Dale spent eight months in the county lockup. He was a muscle head already and so just passed his sentence lifting weights and fighting with the cons. I think they finally turned him out because they were sick of messing with him. He moved into a tenant house on a spread his uncle owned and proceeded to get fired from a series of low-wage jobs for being, well, Dale.

"What's he got?" I asked Kalil.

"TV," he told me. He checked the invoice. "Panasonic."

"The big one?"

He nodded.

"Why in the hell did you let him have it?" Desmond wanted to know.

Kalil gave us the devilish smile we saw sometimes when he was tickled. "So you two could go and pick it up."

Kalil could sometimes be thoughtful like that. Mostly he was a raging screamer, but that's probably why the kind turns he did usually touched us so. They were rare and out of character. He offered us the invoice. We tried to thank him, but Kalil just waved us off.

"Don't get anything broken," he said. "Especially my damn TV."

In a way, it was a lot easier going after Dale than the likes of that Ketner. We knew Dale wouldn't pull a firearm on us. He was too proud of his physique for that. Dale insisted on a fight. He preferred fists mostly, but he'd beat you with a stick of wood or a garden shovel if either one of them came to hand. We usually did the gentlemanly thing and went after him one at a time.

"Me first," Desmond told me as we pulled up before Dale's house.

Dale had bought Desmond's old Geo Metro from the guy Desmond had sold it to, so it was probably seventh-hand by now. The thing was sitting up in Dale's yard sheathed in filth.

When Desmond saw it, he said mournfully, "Aw, baby."

"You hated that car," I reminded him.

"Didn't keep me from washing it."

"Dale can't lift and do that, too."

Dale's weight bench was up by the fuel oil tank with his dumbbells and his barbells scattered around it.

"Going for that prison yard look," Desmond told me.

And that's about when Dale shouted at us through the door screen, "What?"

He knew "What" already. He'd been waiting for us.

"I'm all tingly," I told Desmond once Dale had shoved the door open and stepped out onto the stoop.

He was shirtless, of course. Being a sculpted specimen was about all Dale had anymore. He'd lost his wife and his Grenada girlfriend, his state police badge and his cruiser. Somebody had even adopted his dog. Now it was just Dale and his free weights and his leased-out Panasonic. That made things awfully simple. We'd come to get it, and he wasn't giving it back.

"Why do you want to do this?" Desmond asked him.

We were obliged to go through the motions.

"Think of all the shit I've done for Kalil," Dale said and flexed his biceps. He was always keen for us to see how musclebound he was.

He had done a lot for Kalil. He'd broken his plate-glass store window twice. Once with a punch just to prove that he could and once with the grille of his state police cruiser. He'd been raging drunk both times. Dale had also been the cause of various spectacles whenever he would fight with Patty. She'd be there at the store just doing her work, and Dale would show up to berate her. We'd have to haul him out of there, with Kendell if we were feeling charitable. But sometimes we'd just gang up on him and take him to pieces by ourselves.

Dale's trouble was that he couldn't really fight. He was thick and slow and fancied himself a home-schooled mixed martial artist. He had the six-pack for it and the quads and the lats, but he was the sort of guy who almost thought out loud. When I tangled with Dale, I knew what he was doing before he did. I liked to work my way around him—ducking and dodging—and just flat tear him up.

"You're three months behind," Desmond told him. "You know how that's got to go."

"All right, then," Dale said and pounded his fists together. Then he told us what he always did. "Let's get it on."

The problem was we hadn't really tangled with Dale since his stint in the lockup, where, as it turned out, he'd picked up a couple of moves. He used one on Desmond. It was a showy, spinning kick we'd neither of us seen before. Ordinarily, Dale would just run at you low and hope to knock you over. Then he'd perch on you and show you his muscles, tell you what a girl you were, and flail at you with those weak-ass punches musclemen are prone to. A hard left from Dale was a lot like getting hit with a sofa bolster.

A firm grip on his testicles was usually all it took to get Dale up and shrieking, and then you could pummel him at will. Dale didn't have any stamina. He was just a show pony.

So Desmond walked up expecting the usual, and Dale wheeled around and kicked Desmond in the head. It wasn't a vicious kick or even a little debilitating, because it had been delivered by musclebound Dale.

It was surprising nonetheless, and Desmond got himself in trouble when he turned around to say to me, "You see that?"

Dale kicked him again. This one was a straight blow to the back of Desmond's knee, and Desmond folded up like a church chair and tumbled over face-first onto the ground.

"Hell," he said, "I think I tore something."

That's when Dale piled on top of him and started smacking Desmond on either side of his head. Desmond had too much girth and too little dexterity to reach behind himself to much effect, so he just kept getting punched and wearying of it. Dale gloated that way Dale does, and I just had to stand there and watch it all. Me and Desmond had policies and rules. We didn't like to gang up on people, most particularly if those people were Dale because he was lumbering and slow.

But I made a decision standing there watching Dale drumming on the back of Desmond's head. If he'd picked up the kind of moves in jail that made him more of a danger, then Dale no longer qualified for gentlemanly treatment.

"I'm coming," I told him. "You'd better get up."

Dale tattooed Desmond again. Desmond wasn't bloodied or anything. He was simply irritated.

"Just washed this shirt," Desmond told me. "My damn knee hurts like hell."

Naturally Dale hadn't gotten entirely up by the time I'd reached him. I waited for him to stand, and he took his sweet time. He had stuff to explain to me. He wanted to talk about lines I'd crossed and offenses I'd committed. He also wanted to tell me how humbled I was about to be. Then he tried on me the same roundhouse kick he'd lately landed on Desmond. It only missed me by a foot and a half and left Dale's back to me.

I would have hated to see Dale tangle with the ninja schoolgirl assassin. She wouldn't have needed her Taser. Dale would have worn himself out with his kicks, and then she could have just savaged him with all that vicious shit she got up to. He was lucky, I told myself, that it was me instead of her.

Then I hit him, and he made that altogether satisfying noise he makes. The sort of noise you don't want to make in a fight because it tells your opponent, "Ouch."

He tried another kick. I saw that one coming, too, now

that I knew Dale had picked up a fresh technique in jail. I hit him again, a straight left. Dale smiled and spit a bloody tooth my way.

"I think he's drunk," I told Desmond.

Desmond had clambered up and was testing his knee by then. Dale just laughed and tried to kick me some more, but he was halfway across the yard and so couldn't begin to reach me.

"You all right?" I asked Desmond.

"Feels kind of funny." He worked his knee and grimaced. "Let's get this damn TV and just go on."

"Try it," Dale told us.

He'd gone all John L. Sullivan on me. He had his fists up in front of him in proper nineteenth-century form. I hit his left hand with my right one, and Dale managed to break his own nose. Then I hit him low and hit him high and doubled up everywhere he was open. His arms were down by then, so I was throttling him all over.

Dale gave me that look I'd seen before, the one that says, "I'm falling down now."

He dropped like he always did, tipped forward and landed on his face. You'd think he would have figured out how to use those massive arms to break his fall, but experience has never been much of a teacher with Dale.

I poked him with my foot until he turned his head and groaned and I could be certain that Dale was breathing on his own. Desmond was already gimping up into the house by then while Dale laid there on the hardpan and talked trash to me. Muttered it, anyway, and puffed up little wisps of dust.

He had devastating plans for me, intended to bust me all to pieces.

I tried Kendell's approach. I pointed at him and said to Dale, "Shut up."

Me and Desmond ripped out all of Dale's connections and hauled his TV into the yard.

"You know where to buy it back," Desmond told him.

Dale made another dusty threat.

"Should we drag him out of the sun?" I asked Desmond.

He shook his head. "He'll be in the shade in an hour."

"You're a hard man."

"Fucker kicked me. Better not be nothing tore."

Desmond made me go by critical care before we returned to Kalil's. Paco was still in the waiting room. We thought he was still in the waiting room, anyway, but it turned out he was back in the waiting room. He'd gone out for a burrito, thinking he could keep his place in line without actually being there. Paco had a gaping wound over his right eyebrow, probably an eight- or ten-stitcher that was seepy and crusty and had kind of welded shut.

"What did he hit you with?" I asked him.

Paco shrugged and shook his head. He couldn't really say. "I was barely out of the car, hadn't told him nothing except hey."

I pointed at Desmond. "He got kicked."

Desmond nodded glumly as the door to the back hallway swung open. There stood Kendell with four bright green butterfly sutures on his cheek. His uniform shirt was spattered with blood. He didn't appear too happy to see us.

I let Desmond do the honors.

"Talk to Shawnica?"

Kendell snorted one time, touched his sutured cheek, and told us, "Yep."

THIRTEEN

Naturally, the only place Shawnica would consider retreating to for her safety was the Alluvian Hotel in Greenwood, a swanky Delta spa.

Kendell relayed the message to us at a back table of the Pecan House, where we'd stopped in for coffee and nut clusters once we'd finished with critical care. Desmond had a sprain. That was the considered opinion, anyway, of the doctor who manipulated his knee. Desmond also had high blood pressure and about two hundred extra pounds, which he heard about from the critical care doctor as well.

The guy was giving Desmond dietary advice—he seemed down on Coney Islands—when Desmond put his trousers on and left the examination room.

Paco was jonesing for a burrito, but we convinced him to

stay behind and get sewn up. We told him we'd go out and get him one, but that was just to hold him there.

So it was me and Kendell and Desmond once more talking the whole business over.

"Knife?" I asked him.

Kendell touched a suture. He shook his head. "Stick-on nail."

"Told you."

Kendell sipped his coffee. "Awful short fuse," he said.

"What about Larry and Skeeter?" Desmond asked Kendell.

"What about them?"

"Just leave them there for Shambrough? We're sure to find them beat to shit and dead someplace soon enough."

"They can't take care of themselves?" Kendell asked. It was a sensible question. They'd both been in and out of prison. You'd think they'd have learned how to get out of sight when being nowhere was best.

"They're both kind of clueless," I told Kendell. "Shambrough and that girl of his will chew them up."

"So you'll hide them away, too."

"Us?" I asked him.

"I've got no budget for it. If you want me to take care of Larry and his buddy, they're going right in a cell."

"No more in-laws," I told Desmond. "Ever."

Desmond shifted and winced a little in a play for sympathy.

"Don't want to hear about your knee," I told him. "This is coming out of yours."

"His what?" Kendell asked me. "Share? I know you took

all that crazy meth head's money. Go on. Fess up. What can I do about it now?"

I wasn't quite sure the answer was nothing.

"We're just frugal," I told Kendell.

The Alluvian Hotel, as luck would have it, was packed full of Delta blues tourists and wouldn't have a vacancy for a couple of nights. Me and Desmond had driven over to have a look at the place, see if it was the sort of establishment that could tolerate Shawnica and put up with Larry and his buddy Skeeter. Or rather, I'd driven over and Desmond had complained about his knee all along the way.

When we hit the outskirts of Greenwood, he insisted I stop at the CVS and get him some Tylenol and a cane.

"Can't hope to climb out of here," Desmond said. He'd found a way to be both pitiful and knock my car.

So I went in and bought his aspirin. They had a box of canes, the adjustable aluminum kind. One of them was pink with daisies on it. The thing had feet at the bottom so it would go on standing up even if you toppled over. That was the one I bought Desmond.

I told him when I came out, "Only one they had."

The young lady at the desk at the Alluvian Hotel was wearing a tailored ebony jacket and didn't talk at all like a girl from Yazoo City, which is where it turned out she was from. The hotel trained their people to fit in with the decor, all of it expensive and tasteful and (I guess) ready to be undone by a desk clerk who'd greet guests with a "How y'all?"

Her name tag said she was Tabatha, but when I called her that, she didn't seem to know who I meant. I asked about a suite that would accommodate three people.

"Adults?" she asked us.

Desmond said, "More or less."

"What are your dates?"

"A full week?" I asked Desmond. "Starting tonight maybe?"

That seemed sensible to him, and he nodded.

"We're full up until day after tomorrow," Tabatha told us. "Blues tour."

"All right, then," I said. "Make it Thursday to Thursday."

She needed a deposit for the booking. Desmond handed me his pretty pink cane while he dug through his wallet. I could tell by the way she was looking at us what was going through her head. She was thinking we must be one of those couples that proved that love came in all colors and sizes.

Desmond offered her cash. His mother had ruined his credit standing a few years back. She was smoking rocks at the time for pain she had and ordering all manner of crap off the television with Desmond's Visa.

"We'll need a card on file," she told us, "for incidentals and such." Like repainting the place, I had to figure, once Beluga had put his feet on all the walls.

I gave her mine.

"You're all set," she said just as me and Desmond both heard a familiar voice from an adjacent room.

I pointed toward the doorway. "What's in there?"

"Our lounge," Tabatha from Yazoo City told us.

It was more of a bar, really, with its own variety of bar rat. Big honking white guys in button-down shirts and a few of their shrill wives. The wood was dark. The lights were low. There was mercifully no music, and over at a table against the window was the source of the laugh we'd heard. Kalil was

having his Armagnac with some buddies, a quartet of gentlemen who, along with Kalil, looked like a boozed up U.N.
delegation. One of them was Delta Chinese. One of them was
Delta Hispanic. A Delta Hassidim, and by the paleness of
him, a Delta Canadian I had to guess.

They were having a jolly time of it. When Kalil saw us, he
waved us over.

"Sit," he said.

There was no room for us, and we didn't want to join them
anyway. Everybody scooted and chattered at us, but we just
stayed where we were.

"Got Dale's TV," I told him. "Still out in the truck."

"I know," Kalil said and laughed. "He came and broke my
window."

The whole crowd at the table found this hilarious. They
hooted more loudly than one of the doughy planters at the bar
could stand. He was all gut and entitlement. He shoved off of
his stool and came waddling over to speak to Kalil and his
friends. Me and Desmond, too, I guess.

"Now boys," he said in that southern way that reliably sets
me off, "can't see the need for all this racket in a swanky place
like this."

The Delta Chinese man giggled. He was drinking something with Coke and was loaded enough to find everything,
even this planter gasbag, funny.

That man reached into his pocket and pulled out his cell
phone. I'd seen this act before. It's gotten common in the Delta
with the white privileged class. They'll run into something
they don't like—say, a table of drunk immigrant riffraff—and
show off their phones as a sign of all the people they might

call. Hardheads and roughnecks ready to go, the sorts of guys who'd make Kalil and his friends wish they'd never shown up at the Alluvian bar and made the racket they'd made.

I put my arm around the guy, smiled at him as if I was white, and agreeably pointed, headed in just the way he preferred.

"Hey," I said and leaned in so I could speak low into his ear. "How would you like a pink cane with daisies shoved up your fat ass feet first?"

He drew back and looked at me. I went on smiling at him. We came to an instantaneous understanding.

"I wouldn't care for that," he told me. "Wouldn't care for that at all."

"Then you'd better go on."

He did, too. Kalil hooted. His Delta Chinese friend giggled.

They shouted out to the barman for another round.

"Dale get arrested?" I asked Kalil.

He shrugged. "I called it in. He took four TVs and two big sets of speakers. Said he was going to throw them in the river." Kalil turned toward Desmond. "How did he end up driving your shitty car?"

The Delta Canadian started in on a story before Desmond could answer. Something pressing about a gin cocktail he'd had a few years back. That gave us all the out we needed, so me and Desmond made for the door.

That planter I'd just threatened was outside trying to pour his wife into his Riviera. He turned to me like he had some brand of jowly thing to say.

"I'd keep it to myself," I told him.

They're used to running the world, these planter types. They come from people who got away with just about any damn thing they wanted, people who not that long ago would buy their farmhands and work them to death. Kingly people. Dixie royalty. This homely world doesn't suit them anymore.

That gentleman did the sensible thing. He got in his car and blew his horn as he pulled out past us. He spat out the window toward me and Desmond, his token of outrage. It hit me just then that Lucas Shambrough was a version of the same thing. The son of some fine old Delta planter who was himself a planter's son, and he was keeping up planter appearances in the Shambrough homeplace, which was sprawling and eccentric and going doggedly to seed.

I felt sure that Lucas Shambrough would sneer at Kalil and his friends as well. Their people had been imported to pick cotton, and they'd gone native and stayed. That meant Kalil's ilk could never quite be proper Delta upper crusty. Not like a Shambrough, anyway. Even a treacherous thieving Shambrough. He wasn't just a thief. He was a snob, too. That's why he could be so vicious. The people he went after didn't necessarily count.

We eased up on Shawnica's house, just in case there were Shambrough henchmen about. But I had come to believe that part of the evil genius of Lucas Shambrough lay in his full appreciation of *eventually*. Larry and Skeeter had to know they'd blundered into some fairly profound trouble and that they were sure to be paying for it one way or another. They had a dead friend now. Their tires were gone. Their lives probably weren't worth spit. It hardly mattered where they were—in the lockup or not. The people who wanted them dead would get to them wherever they might be. So now they were left to sit around waiting for it to happen.

I knew if I was either one of them, I'd be having an ordeal. But that, I guess, was the beauty of Larry, and even Skeeter a little. We found them watching a cooking show and eating icebox fish sticks on Shawnica's sofa.

They couldn't even see me when I knocked on the screen door, but Beluga just told me, "Come on in."

The cooking show they were watching didn't require anybody to cook. The people on it just had to argue with each other for half an hour. They seemed to be quarreling about tomato sauce when I stepped over and switched off the set.

"You know your buddy's dead, right?"

Larry went bereaved. He kept eating his fish stick, but he ate it with his head low and chewed in an inconsolable sort of way.

"Shambrough," I told them.

Skeeter and Larry nodded. Larry said, "Figures."

"And that girl he's using is looking for you."

They nodded again. This was something they knew, too.

"And when she finds you," I said and glanced at Desmond.

He picked it up from there. "She's got this thing for killing folks a little at a time. We saw that catfish boy." Desmond shook his head.

"Heard he drowned," Skeeter said.

"Dead going in or near it," Desmond told him.

"And you guys just sitting here watching TV," I said. "Anybody could come up."

"What do you care?" Larry asked me.

"I'm going to hit him," I told Desmond.

I thought he'd tell me not to, but Desmond just said, "Well, all right."

I was still drawing back when Larry dropped to the floor in a heap.

"What do you think that schoolgirl would do with him?" Desmond asked.

"Not much sport to Larry, is there?"

That's when Shawnica came in from the back—she'd been working on her broken nails—to give me and Desmond and Larry and Skeeter one emphatic "Uh-huh."

I don't think any of them quite understood what sort of peril they were in. Partly because they were not the sorts to plan ahead for things. They were all of them accustomed to doing whatever impressed them at the moment as just precisely what they'd like to do. Consequences didn't enter into it. They had impulses they were perfectly happy to act on as if they were actual sound ideas.

That's how Larry and Skeeter usually got indicted and why Shawnica would get in fixes that she'd routinely come to Desmond to straighten out. Talking to them about the future was worse than talking to a child. You could have a more productive conversation with a collie. The future was generic and uninteresting to them. It was just what followed after they had done what they wanted to do.

"Do you know who Lucas Shambrough is?" I asked all of them generally.

Shawnica was bored before I was halfway through. Skeeter nodded. Larry told me, "Tire guy." He started in on another fish stick. "So he's still pissed about that boy with the broken leg?"

"You tell them," I said to Desmond.

"What's that for?" Shawnica asked Desmond, pointing at his cane. "You do know it's pink and shit."

Desmond nodded. "Hurt my knee. Saw Kendell at the doctor's. Why are you fighting with him? He's just trying to help."

Shawnica wagged an index finger at Desmond by way of contradiction. She was the final judge of who was helping and who wasn't. "He don't talk to me like that."

"The man's a Baptist deacon," I said.

"Didn't see you there." Shawnica wagged a finger at me and that was that.

Desmond was as flummoxed as I was. They were all three used to meeting trouble as it came and couldn't be persuaded— even by two beat-up people and another one thoroughly dead—that this was an entirely different class of upset. Larry seemed to think he just needed the chance to explain what had gone wrong, how everything had been an accident and a foolish misunderstanding.

"Damn boy went and got up under the truck," Larry muttered. Now it was all Bugle's fault.

So me and Desmond decided just to appreciate the danger for them and asked them if they'd like to live it up in the Alluvian Hotel for a week. That they understood, but we still had to stash them somewhere for a couple of days while the blues tourists cleared out of the place.

"Pearl likes company," Desmond told me.

I'd been afraid he'd say something like that. I'd imposed

on Pearl's hospitality before with a couple of Delta swamp rats, and she had succeeded at civilizing them a little. Pearl had a gift where it came to people. She was the anti-entitled planter. Pearl treated everybody exactly the same. If you had ears she could pour prattle into, she didn't care what color you were.

Larry was messing with the TV remote and even managed to turn the set back on before I snatched the thing away, took the batteries out, and told them all, "We've got to get you out of here to give us time to straighten this out."

"When?" Shawnica asked me.

"Right now."

"To the hotel?" Skeeter wanted to know.

"Day after tomorrow was the best we could do. We'll put you up at Pearl's until then."

Shawnica's hands found her hips. "That bony white woman you live with?"

"Yeah."

Shawnica did that thing she does with her neck sometimes. She must have picked it up from a rooster. It's always followed by a decisive "Nuh-uh."

FOURTEEN

Pearl saved us a lot of grief with her gold-plated cable package. Her husband, Gil, had been the TV nut, and Pearl had just left everything as it was. She was hardly the sort to park herself in front of the set and watch, but she turned it on when she got up and let it play throughout the day. I didn't know she had two hundred channels, including all the premium stations, but Larry discovered it almost straightaway.

He told me and Desmond, "This'll work."

We weren't even in the middle yet of giving Pearl the lay of the land. Shawnica wasn't helping any. She wouldn't let me talk to Pearl without coming in behind and over top of me to tell Pearl how none of this was her idea. She was all sassy about it, too, the way Shawnica likes to be. Then she stepped over to the refrigerator and started poking around inside.

"You know witness protection?" I asked Pearl.

She nodded and told me, "No."

"They're people the criminals want to get at, the ones who saw a crime or something."

"What did *they* see?" Pearl asked me.

I heard Desmond mutter, "*Iron Chef.*"

"They saw somebody get knocked on the head," I told Pearl. "The police'll sort it out, but they need a place to park for a couple of days."

"Here?" She didn't say it like I would have said it. She said it like I'd just told her the queen and prince consort were passing through the Delta and hoped to hole up for a little while at her house. It was an optimistic *Here?* A grateful *Here?*

Pearl reached up and fooled with her hair, not that she could have done much good since she'd put her curlers in it already. She was wearing her housecoat and her ratty slippers that once had cat faces on them or something. Now there were two beady eyes between them, and one serviceable ear.

"I should dress," she told me.

Just then Shawnica held up a plastic container with something purple and green inside it.

"Miss lady?" she said.

"Trifle," Pearl told her. "You have all you want, sugar."

Me and Desmond tried to warn her off. We shook our heads at her, anyway, but Shawnica peeled off the top and went hunting for a spoon. She'd almost even eaten a little before the smell impressed itself upon her. That item might have been trifle once, six or seven months ago. That was the trouble with Pearl's refrigerator. Archaeological cuisine.

Skeeter and Larry had found some soft-core porn. I could tell by how quiet they'd gotten. Out-and-out pornography doesn't require so much attention as the half-cooked semi-modest brand. It calls for sustained hopefulness. They were watching a spot of congress. We could hear the moaning a little. They were willing it to get more lurid than it was.

"Is this all right, Pearl?" I asked her. "Two nights?"

She laid a hand to my arm. "Those boys in there, don't they look about Gil's size?"

Every man looked Gil's size to Pearl. She was sure to go into Gil's closet and fit Larry and Skeeter into Gil's trousers, Gil's sport coats, his suits. It was the Jewish mother in her, and she was Presbyterian. So you didn't get brisket. You got a seersucker jacket from Pearl and pleated pants.

My phone rang just as I was feeling like me and Desmond had accomplished something, had bought a little time until we could get our Shambrough problem in hand. At that point I didn't care if the whole business ended with Lucas Shambrough in the back of Kendell's cruiser or underneath a swamp somewhere. That went double for the ninja schoolgirl assassin. I couldn't see how this world needed her.

So I had a moment of good feeling about what we were up to, most especially once I looked at the caller ID and saw it was Tula Raintree.

"How'd you get this number," I said to her, giving it back just like I'd gotten it.

She laughed about like I'd hoped she would. "Sorry," she told me. "I was caught in the middle of something, wrangling a couple of shitheads."

"The Lord's work."

I stepped out on Pearl's back porch for a little privacy. I hoped maybe Tula was coming off shift and seeking me out for company. The truth was a little different the way the truth too often is.

"Got some guy here. Says he knows you."

"What guy?"

"We caught him throwing TVs in the river."

I felt a lot less good than I'd only just felt. "Dale?"

"That's the one. He said you'd bail him out."

"He used to be a trooper."

"Told me that, too. He told me all sorts of things. Is he a tweaker or something?"

"Might be these days. I don't know. A stone cold idiot, I can tell you that."

"When did you last see him?"

I checked my watch. "About five hours ago."

"Know where he got the TVs?"

"Got a pretty good idea."

"You anywhere near Greenville?"

"I'm about to be," I told her.

Desmond agreed to babysit. If I'd been thinking at all, I would have taken his Escalade instead of my conspicuous Ranchero. But then I had my A-5 behind the seat and my Ruger in the glove box, my .308 still on my ankle, and a deputy waiting for me in Greenville. So I wheeled straight through town on the truck route, not worried about who might see me. I was focused instead on T. Raintree at the end of the road.

It wouldn't usually pay to notice in the Delta if there was a pickup truck behind you. The place is lousy with them. It's a pickup part of the world, so the one behind me didn't register for the first twelve miles or so. But the fool at the wheel stuck to me so close, I couldn't help but notice in time.

We sped up together. We slowed down together. We changed lanes at about the same time. There were two of them in the cab. I recognized the type. Gritty lowlifes. Self-inflicted haircuts. One of them even had a phone, and he got on it while the other one drove. He couldn't seem to help but point at my Ranchero while he talked about it.

I caught up with a semi hauling chickens as we approached the town of Leland. I rode along in the left lane beside it until we'd closed hard on a turnoff to the right. I waited as long as I dared and then whipped over and turned on the side road. Those boys couldn't get around that truck, and so I bought myself some time. They'd have to go down and make a U-turn. I figured I had two minutes.

I drove into Leland proper and stopped at a Double Quick on the bayou. I parked right out front where those boys were sure to catch sight of my Ranchero. I took the Ruger with me and slipped around behind the place.

They didn't disappoint. They pulled in shortly. I could hear their muffler. That old Ford they were driving dieseled and sputtered when the driver switched it off.

I slipped down the side of the building until I could see a piece of that truck. The back quarter panel. The thing sank and wallowed as the driver climbed out of the cab. I heard the sound of one door slamming. The passenger, still in the cab, said something I couldn't make out.

The driver told him back, "All right."

I gave him time to go inside before I came around the building. I lurked at the corner of the Double Quick. The guy in the truck was smoking a cigarette and fooling with a pistol, an old Buntline revolver, dull and rusty. He kept dropping the cylinder out and slapping it back like he'd seen in the movies. He was so happily occupied that he didn't notice me coming until I'd swung open the driver's door and slipped in under the wheel.

He told me (or maybe just told himself), "Shit!"

I reached over and grabbed his pistol. The cylinder was flopped out, so all I had to do was tilt the barrel up to dump the bullets into his lap.

"Now what?" I said.

He did the typical weaselly redneck move of trying to go everywhere all at once. It's the sort of thing that looks to the untrained eye like a spastic fit with freshets of profanity.

That boy was telling me, "Motherfucker," and reaching around like he had something down by the door to harm me with when I took full advantage of the vintage truck they were driving.

The dashboard vinyl had long since rotted and curled, and the thing was steel underneath. So I reached my hand behind that fellow's head and slammed him forward until he bounced. One time proved enough. The air left him, and he collapsed onto the seat. I leaned him up against the door as if he were relaxing, reached over him, and pulled out the machete he'd been reaching for. It looked like he'd made it out of a mower blade and shaped it on a grinder. The edge was so dull, you couldn't have hoped to cut suet on a hot day.

I left it on the floorboard and ducked back around the building to wait for the driver. He was probably parked outside the men's room and hoping to waylay me there.

I called Desmond. I guess I was warning him, but I was venting a little, too. "I can't believe the crackers they've put on us."

"You all right?"

"I'm damned insulted."

"Shambrough's boys?"

"Probably, but they sure don't speak well of him."

"Need me?"

"No. One down. Just waiting for the other one."

"Why don't you put that thing of yours in the car shed for a week."

"Probably should," I told Desmond. "Think the other one's coming."

He came out of the store and went peeking around the far end of the building. He pulled something out of his jeans waistband. I couldn't quite see what it was. When he didn't find me down there, he came back toward his truck, talking to his buddy along the way.

"Where the hell is he?" He paused to cup his hands and look in my Ranchero. He got the driver's side glass all greasy. That was another mark against him. "Wasn't in the crapper."

His buddy just kept lounging against the door and being unconscious. "Lady at the counter said didn't nobody like him come in."

He'd just drawn open the driver's door when I slipped up behind him. He felt me there. I had to figure he would. "You, ain't it?" he said without looking.

I'd expected to find a gun in his hand—a pepper pot or a Mauser or something—but it wasn't even anything that ambitious. Just a homemade sap instead. He'd fashioned it out of a stiff steel spring with blue electrical tape for a handle.

I told him, "I've never been so irritated with two pinheads in my life."

He put his hands up like we were in a Western. "Got a gun on me, don't you?"

"Put your hands down."

"I ain't making no moves."

"Down!" I told him. He dropped them to his sides.

"He dead?" he asked of his partner.

"Not yet," I said, and he raised his hands again. It doesn't pay to have a thing in this life to do with cracker pinheads. "Down," I told him.

"You the one with the drop."

"For fuck's sake. What did I say?"

He put his hands down.

"Shambrough send you?"

He decided to clam up, so I tapped him once on the back of the head. "Don't you raise those hands."

He told me, "Ow, buddy."

"Shambrough," I said.

"Wasn't him. No sir."

I had to figure he was getting literal on me.

"Did Shambrough tell somebody to send you?"

I had to tap him again.

"Yeah," he finally told me. "Maybe."

"You know where Lucas Shambrough lives?" I asked him.

He nodded. "Been by there," he said.

His buddy started groaning and stirring in the truck.

"Bang him one time on the dashboard," I said.

"I don't want to be—"

I tapped him again. He grabbed a fistful of his colleague's hair and slammed his forehead against the dash. Hard enough to lay him open and make him bleed.

"That do?"

I told him, "Yeah. Now take off your clothes."

He didn't do anything for a moment, beyond getting cracked in the head.

"All right, all right." He stripped out of his sweaty T-shirt. He had enough hair on his back for a throw rug.

"Pants, too," I told him.

He grumbled but kicked out of his shoes and peeled his jeans off. Clearly his mother had never instructed him on the value of clean briefs.

"All of it," I told him.

I got an incredulous cracker glance from over his shoulder. All I had to do was draw back, and he came out of his underpants, too.

"Throw the hat down." It was a blue Dale Earnhardt tribute cap that I'm sure he cherished or I wouldn't have bothered to make him leave it behind.

As he stood there buck naked, an old fellow at the pump island glared over at us and spat.

"What are you going to do?" that cracker asked me.

"Get in the truck," I told him. When he tried to gather up his clothes, I added, "Uh-uh."

He whimpered a little and got on in.

I threw his sap up on the dash. "You go straight to Lucas

Shambrough's. Don't stop anywhere and don't cover up. I'll be behind you. You knock on his door just like God made you. You'll tell him he needs a bigger fucking boat."

"A what?"

I was tempted to hit him again, but I opted for considered self-restraint. "You heard me," I said. "I'm watching. Go on."

He started his truck and backed out of his spot. He cleared the gutter and gained the road with enough velocity to make sparks come off his undercarriage. I climbed into my Ranchero and pulled out the other way. He was sure to suspect every pair of headlights behind him to be mine.

I called Desmond on the way into Greenville to fill him in on what had happened.

"Keep them in if you can," I told him. "He's turned his cretin army loose."

Desmond said that Skeeter was watching TV in a double-breasted blazer and Larry was wearing a pale green linen suit.

"What did Gil do?" Desmond asked me.

"Suffered Pearl," I said. "What's she up to?"

"Shawnica cleaned out her icebox. Now they're making some kind of cake."

"Stay on, will you?"

"Yeah. I called Momma."

"I'll get back as soon as I can."

I'd hit downtown Greenville proper by then. The place was little short of desolate. It was just me and a pair of radio cars out in front of the station house. The officer at the desk was watching what looked like ice dancing on his puny TV.

"Officer Raintree's expecting me," I told him.

He waved me up and went back to his set.

The pew was empty. Teddy must have been out in the wild eating dollar bills. I found Tula at her desk doing the sort of paperwork that had finally drained the life out of police work for me. There wasn't anybody else in the squad room. It was half past nine by then.

"How you?" she asked me.

I thought for a moment. I finally told her, "Grand."

FIFTEEN

I dropped into the chair beside her desk, and we talked about nothing for a bit, which in this case meant we mostly didn't talk about Dale. Didn't talk about Shambrough either, of course, and I wasn't going to mention Larry's dead buddy, so instead we talked about CJ, who was sleeping at a friend's.

"Good kid," I told Tula. "Clean." I was thinking about how he'd scrubbed his hands in the men's room at the restaurant, but before I could explain myself, Dale bellowed from his cell.

"Hold on," Tula said and pushed back to stand up.

"Let me." I followed the sound of Dale's voice into a back hallway and down around a corner where the holding cages were.

Naturally, Dale had taken his shirt off. Since his cell was overlit, I couldn't help but notice he was slick and sweaty and as hairless as an egg. I caught myself wondering if Dale was suffering from the toxic side effects of mixing anabolic steroids and Nair.

"Hey," Dale said as if we'd run into each other at the mall.

"What's up?"

Dale had to think a minute. He glanced around his cell like he was only just coming to grips with where he was.

"What are you doing in here?" Dale asked me.

"You're in," I said. "I'm out."

He must have believed me, because he started bellowing again.

I rattled the door bolt against the keeper like you'd shake keys at a crying infant. Dale immediately fell silent and looked at the door, at me.

"You taking something, Dale?"

"Aspirin sometimes. Doctor put me on it."

"Anything else?"

Dale shrugged and shook his head.

"You know they caught you throwing TVs in the river, right?"

Dale considered this for a good quarter minute. "What river?" he finally asked me.

"Kalil's TVs," I told him. "You busted into the store to get them."

Dale snorted, amused I'd say such a thing. He shook his head and told me, "Naw."

"Yeah," I said. "They want to send you to Whitfield. Let you stew in there for a while."

Even in his addled state, Dale knew what Whitfield was— the big hospital out by Jackson where the head cases ended up. Nuts went in, and dull, medicated people occasionally came out.

Dale made a sort of Scooby-Doo noise.

"You don't want that, do you?"

He watched sweat drip from his shiny bicep. "Uh-uh," he finally told me.

"So how are we going to keep you here instead?"

Dale pointed at the floor.

"Right here," I told him. "Until maybe tomorrow morning when you're feeling better. How are we going to make sure nobody knows to come haul you out of here?"

Dale couldn't say. He tried to, but he just shook his head and moaned a little.

"If they don't hear you, they can't find you. Might forget you're back here tonight."

That made a kind of sense to Dale. He nodded.

"Then I'll come get you in the morning, and me and you'll go see Kalil. Figure out what to do about those TVs."

Dale cleared up enough to say, "K-Lo."

"Yeah. First thing. But you've got to be here when I come. How are you going to do that?"

Dale put his finger to his lips.

"That's right." I pointed at his bunk. "Let me see if I can get these lights switched off."

Then I stood and waited until Dale grew convinced I'd keep standing and waiting unless he went to his bunk and sat down.

"No more racket, right?"

I got an outright nod from Dale.

"I'll come get you in the morning."

I slipped out slowly. Before I got entirely out of sight, Dale had tipped over onto his bunk. I found the light switch at the end of the hallway and plunged the lockup into darkness but for the orange glow of the mercury lights outside.

Tula was just signing off from a phone call when I finally returned to the squad room.

"Just checking on CJ," she told me as she pocketed her phone. "You know," she added. "The clean one."

Then she headed for the door, and I followed her down the steps and out of the station house into the street.

"Glass of wine or something?" she asked me.

"You're off duty?"

"Better be."

"Sure. Where?" I glanced around like I might spot an open nightspot there in Greenville. Aside from the casinos beyond the levee, there wasn't anything open at all. That's when I saw them. There were at least two, sitting in a shiny Impala. It was parked on a side street with the nose out so they could watch the station house door. I caught the glow of a cigarette. Saw their shadows shift a little. Maybe somebody in the back. I couldn't be sure.

"Nothing here," Tula said. "I was thinking you could follow me to my place."

I wanted to, all right, but if I followed her, they were sure to follow me. So I had some responsible thinking to do and no real time to do it. I was half tempted by the noble thing, just begging off for the night. Like usual, though, the noble thing didn't hold much interest for me.

Then Tula reached back and unclipped her hair, gave her head a shake to make it fall, and I was weak against any

course of action but following her after that. I just had to decide how to do it. Did I excuse myself long enough to slip
around to that Impala and have a chat with the gentlemen
inside it, or did I let them trail us to Tula's and take care of
them out there? That would require some explaining, and
I flashed on how Tula might react.

I could be sure, from past experience, that she would put
me in cuffs if she had to. Then I wondered if maybe those boys
weren't even interested in me. It could be that sitting in that
Impala and smoking was their idea of a night on the town in
Greenville. I liked the idea of that and was trying even to believe it when Tula broke the spell by saying, "So maybe another time."

"What? No. Now's good. Just thinking I might need gas."

"Quick Stop," she told me and pointed vaguely toward the
truck route.

I asked her, "Which way are we heading?" like I didn't
know where she lived.

"Toward Leland," she said. "Have you eaten?"

I tried to remember. "Not since lunch."

"I'll pick up something. Meet you at the pump."

I glanced again at that Impala. I nodded. I guess I seemed
distracted.

"Somewhere else you need to be?"

"Know those guys?"

She turned and looked. The driver's arm was hanging down
the door. He flicked his cigarette away, and it kicked sparks up
on the street. He dropped that Impala into gear and pulled
into the boulevard proper, heading west toward the levee, just
creeping along away from Tula and me.

"Nope," she told me. "Why?"

I shrugged like I couldn't really say, but I had to guess she was too good a cop not to have her antennae up by then.

"Quick Stop," she said.

"Yeah," I told her and tried to walk her to her car.

She snorted. "Right. See you there." She left me at the curb.

So I had the chance to lose those boys. I went the way they'd gone, hoping they'd fall in behind me and I could take them across the bridge, tangle with them in Arkansas, and leave them busted up over there. I didn't spot them anywhere. I went coasting all through town. It was a little past ten by then, and there was nobody on the streets. So I headed out Washington and turned east on the truck route. I pulled up to the pump island at the Quick Stop and topped off my tank.

I left the nozzle in and leaned against the quarter panel. I watched what little traffic there was passing on the four-lane. Semis mostly and chromed-up coupes. I'm pretty sure I saw Larry's Tercel. No sign of that Impala, though.

I half thought I was overreacting and it was just a bunch of crackers out for a night, but my earlier run-in had served to key me in to what was up, so I was primed to think everybody who glanced my way had been sent by Shambrough to do me harm.

Tula pulled in with a pizza box on the passenger seat beside her.

"About two miles," she told me, "and then we'll turn right, just past a pair of old silos."

I followed her, checking my mirror. I felt foolish enough after a while to spend most of my energy gaming out where pizza and wine might lead. I didn't want to assume too much, though. Tula didn't strike me as the sort who'd let even an authentic prize of a guy into her affections straightaway, and while I might have been rugged and impeccably well-meaning, I knew I wasn't much of a prize. So I figured we'd eat pizza, drink a little wine, and chat, and then I'd get a chance to run the gauntlet of Shambrough hooligans back to Pearl's.

It was just me and Tula on the road. I signaled when she signaled. I turned where she turned and finally followed her into her drive. Her house was dark. The yard, too. She pulled her service flashlight and lit our way. I heard frogs somewhere and crickets, the yelp of a hound but no car engine. I followed her inside and took a last look before I shut the door.

Tula switched on a couple of lamps and went back to crank up the AC. I was looking out the front window for any trace of car headlights when Tula came in from the kitchen.

"I've got red and red," she said.

"The red, then."

"And you can fill me in whenever you want."

I gave her my *Whadda you mean?* face but for only a couple of seconds. I already knew it wouldn't work on her. She didn't hang around long enough to see it anyway. I followed her into the kitchen.

"You're not going to like this," I told her.

She pointed in a way to indicate all of my peeking and lurking. "I don't like that," she said. "Somebody's husband after you?"

"I wish."

"Oh yeah?"

"At least that'd mean I'd made a different mistake."

Tula fairly tossed a slice of pizza on a plate and shoved it at me across the counter. She poured herself a glass of wine and set the bottle back down, didn't offer to pour me one. She sipped. She waited. I'd had a wife once and so recognized this sort of chill. There wasn't anything for me to do but give her what she wanted.

"You know Desmond, right? Kendell's cousin?"

Tula managed a curt nod. She was especially beautiful irritated. Her eyes were almost black. She was a little short of simmering in her preemptive disapproval, as if she knew Desmond and me well enough to know we weren't up to anything good.

"Know Shawnica?"

She nodded. "Seen her around."

"She's got this brother. Calls himself Beluga."

"The holdup guy? The car thief?"

I nodded. "Been in and out of Parchman."

"Buddy of yours, too?"

"No," I said, and a car went by out front, which stopped me cold. I glanced toward the street even though I couldn't hope to see a thing from the kitchen.

"Me and Desmond kind of lent him some money. He said he had this business thing." I reached for the wine and poured myself a glass.

"What thing?"

"A line on some tires. Was going to get them cheap and sell them dear. Like that."

"Define *get*."

I held up my hands and showed her my palms—the universal gesture for *I feel like a dick in retrospect*. "Shawnica wanted us to bankroll him, which means Desmond wanted us to bankroll him, which means there wasn't much I could do but go along. Family, you know?"

"Kendell told me you two were flush. He said you took off some Acadian meth guy."

"I love Kendell, but sometimes he doesn't know what the hell he's talking about."

"He said you'd say that."

I waited. I breathed. "We gave Larry some money," I told her.

"So you're bankrolling Beluga." She was enjoying herself now.

"Could be we're just thrifty, you know? People save up money sometimes."

She sipped. She nodded. She smiled and said, "All right."

"So anyway, the tire thing's not exactly as advertised."

"Go figure."

"I know. Big surprise. Beluga takes them off a guy who doesn't have much patience for shit like that."

"Vindictive streak?"

I nodded. "Sends some muscle after Beluga."

"I heard it was a girl."

"First one, yeah. Cyborg in a skirt."

Tula came out of her uniform top. She hung it on the kitchen doorknob. She had on a gray Delta State T-shirt underneath. She was all lanky and brown and distracting.

"And the Impala guys?" she asked me.

"Want to . . . ?" I pointed at the dinette. This was all going to take the sort of explaining I thought I'd best sit down to do.

She hit me with the odd question, but mostly Tula let me

talk. About Shawnica and Beluga. About Pearl. About Lucas Shambrough and his ninja schoolgirl assassin. About me and Desmond and why I do for him and him for me. She'd had a female version of Desmond herself, down in Baton Rouge, so she knew all about asking no questions and doing what had to get done.

I told her about the naked guy in the pickup truck in Leland.

"That's just going to make them madder," she said.

"I kind of know that now."

I was leaning her way by then. I was trying to be suave and failing at it, and I'd reached an age where I knew I was failing at it in real time. So I was either going to kiss her awkwardly or pitch over onto the floor. She just sat there and saw me coming. When I couldn't quite reach her, she giggled.

"You could scoot a little," I told her.

"You'll figure it out," she said.

I had to shift my chair and start leaning toward her all over again. I'd raised a hand to steady myself and maybe put it somewhere. Not that I had a clue where it ought to go. She just smiled and didn't help me a bit, and I had closed my eyes a little when the bay window exploded all over Tula's front room.

I was still puckered when she was up fetching a shotgun out of the pantry. I pulled my .308 from my ankle holster. She switched off the kitchen lights, and we both charged out the back door into the yard. I caught the chrome flash of some sort of sedan roaring away with no lights on. I leveled on it, but Tula reached over and pushed my aiming hand down.

We went back inside. Tula's big front window had gone to

shards and bits. A hunk of brick had done the damage, about three-quarters of a paver. There was a message for me, I had to think, scratched on the thing in pencil.

I showed it to Tula. The message read, "Your dead."

SIXTEEN

I slept on the sofa once we'd finally cleared all the glass off of it. I wasn't being noble or particularly gentlemanly, but there was no glass in the window anymore, and any damn thing could have come in.

Tula gave me a pillow off CJ's bed and her pump-action 20-gauge shotgun.

"Want me to spell you around three?" she asked me.

I shook my head and got a kiss on the cheek goodnight.

I only sort of dozed on Tula's sofa. Mostly I'd drop off and come lurching awake, half expecting to find a bear or an alligator or maybe a cracker pinhead in the front room with me. It was not a good night. Not truly much of a good morning either. I was napping lightly when a fellow showed up, some guy in a straw fedora. He was peeking in at me over the windowsill by the time I'd noticed him.

"Hey," he told me.

I went scrabbling for the shotgun.

"Ain't this some shit?" he added, then turned his head and spat.

"Who are you?" I asked him. I could barely see the guy below his ears.

"About to ask you that."

Then I pointed the shotgun. He chuckled and winked.

"You first," I told him.

Instead he just sank out of sight.

"What is it?" That was Tula. She'd come out at the sound of my voice. She was all T-shirt and legs.

"Some guy." I was up by then and on my way to the window. I looked out into the bushes. "What are you doing," I said to the fellow crouching there.

"Didn't much want to get blasted," he told me.

"Dickie?"

"Yes, ma'am," that gentleman told Tula.

She joined me at the casing.

"Saw your window was out," Dickie told us, fighting his way back upright. He was hobbled with arthritis and was either seventy or two hundred years old. I couldn't tell which.

"Dickie lives down there." Tula pointed. I just saw soybeans and a hedgerow. "He doesn't miss much."

"See the boys who did this?" I asked him.

"Chevy," he told me and spat. "Didn't have no lights."

Tula said, "Shit," and picked up her foot. She was bleeding, barefoot, punctured.

I lifted her off the floor and carried her over to the couch. I plucked out the splinter of glass she'd picked up. Cleaned her up with a little spit. "Shoes," I told her. "Maybe pants. A guy needs to keep his mind on business."

She gave me the look without the snort. "Did you make coffee?"

"I'm barely up."

"Po-po." That was Dickie out in the bushes.

I heard the sound of tires on the driveway. Kendell got out of his cruiser and opened the door to let Dale out of the back.

"Did you call him?" I asked Tula.

She shook her head and continued into the kitchen.

"You know Kendell," she shouted my way. "He's a Jedi or something."

Then they were all in the bushes looking at me, their heads just over the windowsill.

Kendell gave me a hard once-over. "Figures" was all he said.

"Guy with a brick," I told him. I picked up the paver and showed it to him.

"What guy?"

"Some scholar. Impala, right," I said to Dickie.

He nodded and spat, told me and Kendell, "Uh-huh."

"We've got to straighten this fool mess out," Kendell said.

They all came in, even Dickie. Dale was quiet and meek, looked a little embarrassed. He stuck out a hand for me to shake it.

"That's right," Kendell told Dale. "Apologize at him for a while."

Dale was deeply and profoundly sorry and had to tell me all about it. He got mousy when he was sorry about something, which didn't happen with Dale terribly much, but it was happening just then. He crowded me and told me with next to no volume how full of regret he happened to be for everything he'd lately done.

"Those TVs," Dale said and shook his head. "I can't even remember what I was thinking."

"What TVs?" Dickie asked Dale.

"Tell *him* about it," I suggested, and Dale crowded Dickie and drew him aside.

"Were you here?" Kendell asked me as he sized up the empty window casing.

I nodded and pointed toward the kitchen.

"What time?"

"Ten maybe. Not sure. We were in there talking."

"But you saw a car?"

"In Greenville. They must have followed us out."

"You ready to tell me what all went on?"

I pointed at the floor like he might mean right there. Kendell raised his index finger and spiraled it around. He meant everything and he meant all over.

"Might as well." I turned toward the kitchen. "Had coffee?"

"Am I coming in on anything?"

"Brick kind of spoiled the mood."

Tula served us all breakfast about like she'd served me pizza the night before. She set a box of Cocoa Puffs on the counter and said, "Bowls are over there."

Only Dale had cereal. He ended up finishing the box. Then Kendell sent Dickie and Dale out to measure the casing for a new window glass once Tula had fished her tape out of her tool drawer.

"Get it right," he told them. "Clean out that channel good."

Dickie looked at his wrist like he had a watch on it. "My show's coming on."

"Be back on tomorrow," Kendell said.

If he'd not been inside, Dickie would have spat.

They were hardly out of the kitchen before Kendell told me, "Let's hear it." Kendell refilled his cup, Tula's as well. He showed me the empty pot.

"Guess I'm fine."

I laid it all out, everything we hadn't told him the day before after the beat-up boy in the catfish pond, which should have been incentive enough to talk.

"Shawnica," I told Kendell by way of explaining why we'd been discreet. He still had a bandage on his cheek and instinctively reached up to touch it.

"Two in the hospital. One in the morgue. I've got to pick somebody up."

"Larry?" I asked him.

"I guess."

"That girl's probably still out at Shambrough's."

"Let's get Larry talking first. I'll get to Shambrough when I have to. That's going to raise a stink around here."

"Why is everybody so damn scared of him?"

"Scared? That's not quite it," Kendell told me. "There are enough decent Shambroughs left, mostly up around Clarksdale and Cleveland, to make picking up the bad ones a little delicate. They close ranks. Hire lawyers. Call governors. That sort of thing. You've got to be squared away before you go after a Shambrough."

"And if she's out there under his roof?"

"We'll get there," Kendell told me, "but Larry first. We wouldn't be sitting here talking about this but for him and . . . who was it?"

"Skeeter."

"You on today?" Kendell asked Tula.

"Noon," she told him.

"I was going to give you . . ." He jabbed his thumb toward the front room and Dale. "Figured you could drive him over to Indianola."

"How's this?" I said. "I'll take Dale. Him and Kalil can work something out. And then I'll bring you Larry and Skeeter, and you can hear it all straight from them."

Kendell thought the way he usually did, with an expression of vague gastrointestinal upset. He finally gave me a nod.

"And you'll make sure she gets a window," I told him.

"*She,*" Tula informed us both, "can handle that herself."

I stood and said to Tula, "I'm sorry about all this."

I did that thing with my hand again. I reached toward her without any idea of exactly what I was up to. Especially there in front of Kendell. His gaze was like a laser sight. So my hand went into my pocket, which earned me the smile and the snort together from Tula.

I slinked straight out of the kitchen, collected Dale, and left the house.

Dale apologized to me all the way to Indianola. Whatever is five miles beyond profuse, that's where he ended up.

"Are you working?" I finally asked him as we were rolling into Indianola.

"My program?"

"No, like a job."

He shook his head.

"What are you living on?"

"Army money. Some disability."

"Disability?" I eyed him for effect. Dale might have been an idiot, but he was a specimen, too.

"Back trouble," he told me. "Sometimes."

"Want to work?" I asked him. "I mean, like, when your back'll let you."

Dale nodded. Sarcasm meant nothing to him. He was reliably tin-eared that way.

"Think you can stay straight?"

"When I'm working my program," Dale told me.

"Your program's clearly shit," I suggested.

"That's what Momma says, too."

"Wise woman," I told him as we pulled into K-Lo's lot. "I can probably get you on here, but you've got to show up and work."

Dale exhaled like he was approaching a five-hundred-pound dead lift. He nodded grimly and told me at last, "All right."

"You know how Kalil is," I said as I slipped out from under the wheel.

Dale nodded. "Talks a lot of shit."

"You ready for that?"

He exhaled again. He nodded.

As broken windows go, Kalil's was appreciably worse than Tula's. There'd been so much more of it to go to pieces, and by the look of the damage Dale had used his car instead of a brick.

"The Geo?" I asked him as we crossed the lot.

"I guess. I'm kind of fuzzy."

"Where is it now?"

Dale didn't know. "Hope it's not with the TVs," he said.

Kalil greeted Dale about like I'd thought he might. "Mother-fucker," he said. "Happy?" Kalil gestured toward his busted storefront.

A couple of glaziers were rebuilding the framing and cleaning up all the busted glass. They'd come all the way from Grenada with new sheet glass on their truck. They looked happy to see us. Anything to get Kalil off of them.

"He's real sorry," I told K-Lo.

K-Lo was standing out in front of the empty storefront that used to be the Hair Den. That's where he always ended up when he needed to smoke and fume, and he was right in the middle of doing both as me and Dale closed on him.

"He wasn't in his proper mind."

K-Lo spat, but not in that utilitarian country way that was common in the Delta. K-Lo always spat like he was punctuating a curse.

"But he's ready to make it right."

Dale was just standing there nodding instead of being helpfully profuse with apologies.

"Now," I told him, "would be a good time for some more apologizing."

That was all Dale needed to set him off, and he went straight up to K-Lo and told him every apologetic thing he'd told me ten times already. He closed so hard and flush that K-Lo had no room to spit, barely had enough space to bring his Merit Light up to his lips.

Desmond pulled in before I could call him. I was hoping

he'd have a full car and so save me the trouble of collecting Beluga LaMonte and Skeeter. That way I could just swap him Dale for the pair and get back on the road heading west. But it was only Desmond, looking unrested and a Coney Island or two short of a load.

"Everything all right?" I asked him.

"I think they'd watch TV all the time if there was a way to do it."

"Oh, there's a way to do it," I told him. "Ask my ex. Are they parked there now?"

Desmond nodded.

"Shawnica?"

"Went to work," Desmond said. "I don't worry about her, but those other two . . ." He just shook his head.

"How's Pearl getting on?"

"Company's company. She just keeps feeding them that mess she makes, and damned if they don't shovel it in."

"Kendell wants them," I told Desmond, and I explained what I'd been up to ever since I'd left him back at Pearl's.

"Lot of broken glass between then and now."

We both watched Kalil and Dale as Dale stood there all hangdog and Kalil unloaded on him. It was prime K-Lo— corrosive profanity delivered while he jabbed a finger at Dale's shirtfront. Those were the occasions when Kalil was most alive.

I left Desmond to wrangle Dale and Kalil and help them straighten out their mess. For my part, I headed to Pearl's to pick up the boys. Her Buick was gone from the driveway, but Pearl was out watering her hydrangeas. If there were such a thing as a Bible study cocktail party, Pearl would have been dressed for that.

"There you are," she said to me. It's what she always said.

"You look nice," I told her. That's what I always said.

"Thirsty," she said of her hydrangeas.

"Don't see your car."

"Boys took it," she said. "You would not believe how Gil's clothes fit the both of them to a T."

"Know where they went?" I asked her.

"Beluga told me," Pearl started in, and I confess I went a little weak. Larry had finally found somebody who would actually call him Beluga. "They had some shopping to do and some errands to run. They said I shouldn't hold lunch."

"Any idea where they were headed?"

"No, sweetie," Pearl said. "Would you?" She gave me the hose so I could coil it for her.

I called Desmond, but he didn't know about any shopping or errands.

"They were watching that damn show about the butler when I left."

I figured I could go out trolling for them, but Pearl's car was a gray Buick Regal. Somebody must have bought a fleet of them and sold them to all the canasta-playing Presbyterians, because whenever Pearl was hosting cards and the ladies all rolled in, it tended to look like a gathering of the clan.

The only chance I had was Pearl's cell phone. I'd bought her one for when she drove, and she'd gotten to the point where she never took it out of her cup holder. It was plugged into her lighter. I'd tried to teach her how to use it, but she'd never quite gotten the idea of the CALL button down. So she'd punch in the number she wanted and quit. She'd say, "Hello!" into the phone, wouldn't hear anything back, and would clap it shut and put it back in her cup holder.

I knew if I called Larry and Skeeter on Pearl's phone, they'd see who it was and surely wouldn't answer, but I also knew whose call they wouldn't dodge.

Shawnica wasn't delighted to see me. She was never delighted to see me, but on this day she was more conspicuously less delighted to see me than usual.

I'd swung by the veterinary clinic where she worked. The place had a CAT door on the east end of the building and a DOG door on the west end, but they both dumped the customers out into the very same waiting room, and I walked in on a kind of cross-species bedlam. There was an ancient ill-humored spaniel that was barking and snapping in a general way, and a mongrel puppy was peeing on the linoleum. Four cats in carriers were hissing and yowling, and some kind of miniature goat was raising a fuss.

The man with the miniature goat was just the type he had to be. He was a miniature goat promoter by nature, wanted everybody to have one. He was intent on proving how civilized a miniature goat could be. To that end, he kept setting his down on the floor so it might show off its manners. All it did, though, was slip on the floor tiles, get terrorized by the puppy and driven into the vicinity of the snapping spaniel or the hissing cats.

"Hold on to him or wait in the lot" were the first words I heard as I entered.

Shawnica had gotten up out of her seat and was pointing a glitter-nailed finger at the miniature goat guy, who just wanted a chance to bring her around to the charms of miniature goats.

"Right now!" Shawnica told him.

He snatched up his goat. What else could he do? He seemed to want to tell her how sweet the thing was and how it served as a comfort to him. Maybe how it had saved him from buying a mower or finding another wife. Shawnica made him think better of all of it. He held his tiny goat under his arm and parked in one of the plastic chairs.

That freed Shawnica to look at me, sneer, and tell me, "Uh-huh."

I explained what I was up to. I'd written Pearl's number on a scrap of paper, and I tried to keep the whole enterprise as simple as I possibly could.

"I ain't," Shawnica told me. That was usually her opening bid.

"You know where they went?"

"Do I look like I know where they went?"

She looked like she wanted me deboned with violence.

"Kendell wants them," I told her, "and he's going to get them one way or another. Might be better if me and Desmond take them in."

Shawnica leaned forward so she could whisper at me. Her whispering tended to carry as well as her regular shrieking did. "First some crazy bitch is going to kill us all, and now *they* going to jail."

She sounded profoundly skeptical about my whole afternoon's worth of plans.

"It's kind of a mess. I'll give you that. But it's Larry's mess, and it's Skeeter's mess, and they've got to explain it to Kendell. You know how he is."

She did. We all did. Kendell was like God. You always had to atone in the end.

"Uh-huh," Shawnica told me.

I offered her my scrap of paper again. She reached out with her glittery fingers and snatched it from me.

"Just find out where they are, and don't tell them I'm coming for them. Probably better I should explain it all face-to-face."

"What did I say?" Shawnica was talking past me to the gentleman with the miniature goat. He couldn't give up on selling the other customers on its virtues, so it was slipping again on the floor tiles and getting a rise out of the spaniel, causing the puppy to pee again on the floor.

When that fellow started making goat justification noises, Shawnica went over and held the door open for him. She pointed to a shady spot in the far corner of the lot. There wasn't a thing in this world he could do but go.

We followed him out. Shawnica called Pearl's cell number from the front clinic landing. She didn't get an answer—I imagined Skeeter examining the phone—so she called back and raised the pair of them.

"Where are you?" She listened, pointed toward the truck route. "Then where?" More listening and pointing. "All right." She ended the call. "RadioShack. Then the Walmart. Over in Greenwood."

"Thanks," I told her.

I got a Shawnica "Uh-huh."

SEVENTEEN

Greenwood was a good half hour east from where I was. Living in the Delta is all about driving to hell and back in a regular way, so I just switched on the radio to the Valley State gospel station, worked my way over to 82, and went.

At least the Walmart was on the near end of town. The RadioShack was, too. It was one of the few going businesses left in a sprawling shopping plaza where the department store had folded and the Shoe Show had given up. There'd been a pharmacy there for a bit as well, but the Walmart had done them in. So now there was the RadioShack, one of those edible florist shops, and a big junky fell-off-the-truck store that didn't even have a sign out front. There was also enough parking for a municipal airport or two.

I tried the RadioShack first. They'd been there, all right.

"A couple of guys in ugly suits," I said to the fellow working the counter.

He nodded immediately. "Bought a universal remote."

"How long ago?"

"Half an hour."

It was a short hop over to the Walmart, where I found Pearl's Buick in the lot. At least I felt reasonably certain the Regal I found was, in fact, Pearl's. She had a talent for banging it at every corner, being a contact parker, but I'd lately noticed a few of her friends were fond of the same technique. It was a gray Buick Regal with shoes on the back floorboard and a big-buttoned phone in the cup holder. I went ahead and decided to feel encouraged.

My optimism evaporated shortly because I wandered through the whole damn store without running across Larry or Skeeter. I went straight back to electronics first, what with the universal remote and all, but there was just a large woman there in with the TVs complaining about her reception and an employee informing her every chance he got, "Yes, ma'am."

I checked out the automotive section. The hardware section. I even went into the grocery end. Since it was the middle of a Wednesday, there weren't that many customers to speak of, and Larry and Skeeter in Gil's old sport coats would have fairly leapt out at me. They weren't anywhere. I even had a wander through menswear and ducked into the eyeglass shop. Then I went back out to the parking lot to see if that Regal had gotten gone.

It was sitting right where it had been. I took a harder look this time and spied two pair of espadrilles under the passenger seat. It was Pearl's, all right, so I had a look around the lot. Nothing special there, just the usual trucks and 4 × 4s and bug-encrusted sedans. I headed back into the store determined to be organized and systematic. I started over with the pharmacy against the front wall and figured I'd work through from there.

I almost didn't see her because I wasn't looking for her and because she was wearing what they used to call a shift. At least that's what they called them back when my sister wore them. So she looked a little like she'd stepped out of 1972. Her jumper had daisies in the pattern and bright green stalks of grass. She was wearing white tights and shiny black patent leather shoes. Her inky black hair looked freshly combed. She was walking away from me down an aisle, the one with the toasters and waffle irons and six different styles of coffeepot. I glanced at her and kept on going. I was two aisles past her when I stopped.

I couldn't have said at the time what caught my attention. I've thought about it since, and there was something in the way she walked that contradicted how she looked. She had the girlish clothes, but something in her stride . . . It wasn't swagger exactly. It was confidence. Assurance. A sense of security that actual adolescents never give off. They're always faking it at best. This was the genuine thing. So I backed up for another glance, but she was out of the aisle by then.

I hadn't noticed the tattoo or the stitches I'd caused her, but I was dead certain I'd just seen the ninja schoolgirl going away. I hustled down her aisle to look for where she might have turned and found myself in the notions section or the sewing department or something. There was some guy standing there by the thread rack. He turned and took me in. He was comparing two spools of sage green thread like he truly meant to buy one.

It was an odd enough sight to distract me a little. The guy smiled, and he had about twelve too many teeth. They were turned all which way. I felt sure I was looking at a couple of them on end.

He held up the spools so I could see them. He said to me, "Huh?"

I think that's what he said, anyway. The clatter kind of drowned him out. It turned out to be the sound a toaster oven makes when it hits me in the head.

Lucky for me I'd caught the flat part, and I told anybody who cared to hear it, "Ow. Shit."

I felt sure she was behind it, but I turned to see it wasn't her. It was some Latin guy in a green sequin shirt and white jeans with scarlet piping. He had his hair slicked back with greasy pomade and a perilously thin mustache riding his upper lip. His belt buckle had both turquoise and rhinestones on it. He looked like the emcee at a West Hollywood rodeo.

He blew a bubble with his gum and giggled at me like a forties starlet. Then he swung that damn toaster oven and tried to hit me with it again. I picked up a bolt of the ugliest yellow fabric I ever hope to see and swung it like a fungo. I caught him just under the chin. His teeth clapped together and he groaned and staggered. I would have enjoyed it more if the guy with thread hadn't decided to join in. I was expecting him sooner. He came up behind me and hooked an arm around my neck.

He was wearing cheap sneakers on his massive feet, so

there wasn't a lot of aiming required. I just stomped until I hit one, caught it right below the ankle. Everybody in that end of the Walmart heard his foot bones fracture and snap. He didn't scream, but he sure sucked lively air through all those teeth of his. I gave him an elbow in the throat, and that sent him hobbling back.

Just in time, because the other one was coming at me again by then. He was bleeding all over his sparkly shirt, and he'd pulled out a knife in the meantime. He whipped it around the way his sort will while licking blood off his lip and giggling at me. He seemed just the sort of fellow batty enough to cut me into stew beef.

I picked up a box with a sewing machine in it and tried to use it as a shield, but it was a flimsy thing and didn't have any heft to speak of.

I backed into one of the main aisles, hit a pallet of deep-fat fryers. I worked my way around them while that sparkly fellow lunged at me and the other one hobbled along behind him like some redneck Frankenstein. A customer with oxygen tubes in his nose perched on an electric cart rolled up between me and those two guys and made for decent interference. When they jostled him as they tried to push past, he supplied them both with a scrap of advice. Something to the effect they should watch where the fuck they were going. That he'd kick the shit out of them, even with his emphysema. He'd been in the goddamned air force. He'd make them sorry they were born.

I thought the sparkly one might slice him up there for a second. But he just licked more blood and giggled. The other one wheezed through his teeth while I backed into an automotive aisle. I didn't find much help there. Just assorted wiper blades, oil filters, and aftermarket floor mats. I rounded the end cap and headed up the next aisle as the boys behind me got wise. The one with the broken foot went back toward the fryer pallet to head me off on that end while the sparkly one kept after me to drive me into his partner's arms.

So I'd be obliged to make my stand in among a display of chrome wheels, trailer hitches, and a pair of heavy-duty garage jacks that mercifully came with heavy-duty handles. I grabbed one out of its socket. Four feet of tubular steel with a rubber grip on my end and just bare metal on the other. I decided to go for knife boy first, and he giggled his way right into trouble.

I gave him a lesson in not bringing a knife to a Walmart jack handle fight.

As he rounded the corner into my aisle, I tapped him flush on top of his head. That stopped him from walking and giggling both. He staggered a little and moaned. Since I wasn't looking to crush his skull—that would involve a lot of explaining, maybe some of it in open court—I just tapped him again. That's what I'll call it, anyway. It was enough to reduce him into a Larry pile, which freed me to pivot around and pay my full regard to his partner.

He had nothing but a broken foot, far too many teeth, and free-range animosity. He snatched up a lug wrench out of a hopper at the end of the aisle, but it was one of those stunted useless ones. Not good for changing a tire and certainly nocount where it came to a fight with a man with a steel jack handle. I tapped him as well, sort of like I was knighting him but with a hell of a lot less ceremony and fond regard.

He told me, "Uh," and staggered back into the wide aisle with the pallets. There was nothing but fryers and coolers and throw rugs out there.

I gave him kind of a line drive swing. He blocked it with his arm and then appeared to wish he hadn't. He threw a fryer at me. I think I hit a double with it. We were attracting both associates and customers by then.

Some management type in a vest came stalking up to straighten us out. I didn't even have to talk to him. My buddy clubbed him with a cooler, and he hit the floor crawling and squirming and rethinking his career.

The customers, ladies mostly, were profoundly scandalized and gathered in clumps to tell each other all about the sorry state of people while I beat everything my guy picked up directly out of his hands. Knife boy revived enough to make another stagger at me. The ladies raised a mortified fuss when he came pitching into the main aisle, so I knew to whip around, and I smacked him one more time. He landed on his face. I couldn't make out any giggles. I had to doubt that he'd be getting up.

The other one with the busted foot made a bid to slip away, but he wasn't quite agile enough for that. I softened him up with a blow to the ribs, and when he groaned and turned my way, I dropped my jack handle and punched him. A fist to the jaw was enough to send him into a bin of rubber dodge balls. The brick red ones with the pebbly texture like they used when I was in school.

I knew the Greenwood cops would be showing up shortly, so I ducked down the towel aisle. I tried to look a little like I was shopping while I kept an eye out for the schoolgirl assassin and Larry and Skeeter as well. Everybody else was moving toward the upset in the fryer aisle.

So the deeper into the store I got, the more I had the Walmart to myself. I didn't see anybody, aside from the people at the checkout. Certainly no ninja assassin, and not Larry or Skeeter either. Then I drew up in the men's department so I could reconnoiter. I was standing there by a rack of twelve-dollar Puritan trousers, the pleated kind that pass for dress slacks in the Delta, when I thought I heard somebody. I picked up something that sounded like sniveling.

I'm sensitive to sniveling. I tolerate whining better than most, but sniveling tends to set me off, particularly from adults. Working in law enforcement back in Virginia and doing repo for K-Lo, I'd run across an awful lot of sniveling, had even been the cause of some. It's two steps past pleading, downslope from whining. When you're sniveling, you're both quitting and making a plea for sympathy. It's like coming out and saying, "I can't even be bothered to whine."

I've kicked a sniveler or two. I'll admit that. Partly to buck them up and partly out of exasperation. Snivelers are always trying to explain themselves, and it mostly comes out snot and bubbly saliva. I just happen to react to sniveling the way some people react to snakes. It's an instinctive thing. I always want to reach for a shovel or a poleax.

The longer I stood there by the trousers, the surer I grew that I heard sniveling. I didn't see anybody, and there wasn't a conventional place for a person to be. Just racks of knit shirts and pants and sweatsuits and underwear and socks. I froze there and listened. It was sniveling, all right. With spit and snot and laced through with self-pity.

I crouched and looked under the display racks. There were feet in with the sweatsuits. Somebody was cowering back under the rack. I stepped over and stood there, listening some more.

"Larry?" I finally said.

He said something gurgly to me.

I reached down and grabbed an ankle and dragged him out.

He had on one of Gil's blazers. I'll call it deep peach. The color was close to a ghastly postcard sunset. He must have been wearing Gil's pants as well. They were nappy blue velour.

When I let go of Larry's foot, he crawled back in to where he'd been. Combined with the sniveling, that truly set me off.

"Get the hell out here," I told him.

"Uh-uh."

I grabbed him again and pulled in such a way as to let him know I didn't care if his leg came off at the hip or not.

Even then he tried to crawl back. He made me all but pick him up. Then he bent low and peered around like he was being stalked by a tiger.

"Did you see her?" I asked him.

He nodded.

"Where?"

He pointed back toward the electronics department.

"She come out of nowhere," he told me.

"She does that. Where's Skeeter?"

Larry shrugged. "We both took off."

Larry pulled up his blazer sleeve and showed me a scrape on his forearm. "Bitch hit me with a goddamn tennis racket."

We heard sirens out front. The Greenwood PD finally rolling up.

"What's that about?" Larry ducked again. He had a con's natural aversion to cops.

"Come on," I told him. "Let's find Skeeter and get out of here."

Larry followed me. He stayed right behind me with one hand on my back as I headed deeper into the store, past the ladies' underwear, the religious book section, the DVD bins, and full into electronics.

"Saw her here?"

Larry nodded. He pointed. She'd waylaid them by the iPod display.

We continued full to the back TV wall, where I could see the entire breadth of the store in both directions. Nobody. But there were some sort of tracks on the floor at the layaway alcove.

It was blood, all right. Slender feet had stepped in a pool and tracked it. I followed the footprints down a corridor to where the restrooms were.

"Stay here," I said and parked him against the wall.

The footprints came out of the men's room. I listened at the door but didn't hear a thing. I eased it open. More blood inside. Not pools but streaks and splatters. I stepped entirely into the room. I could see Skeeter's legs underneath the stall wall. There was a severely dented and bloody tennis racket on the floor.

I pushed the stall door open. Skeeter was sort of laid back on the toilet. He was a bloody mess from the crown of his head down. Just red and black all over until he opened a lone eye.

"Jesus, I thought you were dead," I told him.

Skeeter made a noise in his neck.

I didn't even hear the bathroom door open, but suddenly I had company. I glanced around and there he was, a huge black guy in a Greenwood city patrolman's uniform. He had his service revolver—a big black Ruger—pointed at my head.

"Hey here," he told me.

What could I do? I raised my hands and told him, "Hey."

EIGHTEEN

The interrogation room at the Greenwood police station was fragrant in an unsavory sort of way. Not Dupont fragrant but more like a Turkish prison's men's room after a sorority mixer. Like a sweaty, unkempt fellow who'd been dipped in a septic tank. It was a powerful stink. A staggering bouquet. I couldn't for the life of me understand why the cops didn't seem to notice it.

The big black one who'd arrested me—his name was Officer Earl—was the guy who hauled me into the station and cuffed me to the interrogation table.

"Sweet creeping Christ," I said. "What is that?"

He shook his head and asked me, "What?"

They'd put Larry next door. I could hear him sniveling. He was going on at some length about how he hadn't had his lunch. It was too hot in his room or too cool or too bright or too dark or something, because he seemed to be complaining about all of that as well. Then there was a sharp, concussive sound, and Larry didn't say much after that. I made a mental note to thank the cop who'd hauled off and smacked Larry. I hoped it was Officer Earl. He'd seemed decent enough.

I would have arrested me, too. Skeeter was in foul shape, and I was handy, and then there was the pair on the far end of the store, and they were in tough straits as well. So there was plenty to sort out and just me and Larry available to sort it. I'd tried to get Officer Earl to look for the ninja schoolgirl assassin, but he'd just slapped a pair of cuffs on me, walked me to the lot, and advised me to watch my head as I was banging it on the cruiser frame.

The guy who came in to question me was dipped in sandalwood cologne. It was sweet and spicy and married poorly to the septic stench.

He asked me to call him Donnie. He was a conspicuous idiot. "Now, mister," he kept saying, "I might not know much, but don't none of this seem right."

Except for the badge and the gun, I would have guessed he'd dropped in from the barbershop and was just having a bit of a hoot at my expense. He spent a solid minute trying to figure out how to work his pen. Did you push it or did you twist it or did it have a button or something? It was like he'd fallen out of the mother ship. On his head.

"Why don't we run through this thing," Donnie suggested. "Go on. Let's hear it."

"All right."

Donnie fooled with his pen some more. He snorted and

brought up something. He told me, "Hold on," got up from the table, and spat in the trash can in the corner. Then he groaned and muttered like he'd just come in from plowing behind a mule. He dropped back into his chair. He fooled with his pen. "Go on," he told me.

"Ran out of floss. Went over to get some."

"To the Walmart?"

"To the Walmart," I told him. "Drugstore's probably a dollar more."

"I hear you," Donnie said. He went digging in his ear and then noticed a crusty stain on his shirtfront and scratched at that with his nubby finger. Donnie was thick all over, like he'd been living on bacon and beer, and his clothes hadn't quite kept up with all the swelling. His shirt buttons were under some appreciable stress. I half expected one to fly off and put my eye out when he shifted.

"I like the minty waxed kind," I told Donnie.

He said, "I think we've covered the goddamn floss."

"You said every last thing."

"I know what I said, but I don't see no floss. Got your keys and your billfold and shit. Even got a gun off of you."

"I've got a permit for that," I told him.

"Didn't see no goddamn floss!"

"Didn't get to it," I said to Donnie. "Saw a guy I know."

"That one," Donnie said and jabbed his thumb toward the wall behind him. We could both hear Larry chattering in the next room over. He was talking like somebody would cut off a finger every time he stopped. I couldn't quite hear what he was saying, but, knowing Larry, it was a potent blend of spirited shinola and single malt horseshit.

Donnie checked a document in front of him. It looked like Larry's rap sheet.

"Lawrence Carothers." He read the name.

"Beluga LaMonte," I told him.

He looked up at me, back down at the sheet.

"Changed his name in Parchman," I said.

Donnie found the pertinent line on the form. Laid a finger to it. "Oh yeah," he said. Then he looked my way like I knew he would and said to me, "Beluga?"

I shrugged.

"Ain't that a fish or something?"

I nodded. "Or something," I told him.

Then he shook his head and snorted, and he seemed to expect me to do the same. It was the white high sign for *I'll never, as long as I live and breathe, understand your coloreds.*

I just sat there and waited, didn't join in.

"How exactly," Donnie finally asked me as he made a show of studying Larry's rap sheet, "did that boy in there get to be a friend of yours?"

"I know his sister. He kind of came with her."

"What are we going to find when we look you up?"

I shrugged. "Shitty credit. What do you want to find?"

"You been locked up with him?" He jerked his jowly head.

"Nope."

Just then the door opened, so we got a draft of slightly fresher air from the hallway. It came with another Greenwood detective. This one was rail thin and Delta Italian or something. Dark and with an eyebrow that extended straight across. He had jet black hair and a widow's peak and hands the size of dinner plates.

"Used to be a cop," he told Donnie and shoved my particulars his way.

Donnie perused my sheet, his lips moving. He looked up and said to me, "Virginia?"

I nodded. "Just past North Carolina. Cradle of democracy and all."

That irritated Donnie a little more than I'd expected. He looked like he was about to tell me he hailed from the Shenandoah Valley or could trace his family lineage direct to Grandpa Walton. Instead he just bristled and sneered at me. He said, "I seen a map."

The dark, wiry guy sat down as well. His name was Kevin, and he looked the part. Half Chicken Shack night manager, half real estate appraiser. He was far too antsy and transparent to hope to make for much of a cop.

"What you doing down here?" Kevin asked me. Then he chewed on the end of his thumb.

"Live here."

Donnie went back to my sheet. "Not seeing nothing local."

"Indianola. Been here about a year."

"Doing what?" Donnie asked me.

"Repo mostly. Rent-to-own store."

"On the truck route? That Arab?" Donnie asked me.

"Lebanese," I told him.

Donnie said, "Well," like that was about as close to Arab as a fellow needed to get.

Just then Larry let out a yelp from next door like he was having battlefield surgery. Donnie and Kevin both glanced at the wall separating us from him. They exchanged grins.

Kevin turned my way and told me, "Jasper."

I knew Jasper a little, had met him, anyway. He'd once been a buddy of Dale's before they'd had some falling-out at the gym, arguing over weight supplements or something. Jasper was, if anything, a little dimmer than Dale, but that all gets pretty negligible when the light's that low to start with.

"He's got a way with cons," Donnie told me. "That boy'll spill it all."

"Then talk to him," I suggested to them. "I was just in there for floss."

"Fellow in the bathroom a friend of yours, too?" Donnie asked me. Kevin sat beside him nodding like he would have asked me just the same thing given the chance to do it.

"Friend of Beluga's," I told them. "I met him a couple of weeks ago. Don't know much about him at all."

"Play much tennis?" Donnie wanted to know.

"Never went in for it."

"We going to find your prints on that racket?"

"Don't see how. Didn't touch it."

"Whose, then?" Kevin wanted to know. "Somebody touched it all to hell."

"How's Skeeter?" I asked them.

"Stomped pretty good and busted up," Donnie said, "but they say he'll make it. Them other ones, too."

"What other ones?"

Kevin and Donnie had a good laugh about that.

"People seen you," Kevin told me.

"Doing what?"

"Beating them two."

I squinted like I was giving the entire proposition some thought. "No," I told him. "Doesn't ring a bell."

"Now that's a pair," Donnie said. He had paper on them as well. "That funny one come all the way from Memphis to get beat to shit down here. You broke the other one's foot in a half-dozen places."

"I was just in there after floss."

"Funny one's got a concussion or something. He's a sweetheart. A warrant out for him in Kentucky. Sliced a guy clean open."

"So you're closing cases. Got to feel good about that."

"Somebody sure is," Donnie told me. "But you were just in there for floss."

I nodded.

Donnie and Kevin consulted with glances. They both pushed back from the table.

"Jasper," I said.

Donnie gave me his more-in-sorrow-than-anger look. "Half hour with him ought to do it."

Kevin snorted with laughter.

"Don't I get a call or something?"

"Naw," Donnie told me. "Works a little different down here."

They gathered up their papers and both went out, so I was left with just the stink and the ceaseless drone of Larry talking from the room next door. I wasn't savoring the prospect of getting softened up by Jasper. He was the PD's version of a hockey goon, with no investigative chops to speak of. Jasper just menaced people and busted them up when the menacing didn't work. He was built about like Dale but quicker and meaner. Dale mostly liked just having muscles. Jasper mostly liked using his for harm.

I heard Donnie, I had to think it was, stick his head in the room next door and acquaint Jasper with the treat that was waiting for him. He had to be ready for a change by then, given Larry's talent for collapsing and piling up. Jasper liked the illusion that he was battling whoever he was beating up. Just kicking Larry while he was drawn up whimpering on the floor wasn't likely to be satisfying for Jasper.

I took the opportunity to size up my options. It seemed unlikely Kendell or Desmond would drop by to help me straighten stuff out, and I wasn't much tempted to clue in Donnie and Kevin on Lucas Shambrough since I couldn't be sure where his tentacles reached. He was certain to have a badge or two in his pocket. At this point, I trusted Kendell and Tula and nobody else on a county payroll.

That lead me, of course, to think about Tula and be glad she couldn't see me. Cuffed to a table in a stinky room waiting for a no-neck deputy to drop in and scuff me up.

"I'm not," I told myself out loud, "having the week I'd hoped to have."

I was fully decided to let Jasper come in and do his worst. I figured I could cover up well enough and take it. Larry could tell them whatever he wanted to, but I'd just stick with floss. It was a good plan, but then Jasper spoiled it all when he came storming in and hit me.

It was more of a smack really, but there wasn't any foreplay at all. Jasper didn't ask me if I'd rather just confess or if I had details I might want to volunteer about what had gone on at the Walmart. He just charged through the door, flung it shut behind him, and came straight over and clapped me across the ear with his open beefy hand.

"Shit, Jasper!"

Jasper laughed. I guess he was laughing. He opened his mouth and made a noise, and there was a brand of delight in his eyes like he'd discovered a basket of doubloons.

"Donnie says you're an asshole."

"Donnie doesn't really know me."

Jasper popped me again with his open hand. It was like getting hit with a sack of gravel.

"Can't we talk about this?"

"Uh-uh."

Jasper made a fist and swung. I managed to get my free arm up but punched myself from the blow.

Jasper laughed—I'm extrapolating again. "Ain't you some friend of Dale's?"

I kind of nodded. I wasn't sure if that was a good thing or not.

Jasper told me, "Fucker," and swung again. I had to figure not.

Now it's one thing to tell yourself you'll just take a beating, especially from a muscle-head dope like Jasper, and it's something else entirely to actually sit there and take it. Every scrap and fiber of me was desperate to punch him back, so I was dodging him and fighting me, but I soon knew what was coming.

"We'd better talk about this," I informed Jasper.

He grunted and spat onto the floor. Jasper gave me a right to the kidney. Then he asked me, "Why?"

The trouble with people generally is they're not detail oriented. That's particularly true, I've discovered, in the Deep South. There they'd gone to the trouble to drill a hole in a perfectly good tabletop and had positioned it so you could lock a regular handcuff bracelet through it. But nobody had bothered to fix the table to the floor. It was a smallish table but stout. I knew I could pick it up. I'd tried already as soon as Officer Earl had locked me in. So while Jasper had his fists and his sculpted physique, I had the biggest nunchuck a fellow would probably ever need.

"Tell me what you want to know." I was all about giving Jasper chances.

"Guess I want to know how this feels." He swung at me again. This one would have surely broken my jaw if I hadn't managed to dodge it. Then the instincts just took over, and Jasper turned into table meat.

I picked that table up level and whipped it around. Jasper's shoulder broke off the near leg as the table edge met the side of his head and knocked him into the wall. I rammed the whole thing into his midsection. Jasper was still a little stunned. Then I wheeled around with it and hit him again, and it started breaking apart.

The top was pine, and the planks separated as the banding and the legs busted free. So I was loose enough soon to grab up a leg and raise it over Jasper, but there at the last second I decided just to punch him in the face instead. A couple of blows and Jasper went still and silent.

I fully expected Donnie or Kevin or Officer Earl to come rushing in. Me and Jasper, after all, had been making quite a lot of racket and then suddenly and comprehensively we weren't. So I just sat back down and waited, prepping my explanation. I tried out various versions of "Jasper slipped."

A good ten minutes passed. I couldn't hear anything in the hallway or so much as a lone snivel from Larry's room next door. I was down to just my cuff by then, had gotten rid of all the splintered table, so I went to the door, opened it a crack, and peeked out into the hall. There was nobody anywhere I could see, and the air sure was inviting. It smelled a lot less like an active sewer out there.

Jasper was groaning a little by then, so I punched him again before I left and then slipped into the hallway and eased next door. I couldn't hear any voices from inside. I opened the door a crack and thought the room was empty at first. Larry was back in the far corner curled up on the floor. He was unconscious after a fashion but only because he was asleep.

"Hey," I said and nudged him with my foot. Larry didn't look so good. Jasper had caught him a flush one to his left eye, and it was already puffy and swollen nearly shut.

I couldn't really blame Beluga for waking up sniveling. "I don't know nothing about it," he said even before he looked to have quite figured out where he was.

"Get up," I told him.

"Are we done?"

I put a finger to my lips and nodded.

I went back to the door and checked the hallway.

"Where's that big motherfucker?" Larry asked me. He'd yet to move from where I found him.

I dragged a finger across my neck. "Get up," I said.

Larry also was cuffed at one wrist, so we made kind of a conspicuous pair. But Larry was wearing Gil's peach sport coat, which meant he could shove his handcuffs up the sleeve and so look like a civilian with awful taste in clothes. I was wearing a short-sleeve shirt, so there wasn't much I could do but look escaped and shady.

"This way," I told him and held the door so Larry would follow me into the hall.

We moved down to the right and away from the general racket of the squad room. We found a stairwell at the corridor's end, went down a flight to a basement landing. There was a furnace, a bunch of file boxes, and a door that gave onto an alley. It had a lone throw bolt and was swollen in the jamb, but once Larry and I had bucked against it, the thing opened enough to let us out.

The station house backed onto a big square Methodist church downtown. Me and Larry slipped over to the cross street and turned west toward the Yazoo River. I figured we'd find a phone at one of the service stations on Grand Boulevard and just park somewhere discreet until Desmond could pick us up.

"They didn't know shit about nothing" was the first thing Larry told me. He might have looked like hell, but he sounded proud.

"Did you only talk to Jasper?"

"The big one?"

I nodded.

"Just him," Larry told me.

I had to break it to him that Jasper didn't know shit about nothing for a living.

"Didn't ask me about no tires, or that boy Bugle with the broken leg. Didn't ask me about none of that. Kept going on about some shitheads in the Walmart. I didn't see no damn body but her."

"She had friends," I told him. "A couple of guys."

"You get into it with them?"

"The only way they'd have it."

"So what are they all over us for?"

"Me and you were handy and awake."

"I'd be looking for her if I was them. Got those dead eyes like she's not even in there."

We crossed the river on the steel bridge and cut over to the Sunoco. They still had a pay phone out on the wall between the drink box and the bathrooms. They had everything, anyway, but the handset that somebody had made off with.

"Car's at the Walmart," Larry told me. "Skeeter had the keys." He pointed in precisely the wrong direction. "Think it's over there somewhere."

I had a spare Ranchero key in a magnetic bumper box, so if we could get to the Walmart parking lot, we'd be good to go.

"Give me your shirt," I said

Larry made like he was going to argue about it until I gave him, I guess, a Jasper look, when he came straight out of his sport coat, peeled off his shirt, and handed it to me. I fashioned it into a sling that I could hide my handcuff in. Larry slipped Gil's seersucker jacket back on over his naked torso. Together we didn't look like a pair decent people would tolerate loose on the land.

"You go straight up Grand. Left up there at the light. Then cut back through behind the drugstore, and you'll see the car lot and the Walmart." Larry gave me his skeptical look until I added, "Just walk."

To his credit, he did. I cut over first and then went west. I saw a cruiser a block beyond me heading the other way, but not with any frantic purpose like they knew we were out and loose. It must have been midafternoon by then and too hot for people to be stirring, so it was just me strolling down a residential street in Greenwood like I was taking my broken arm for an airing. I wouldn't have paid any notice to me either. I was just another guy without a car.

I crossed Park at the grocery store, cut past the school behind it, went around the nursing home, where I could hear a fellow yelling from inside. He didn't like something. He didn't sound sure what it was, but he knew how he felt. I came onto the Walmart lot past the garage bays and over by the gas pumps. I didn't go straight to my Ranchero but stopped at a truck first just to see what was what and who was where.

There were still a couple of cop cars and an EMT truck in the fire lane. Two deputies were crowding the shade by a trash can, passing the time and smoking. They didn't seem to be paying much attention to anything out in the lot at all.

"Hey."

Larry had slipped up on me, and I almost wheeled around and decked him.

"Want me to go see what's up?" he asked me and pointed at the cops.

"We know what's up," I told him.

"Maybe they grabbed that girl or something."

"Maybe they'll grab you."

"Maybe," he said.

"Come on." Larry followed me halfway across the lot to where I'd left my Ranchero. I felt around the muddy fender well until I found my magnetic key box, and we eased out of the Walmart as inconspicuously as a calypso coral truck thingy allows.

NINETEEN

"What happened to you?" K-Lo asked me and pointed at my arm. That qualified as a misty display of compassion for Kalil. Then he lit a Merit menthol and forgot to wait for me to say.

I pulled my arm out of my shirt sling and showed Desmond the dangling handcuff.

"Figured you were gone for longer than you needed." It was hard to excite Desmond. "Who'd you get loose from?"

I liked the way he couldn't be bothered to ask me what I'd done. I preferred to believe he just assumed it was something that needed doing.

"Jasper," I told him.

Dale heard me from inside. He came walking out the door with a broom in hand to tell us all, "That son of a bitch." Then he turned around and went straight back inside.

"She was at the Walmart," I told Desmond.

"Ninja girl?"

I nodded.

"Tore up Skeeter something awful," Larry said.

"How bad?"

"Haven't seen him," I told Desmond. "Talked to some cop named Donnie. You know him?"

Desmond didn't.

"He said Skeeter'd pull through, but he looked like hell. She beat him with a tennis racket."

"In the Walmart?" Desmond asked me.

I nodded. "Had some buddies with her, too. Guy with a knife, snakeskin boots, little Kid Creole mustache. Came down from Memphis, according to Donnie."

That didn't ring a bell with Desmond. He shook his head and glanced at K-Lo. Since this had nothing to do with his income, Kalil wasn't even listening to us.

"Other one was a big guy. Teeth all sideways."

"Lazy eye?"

I squinted to picture him. "Could have been, now that you say it."

"He's a Hoyt," Desmond told me. "Whole gang of them out by Blue Hole. Big. Dumb. Usually got teeth enough for two people. Been working for Shambroughs a long time."

"He was a sight," I said.

"So the cops picked up you two?" Desmond looked from me to Larry and back.

I nodded. "She cleared out somehow. Nobody else was in any shape to talk."

"And you busted out?"

"Kind of. Goddamn Jasper."

Dale stepped out with his broom again and told us, "Son of a bitch."

K-Lo didn't want us using his good saw. He'd just bought new blades, and he was convinced anyway that his bolt cutters would take those cuffs straight off.

"The chain maybe," I told him, "but the bracelet?"

"Oh yeah."

That stopped me a little. I'd heard K-Lo say "Oh yeah" about all sorts of things he'd made a hash of. Like when he told us he knew how to wire-weld hinges so that nothing around them would catch fire. It's a wonder he hadn't burned the store down and the rest of the shopping plaza with it. So I had reason to think that "Oh yeah" meant *I've got no fucking clue.*

"Hey, Larry," I said. "Come here. K-Lo's going to take your cuff off."

When Larry saw that mine was still attached, he immediately got suspicious, but it was too late by then since me and Desmond had a grip on him between us.

"Shit, man," he said as we turned him over so K-Lo could get a good angle. He worked the bottom jaw of his loppers in between the bracelet and Larry's wrist. Then he squeezed the handles together to limited effect. Limited effect on the steel, anyway. The effect on Larry was all but boundless.

He yelled like Kalil was cutting through bone. A glazier even came over to look. Not look like *Does this guy need my help?* but more like *Get a load of this shit.* Those boys were having a livelier day than they would have known in Grenada.

"Turn it a little," Desmond suggested. "You're going off sideways. Straighten it up."

"How would Jasper do this?" I finally asked Dale.

He threw down his broom and his dustpan and came stomping over to us.

"Give me that." He grabbed the bolt cutter away from K-Lo, worked the blade underneath the bracelet again, and sliced right through the steel.

"Once more," I said to Dale, showing him my handcuffs. "Jasper," I added, and he had me free of that bracelet in a couple of seconds.

"Think they'll come here looking for you?" Desmond asked me.

"They've got my wallet and my phone. Might figure out where to go after a while."

"Want to get Kendell to talk to them?"

"He won't like it. They won't either. If we can find the ninja girl and take her in, that'd smooth things out a lot. They'd probably forget all about me and Larry if we could give her to them."

"Think she was following them or just ran across them in the Walmart?"

Larry was sitting on one of Kalil's sofas with a hand on his puffy eye.

"Did you and Skeeter go anywhere before the RadioShack and the Walmart?"

Larry thought for a moment and then listed a good half-dozen other places. In Indianola. In Moorhead. In greater Greenwood as well. There wasn't a ninja assassin on the planet who wouldn't have gotten wind of them.

"You realize the people looking for you would sort of like you dead," I said to Larry.

He gave me his *whatever* shrug.

"We could just drive him over to Shambrough's and put him out in the yard," I suggested to Desmond.

Desmond groaned and said, "Shawnica," just like I knew he would.

When we couldn't figure out what else to do with him, we decided to take Larry with us. He was clearly going to be a hazard for any decent civilian to keep. Either you'd get a visit from a ruthless girl assassin or Larry would sprawl on your sofa eating microwave popcorn and watching Spike TV at full volume. It was one of those lose-lose situations, so we packed him into Desmond's Escalade and headed straight for the Indianola Sonic to settle Desmond's nerves.

Once the tray was fixed to the driver's door and the girl had brought our iced teas, me and Desmond started explaining to Larry how he would be spending the coming days while he held his cup to his puffy eye and did a fine job of not sniveling.

"Can we go see Skeeter?" he asked us.

"We'll call first," I told him. "See what kind of shape he's in. Might not be the best place for you and me to show our faces."

"Oh, right," Larry said like he'd forgotten about the whole handcuff and Jasper thing. "They got chicken fried steak here?" he asked me and Desmond.

That was the fundamental trouble with Larry. Nothing made a special impact on him. A ninja schoolgirl assassin and chicken fried steak were of equal interest to Larry, and you couldn't really count on him staying focused on the one once the other had popped into his head. I wasn't sure what Desmond and I could do with him beyond keep him in the car. We couldn't have him watch our backs when we were tangling with that Shambrough. Larry would forget what he was up to and start wondering about curly fries or clouds.

Desmond's phone rang. He was still using Barry White.

"It's Kendell," he told me.

"Just play dumb. See what he knows."

Larry started chattering about muskrats or something.

"Zip it," I told him.

Desmond answered the call. He barely got out "Hey."

Kendell's not a yeller ordinarily. He's too Baptist and deliberate for that, but he uncorked some high feeling Desmond's way. The racket even caught Larry's attention.

"Did what now?" Desmond asked. He was awfully good at dumb.

More high-velocity talk from Kendell.

"I've been trying to get Dale and K-Lo straightened out. I don't know anything about it."

Kendell dropped a couple of octaves, but Desmond glanced my way and shook his head to let me know that Kendell was still hot.

"Where now? Greenwood?"

He listened some more. Kendell was as close to barking at Desmond as Kendell ever got.

"Who did that?"

Kendell cranked it down now that he was on the details.

"They catch her?"

Kendell talked some more. He didn't sound too anxious to sign off until he'd fully filled Desmond in.

"Jasper's that buddy of Dale's, right?"

Kendell explained some more.

"What do you want me to tell Nick?"

Kendell had some ideas.

"He'll never go for that. Larry might."

Desmond listened some more.

"What surgery?"

Kendell elaborated.

"But he's going to be all right?"

Kendell rattled on. That was about as much talk as I'd ever known Kendell to spill out in one sitting.

"Yeah, a little. With the lazy eye. What's he got to do with this?"

Kendell clearly had an expansive idea about that Hoyt and his sparkly colleague. Desmond heard him out, just threw in the occasional "Uh-huh."

"I'll tell him if I see him," Desmond informed Kendell. "You know Nick. If he beat down Jasper, he had good reason to do it. I wouldn't have hung around either. Cops get crazy about shit like that."

Kendell, being a cop, had to try to straighten Desmond out a little. He was right in the middle of it when the girl came with our food. She was hopelessly chatty and was prattling about everything she'd brought, which prompted Larry to point at Desmond and tell her, "My man's on a call."

Desmond shouted, "Kendell," a couple of times into the phone. "Lost you," he said and hit the END button to switch the damn thing off.

"If Kendell's anywhere around here," I told Desmond, "he'll know just where to find us."

Desmond plucked up a relish packet and shook it like he always did. Four times and then he flicked it with his finger before he tore off the front right corner.

"I'm eating my Coney Islands," he said, "and I'm doing it right here."

So Desmond and Larry ate late-lunch hot dogs—there's no chicken fried anything at the Sonic—while I nibbled a little at a Sonic burger and kept an eye out on everybody around us. Once you've been attacked in a Walmart by a sparkly giggler and a hulking guy with too many teeth shopping for thread, then the world looks less congenial to you as a general thing.

"Wonder if she eats," I said as I was looking around the Sonic lot.

"Who?" Desmond asked me.

"Ninja."

"Everybody eats."

"She's all muscle and veins and sinews and shit. She might just get by on venom."

"I'm having lunch back here," Larry told me. "Don't want to be thinking about her."

"I'm just saying she's not like us."

"She ain't like anybody. When did you last beat a guy half to death with a tennis racket? Maybe she's some little guy in a dress."

"No," I told Larry. "There's a girl in there somewhere. The question is, what do we do about her? And what do we do about Shambrough?"

"Can't they pick her up for Skeeter?" Desmond asked me.

"I don't know if we can wait until then."

"Think she was even trying to kill him?" Desmond wanted to know. "She beat up Izzy and that woman, too. They're all broken to pieces, but they're still here, and Larry's guy down in Belzoni proves she knows the difference. Wouldn't Skeeter be dead if that's how she'd wanted him?"

"I don't know," I said. "She might be saving Larry for that."

That prompted a spasm from Larry. "It wasn't nothing but tires!" he told us. "How in the world's that something to get dead over?"

I let Larry snivel for very nearly an entire minute. He made me and Desmond understand that he didn't want to die.

"I ought to tell Tula something," I said to Desmond.

"What's going on with you two?" he asked me.

"I get her thinking she likes me a little and then I go and fuck things up."

"Yeah," Desmond decided. "You ought to tell her something."

He gave me his phone, and I went with it over to one of the picnic tables and perched on it. The one back in the slash pine hedgerow where you couldn't see a thing and nobody had a clear view of you. It didn't mean I couldn't still hear Desmond telling Larry to shut up or smell the fryer oil exhaust from the massive Sonic vent. But it was a little private, as the Sonic went.

I was planning on what to say and just coming to the realization that I didn't know Tula's number. It was in my phone, and my phone was still over at the Greenwood PD. So I was irritated about that when a gentleman came to join me. He didn't have any food with him, but he had thought to bring a shotgun. The barrel was rusty, and the stock looked like somebody had driven framing nails with it. This was not a man who gave a happy damn about his guns.

"Get up," he said.

I turned to look at him. I was sitting on the table with my feet on the bench.

"I'd be killing you now, but somebody wants at you first."

He was whiskery, and his dungarees were slick from wear and filth. He had too many teeth, and the bulk of them were turned sideways.

"You a Hoyt?"

That stopped him a little. "Maybe."

I went to shove Desmond's phone into my pocket, and that fellow jumped a half foot into the air.

"Easy," I told him.

He didn't like that much. He jabbed me with the end of his barrel. "Come on."

"Can't I pick up my lunch?"

"What the hell do you think?"

"I think I paid for it already."

He poked me again. "Come on."

"There's probably enough for you."

"Got the gun here, don't I? I'll eat the whole damn business."

"Oh," I told him. "Right." I eased up off the table and stood on the concrete slab.

He poked me again and grunted.

"Easy now. Let's you and me go to the window and pick it up."

I stepped toward a gap in the pine trees, didn't wait for him to talk. He came behind me, shotgun leveled still.

"Might want to drop that a little," I told him. "Don't want people to think what they'll think."

That seemed sufficiently reasonable to him. He lowered the barrel and went all casual like he was coming off the skeet range, and that was really all I required.

The trick to this sort of thing is commitment. That's my theory, anyway. I always go in full bore, as hard as I can. I never pull a punch, and I exploit every opening. You can't be both wailing on a guy and worried that you're hurting him. It's best to be decided that hurting him is what it's all about.

So I whipped around on that Hoyt, held down his shotgun barrel with my left hand, and flattened his nose with a straight right to his face. It's the sort of punch that usually causes a man to forget just what he's up to. He's suddenly blind and in too damn much pain to care about you anymore.

That Hoyt let go of his gun as he reached for his nose. It hit the cement and broke in about six pieces. I can't imagine the thing would have even fired. The lone shell in the breach was rusty, too, but I couldn't let that stop me, so I throttled him some more. He took a few wild swings before I caught him low and high and low, which earned the noise I like to hear when I'm having to scuff up a guy.

In keeping with my practice, I hit him one time further, a left to the jaw that sent that Hoyt sprawling onto the picnic table. I dragged him all the way up and left him there, took his trigger assembly with me just in case he came to with more gumption than I had to suspect Hoyts had.

"Get her?" Desmond asked me.

I showed him my chunk of shotgun. "They're coming at me from all over."

"Who?"

"Another Hoyt."

Larry went twitching like his head was on a swivel. "Where?"

I country pointed nowhere much with my nose.

Larry whimpered a little. "Don't never want to see another tire."

"I'd say it's like the zombie apocalypse," I told them both, "if I thought that was fair to zombies."

TWENTY

We loaded that Hoyt up and took him with us over Larry's objections. Larry thought we ought to kill him. He thought I should kill him, anyway. And he thought I should kill him over on the picnic table where he wouldn't have to see it.

I shoved that Hoyt into the wayback with Desmond's spare tire by way of saying no.

We taped him good, me and Desmond did. Desmond always had plenty of tape. But for duct tape, Desmond's mother's house would have long since fallen to pieces, and the Geo Desmond had sold to Dale had a blue duct tape interior because Desmond was hard on upholstery and tape was close to Kevlar in Desmond's view.

The roll in the Escalade was red and made that Hoyt look decorative. We'd backed up as close as we could to the slash pine hedgerow and the picnic table, but some of the Sonic clientele couldn't help but see what we were up to—pitching a grimy, unconscious fellow into the back of Desmond's car and binding him up at the wrists and ankles, covering his mouth as well. They just kept on eating like we were a typical Sonic sort of thing.

"Where to?" Desmond asked me.

It was midafternoon, and we needed some sort of hideout.

"Remember that place down by Mayersville?"

"At the landing?"

That was it. I nodded. Me and Desmond had gone down to pick up a settee from a guy in a trailer near Mayersville. We discovered he'd bugged out and had done us the kindness of leaving his sofa in the yard, where his chickens had taken it over and had fairly well spoiled the thing. We took a snapshot of it and left it there.

After that, me and Desmond dawdled. We rode up to a place called Miller's Landing that was hard by a bend in the river. There was a fine old rambling house out there somebody had refitted. It had a new metal roof and what looked like new windows. The siding had been painted. There was a lake next to the property. An old guy was fishing there. He was jolly and caramel colored and wearing a coolie hat. It was about as big around as a trash can lid.

He saw us standing at the plank fence looking at that house.

"Ain't home," he shouted. "Ain't never home."

We went over to where he was sitting.

"Who owns it?" I asked him.

"Folks from up north. Think they said Cleveland or somewhere. Thought they'd come in the winter or something, but it ain't really no better down here."

"Nice place," Desmond told him.

He spat and allowed, "It's all right." Then he pulled up his stringer to show us a carp he'd caught, a tubby old thing with whiskers. It must have weighed ten pounds.

We swung by Pearl's first. I had Desmond stop a good block or two away, so I could slip up on the place and take in all the possible perils. I lurked in the neighbor's backyard for a time until Pearl came out off her back porch and went puttering in her flower bed. She didn't look like a woman put upon by villains and louts, so I slipped up to where she was weeding and piddling.

"Hey," I told her.

She jumped a little.

"Anybody been around?"

"Debbie," she said.

Debbie sold cosmetics out of her car, and once Pearl had said her name, I noticed the face that Debbie had put on her. Pearl's cheeks were a little more scarlet than normal, and her eyelids were a shimmering blue. The lip gloss kind of stopped me once Pearl had turned to face me full. It was a two-tone job with stark red in the middle and a border penciled in.

Pearl had been deadheading petunias and went back to it while I watched.

"I'm going upstairs for a minute," I said and pointed toward the car shed, "and then what do you think about going for a little ride?"

Pearl was always up for a ride. She was like a spaniel or a toddler that way, and she never seemed to care exactly where you might be heading. A car trip for her was a social occasion on wheels.

"Can't go in this," she said and went inside to change while I eased up the stairs to my apartment. The door was still properly latched. The apartment was just like I'd left it. I went to the knee-wall door and fished out my duffel. It seemed sensible to bring all the firepower I had left. I'd left my A-5 and the Ruger both back at Kalil's in my Ranchero, so I'd have to make do with my SIG SAUER and the MAC-9 I'd taken off a guy up in Ruleville.

Pearl came partway out in some kind of frock but changed her mind about it and so ducked back in before I could hurry her along. She reappeared in some muumuu-shaped thing but caught sight of her reflection in one of the kitchen windows.

"Oh my goodness," she said in a tone that was bound to trump anything I could manage. So she went back in, and I called behind her, "Kind of in a hurry."

I should have known better, because when Pearl speeds up she effectively slows down. She gets all flummoxed in high gear, and I could hear her muttering in the house. She couldn't find anything in a color or style to suit her. In about a quarter hour she came back out in the clothes she'd had on in the garden—her usual blouse and slacks and espadrilles—and her Debbie-applied face.

Desmond was lurking down around the corner. He could see me in Pearl's driveway and came up when I waved him over. Pearl got in the back with Larry, whose left eye was swollen shut now. When Pearl asked him what happened to his face, Larry asked her what happened to hers.

Then the Hoyt in the wayback groaned and fidgeted, and Pearl told us all, "Oh my."

"A guy we know," Larry informed her by way of explanation.

Pearl leaned toward Larry and whispered at him, "He smells."

Did he ever, and Pearl's gardenia perfume didn't help, about like lighting a scented candle in the stockyard.

"What are we going to do with him?" Desmond asked me.

We were on the truck route by then, heading over to pick up 61 out by Leland.

Beluga LaMonte leaned forward to tell me and Desmond both together that we could take that Hoyt and fling him in a swamp. Not that he'd want to see it or have a hand in it at all, but Larry couldn't imagine there was a Mrs. Hoyt at home and little Hoyts primed to miss him.

"Looks like he lives in a hole somewhere."

"Let's just see what he knows," I said, and then I swung around and told Beluga, "I'm not about to go to Parchman for a Hoyt."

"Are we going to the buffet?" Pearl asked me.

She'd plainly noticed we were heading toward Leland, where a couple of Greek brothers ran a Chinese place that was all steam table fare. Pearl had decided their food was slimming. I can't imagine why. The teriyaki was treacly enough to sweeten your coffee with.

"We ate already," I told her. "You hungry? We'll stop and get you something."

"Peckish," Pearl informed me. She'd never own up to more than that.

Before I could instruct Desmond, he said to me, "All right," and drove us straight over to the Savros brothers' Feast of Peking restaurant, where they opened at ten in the morning and stayed that way until ten at night since once you had the steam table heated up, there wasn't much point in dialing it down.

There was a state police car in the parking lot and a couple of Washington County cruisers, which meant Desmond would have to go in to get Pearl whatever food she wanted. Pearl had been raised to believe that picking up takeout spoke poorly of a woman, while me and Larry were active fugitives from the law.

"Just make me a plate," Pearl told Desmond and then listed precisely what she wanted, which was everything I'd ever seen in there plus fritters and corn muffins.

Desmond gave me one of his grunty groans as he flung open his door. The Hoyt in the back started raising a ruckus. I was afraid we'd have to conk him, but he somehow made Larry understand that he wanted fritters, too.

"That's not Kendell's, is it?" I pointed at the cruiser.

"Too dirty," Desmond told me and went stalking across the lot.

Pearl passed the time telling me and Larry and that Hoyt (I guess) about Gil. She'd been reminded of him by the sport coat Larry had on. She remembered an Easter dance he'd squired her to at the Grange Hall in that blazer.

"We tangoed," Pearl informed us. She even turned to look at our Hoyt. "They had a band from Memphis," she told him so he wouldn't feel left out.

Larry shoved a hand in his jacket pocket and came out with a hair clip. Him and Pearl together studied the thing there on his palm. It was one of those old spring-loaded ones women used to wear. Women, apparently, other than Pearl judging from how she looked at it.

When Pearl finally uttered another word, it was only "Oh."

Then she sat in silence for a bit. I blamed Beluga a little. He tinkered with that hair clip until I reached back and took it from him. I opened my door enough to pitch it out into the lot.

"Isn't she a pretty thing?" Pearl said.

That's when I saw Tula. She was coming out of the restaurant holding Desmond by the elbow, Desmond who didn't look altogether pleased to be escorted. They were walking right toward us. What with the Hoyt all taped up in the wayback and Larry just as wanted as me, I did the only thing I knew to do. I climbed out of Desmond's Escalade, slammed the door behind me, and headed off Desmond and Tula out in the lot.

"Whatever you heard," I told her, "that isn't how it happened."

"What did I hear?"

"I slugged a cop. Just Jasper," I said. "You've got to know what he's like."

She did and didn't seem too terribly disturbed that I'd punched Jasper.

"Heard more about those boys in the Walmart," she told me.

"Came at me." I shrugged. What was a fellow like me to do?

"Tell me something." She was talking to Desmond now. "Does he always draw trouble like this?"

Desmond surely could have thought about it longer than he did before he nodded and said to Tula, "Yeah."

"They all looking for me?" I asked her.

She nodded.

"How about you?"

"Depends."

"On what?"

"Us having a conversation." She worked her finger in a circle to make me understand she meant everybody. The crew in the Escalade, too. "You're going to tell me everything that's going on and why."

"Or?"

She reached back and plucked her handcuffs out of the holster on her belt. I'd been in those already. She didn't use them with much compassion.

"Where?" I asked her.

Tula jabbed her thumb toward the restaurant. "Big table in the back. On me."

I stepped over to Desmond's car and swung open Larry's door.

"It looks like we're dining," I told him and Pearl.

"Just ate," Larry said.

"Want to tell her that?" I asked him of Tula.

He gave her a good look. "No."

Pearl was considerably more enthusiastic. She climbed out and straightened herself. This was more of an outing than she'd dared hope for.

"Maybe they have those peas," she said to me, "with the little onions."

She headed toward the restaurant, pausing by Tula to tell her, "Aren't you the prettiest thing."

Tula made her manners and thanked her. She was a little

less cordial with Larry. She'd been around the badge enough
to know a con when she came across one.

"That all of them?" she asked me.

I almost said, "Yeah," but I didn't get to it quick enough,
so Tula knew to come over. Desmond came with her while
Larry and Pearl went on inside the Feast of Peking.

I raised the glass and lowered the tailgate. Our Hoyt mumbled through his taped mouth and wriggled around enough to
stink.

Tula looked at him. Looked at us.

"He tried to shoot me," I told her.

"Any particular reason?"

"We might can get to that inside."

I went to raise the gate, but Tula stopped me.

"Bring him."

"Stinks something awful," Desmond said.

"Bring him," she said.

I yanked the tape off that Hoyt's mouth and left a slick,
clean strip that he yodeled about at first before he moved on
to other complaints.

"They snatched me!" he shouted at Tula. "Right off the
damn street. That one there"—he nodded toward me—"done
busted me in the head. Got me all tied up like a goddamn
pig. Ain't fit back here for nothing."

I pulled a fresh strip of tape off the roll and laid it over that
Hoyt's mouth. That chafed him pretty good. He was wrig-
gling and mumbling so that I had to raise the tailgate and
lower the glass on him just to hear myself think.

"He's a Hoyt," I told Tula. "Just like one of those Walmart

guys. Desmond says Shambrough's got an in with them some-how."

Desmond nodded. "Does."

"Bring him," she said once more of our Hoyt. He was rais-ing a ruckus, shouting through his tape and kicking the tail-gate.

"Can I hit him sometimes? It's all they understand."

"Open up," Tula told me.

I raised the glass and dropped the hatch. Tula had pulled out her Taser by then. She showed it to our Hoyt as if she had every hope of using it on him. He got still and quiet like a man who'd had a dose or two of voltage before.

I ripped off his fresh strip of mouth tape and yanked out a few more whiskers. Desmond freed his arms and left that Hoyt to work his ankles loose.

"We going to jail?" that Hoyt asked Tula.

She holstered her Taser. "Dinner," she told him.

He stood up off the tailgate and tucked in his shirt. Tidied the front of his jeans.

"I ain't got no money much," he informed us, "and this one here broke my gun."

"Nose, too," I said.

His hand shot straight to the swollen bridge of his nose. His right eye was black already. His left one would be soon.

"Guy in the Walmart one of yours?" Tula asked him.

He made like he couldn't be troubled to say until she'd reached around toward her Taser, when he nodded and told her, "Yes, ma'am."

"Let's chew all this over," Tula said and gestured toward the Feast of Peking.

I tried to sidle up to her and make some sort of all-purpose apology, but she just shook her head. In a low sort of sultry whisper, she told me, "Fifty thousand volts at five-second intervals for a minute."

I'll confess it was a little stirring in its way.

TWENTY-ONE

The general Feast of Peking aroma always puts me off a little. It might be scorched peanut oil or expired oyster sauce, but the place always smells to me like they've just barbecued a goat. Not a young, tender goat but an ancient billy with all his glands in place.

Gus, the host and one of the owners, shoved a laminated menu my way and told me, like he always did, "Hey, y'all."

I'd previously only ever come with Desmond, who had a thing about the ribs. It was a bimonthly thing for the most part. I'd order the egg foo young, which at the Feast of Peking was just an omelet with canned button mushrooms in it, scallions if any were handy, and maybe a water chestnut or two.

Larry and Desmond and Pearl and that nasty Hoyt were crowding the buffet already. The way they were chattering and laughing, you'd have thought they were a church group on an outing. I followed Tula to the big back table in a room all by itself. We had a view of the kitchen, where the chef and the dishwasher were yelling at each other. The chef wasn't Greek, like Gus and his brother, but he wasn't Chinese either. Filipino maybe or Malaysian, but way back in the distant past.

His people were all from Rosedale, and he and the dishwasher—some black kid in two-hundred-dollar sneakers—were arguing about a wide receiver the Titans had lately drafted. Some lanky jackass from Auburn known for his end zone dances. The kid approved. The chef didn't have much use for that kind of thing.

"This isn't what it looks like," I told Tula.

"Do you even know what it looks like anymore?"

"I'm caught in the middle. Desmond's got in-laws, and me and Desmond are as good as brothers, so I've got in-laws, too."

"What is it with you and him? He take a thorn out of your paw?"

"He's saved my ass a couple of times. I wouldn't be here but for him, and that buys him everything he needs from me."

I looked through the double doorway into the main dining room, where Desmond, his massive back turned toward us, was still freighting his plate from the buffet.

Tula thought well enough of my loyalty to Desmond to just tell me, "All right."

Pearl was her bright, chatty self now that she had a plate of food in front of her. She identified for us each item she had spooned up for herself, and then she had a word with our Hoyt, who'd gone exclusively for ribs.

"Where's your greenery?" she asked him.

He leaned toward the table and corralled his plate with his

arms the way inmates tend to do. He mumbled something back at Pearl, the low-grade inarticulate version of "Why don't you mind your own damn business, lady?"

You couldn't shunt Pearl with mumbling or even a crisp, corrosive insult. There was greenery in that Hoyt's future whether he wanted it or not. It turned out to be broccoli that Pearl forced on him. She was diligent that way. If she had a thing you didn't want but she wanted you to have it, you were sure to end up with it no matter what.

So that Hoyt got broccoli, and we all got invited to join hands and hear Pearl say grace. She gave encyclopedic thanks and closed off with a spot of ecclesiastic mumbling before we all got to join her in a rousing "Amen."

"So," Tula said to all of us at the table, "does everybody know what's going on but me?"

Pearl certainly didn't, but she had her fried rice to distract her and what looked to me like mashed potatoes with some kind of ginger gravy. "Yesterday's fritters," she told me and pointed to the half-eaten one on her plate.

With a mouthful of rib meat and a few too many teeth, our Hoyt spoke up and informed Tula, "They done opened a sack of snakes."

"Who?" she asked him.

He pointed with his knife at me and then at Larry.

"What about him?" I asked of Desmond.

Our Hoyt shrugged and told me, "Don't know. The way I heard it, it was you and that one." He pointed at me and Larry again.

"Heard from who?" Tula asked him.

That Hoyt fairly stoppered himself with ribs. He made a

noise, but he might have just been choking. It didn't sound responsive.

"Did Shambrough order you up?" I asked him. "Send you after me and him?"

That Hoyt swallowed and reached for something to sop with. Desmond grabbed him by the sleeve. "Talk to the man," he instructed that Hoyt.

"Ain't got nothing to say about him."

"Shambrough?" Tula asked that Hoyt.

"Nothing," that Hoyt told her.

"Any way I can fix that?" I asked him. I even smiled a little.

"I'm eating," that Hoyt told me like that would be enough to spare him. He grinned as if he'd just informed me he was radioactive.

"It's not like you're using all those teeth."

That Hoyt grinned. It wasn't pretty.

Tula reached around and pulled out her Taser. She laid it on the table next to me as an offering. "In case he won't hold still," she said.

That prompted Desmond to reach in his pocket and pull out the Taser I'd taken off the ninja schoolgirl assassin. He reached it across the table and laid it next to Tula's model. "Don't want him squirmy," Desmond allowed.

That Hoyt caught on and went slack a little. He told us all, "All right now."

"Isn't that cute," Tula said. She picked up Isis/Mako's Taser and pointed it directly across the table from her, where our Hoyt sat.

"You ain't supposed to be caught up in this," he told her. "You the law and all."

"Went off at three," Tula informed him. "I'm not the law again until tomorrow."

I pushed back from the table. "Come on," I told that Hoyt. "Let's get this over with."

"You going to tell us about Shambrough?" Tula asked that Hoyt.

"Naw," he assured her. "Beat or not won't make no difference."

"All right." I stood up. "Come on."

"I told you. Won't do no good."

I was going to tell Desmond to give our Hoyt a slap, but it turned out I didn't need to. He was busy cleaning a rib bone but had a hand free for a pop and gave our Hoyt one right on the back of the head.

"Shit! Ow!"

"Let's go," I told him.

He looked from his plate to me. He clearly wasn't afraid of a beating. That sort of thing seemed to be bred into Hoyts. It apparently came with the teeth. For that Hoyt, the trouble with a beating at the moment was the inconvenience of it. He had what they call in the Delta a rising appetite. Eating a mess of Chinese ribs had only made him hungry for a mess or two more.

So that Hoyt did some calculating and his version of deep philosophical thinking. He sat there for a moment with his face all pinched. I suspected he looked just the same way on the toilet.

"Can we go back?" he finally asked me.

"It's all you can eat," Tula told him.

"And she's paying," I said.

"*You* come on then," that Hoyt said to me, and I followed him to the steam table.

"My people," he told me as he reached into the rib pan with his bare nasty hands, "been working for Shambroughs since way back."

"That's what I hear."

"Used to be planters. A few of them still are, but past a couple of tractor drivers, they don't need us anymore. Mr. Lucas is something different. Not the sort to plant a crop."

"What do you do for him?"

That Hoyt licked his fingers in a hygienic way before reaching into the fritter pan for a fistful of stale fritters.

"Nothing strictly proper," that Hoyt informed me, "but me and mine stay away from the worst of it. We'll do a little collecting or maybe—"

I held up my hand to stop him. "Save it," I said and pointed at the table. "She'll need to hear it, too."

"Friend of yours?"

I nodded.

"She going to run me in?"

"Tell us what we need to know and she won't."

He loosed a breath and nodded. "Get a plate."

"Not hungry."

"Don't need to be. Pile it up." He pointed at the hotel pan, just a quarter full now of ribs. "Before that fat boy gets here."

I grabbed a plate. I piled it up. I followed that Hoyt back to the table.

He was one of those guys who, once he'd decided to do a thing, did it full out. He told us everything he could possibly dredge up and think of about the Shambroughs. It took him a quarter hour to even arrive at Mr. Lucas. There were other Shambroughs he chose to set the table with instead. Uncles mostly and a cousin or two who'd put Hoyts to honest use back before the laser-guided tractors and the mechanical picking machines.

"Dirt farmers. That was us," our Hoyt said. "Times changed. Shambroughs changed. Some of them, anyway."

"What's he into mostly?" Tula asked him.

"Mr. Lucas?"

We all nodded. Even Pearl. She found delving into other people's bone-filled closets about as fascinating as anything on earth could be.

"Hard to say." That Hoyt reached for the hot sauce and doused his ribs with it. "People pay him. I know that. For one thing and another. He only usually calls us out when somebody won't or can't."

"Pay him for what?" I asked.

"No trouble, I guess. Because when they don't pay, they get a mountain of it."

"Who pays him?" Tula asked.

"Slew of folks. Clean up to Memphis. Clear down to Baton Rouge."

"Sounds like standard-issue protection," I said. "They pay or get beat up, burned out."

"Hardly ever gets that far," our Hoyt said. "We just jostle them a little and point a gun or two their way. That's usually enough to shake something loose."

"What do you know about Larry's tires?" I asked him.

That Hoyt shook his head. "Don't know about no tires, but Mr. Lucas is a bad one for making off with all grades of shit."

Then even that Hoyt turned toward Pearl and was quick to tell her, "Sorry."

"So he's collecting protection," Tula said, "and stealing every stinking thing."

Our Hoyt nodded and shoved his empty iced tea glass my way. "I like the sweet," he told me.

I pointed at Larry. He looked like he wanted to tell me he didn't fetch tea for any damn body, but Desmond made an authentic fist, and Larry hopped up from the table.

"What about that girl?" I asked our Hoyt. "Black hair. Tattoo." I pointed to my neck and then picked up the Taser I'd confiscated and showed it off. "Hers."

"Seen her once," that Hoyt said. "She's out of Louisville or somewhere. I heard Mr. Lucas say one time that folks never saw her coming."

"Does he use her much?" Tula asked.

That Hoyt nodded. "Hard cases, I guess. And him and her got this thing."

"What thing?" I asked him.

"You know." He then made an altogether vulgar dumbshow in a bid to describe sex to us. He used his greasy hands. He flopped his tongue out while he panted.

Larry showed up in time to see it. "Hell, buddy. It's only tea." He set the tumbler down with a show of distaste and retired to his chair across the table.

"I think we've got it," Tula told our Hoyt. Then she pointed at Pearl by way of instruction.

Somehow that Hoyt knew just what to do. He told Pearl, "Sorry, ma'am."

"She ever killed anybody that you know of?" I asked him.

"Heard stuff," he said.

"Lately?"

He nodded. "I've got people around Belzoni. Talk down there about a guy."

"Catfish pond," I said.

I got another nod from our Hoyt.

"Who are we talking about?" Tula asked me.

Me and Desmond described what we had seen down by Belzoni. Tula had heard a little of it on her radio, but she hadn't run up on Kendell long enough to get caught up.

"Her?" she asked us.

We nodded.

"Would Shambrough go with her?" Tula asked that Hoyt.

He was quick to nod. "Mr. Lucas likes to watch."

"Does he help?" I asked.

"Maybe. Sometimes. I don't know." That Hoyt tossed a scoured rib bone onto his plate. "The way I hear it, he likes to be over in the bushes, tugging on that thing."

We got another dumbshow, a vivid demonstration of the sort of self-pleasure Lucas Shambrough got up to when his ninja schoolgirl assassin got busy scuffing somebody up. The tongue came out. He panted some more. We all turned out to have grunty groans.

At least when he finished that Hoyt knew to turn to Pearl and say, "Sorry, ma'am."

TWENTY-TWO

Tula was the one who decided to leave Kendell out of it for the moment. We reconnoitered in the lot, me and Tula and Desmond, while Pearl and Larry and our nasty Hoyt got take-out from the Feast of Peking. They'd all agreed they needed hideout food if a hideout was where we were headed. Pearl was more than a little worried about the crockery that might be on hand, and I'd already promised her we would stop for napkins and toilet paper and Sanka.

"Anybody been out to Shambrough's yet?" I asked Tula. "Just for a conversation?"

"Last I heard, they're working up to it. Those people have a lot of juice around here."

Desmond laughed. He'd been in the Delta all his life, but even he was hard-pressed to make much sense of the sway that Shambroughs held.

"They ain't been nothing forever," he said, "and here they are still getting their way."

"I saw her in his house," I told Tula. "The ninja schoolgirl's living with him. Doesn't sheltering a fugitive count for something?"

"So that *was* you in there cracking heads."

I gave her my best contrite look.

"If I tell my boss she's out at Shambrough's, he'll ask me how I know it," Tula informed me, "and then he's sure to have me pick you up. We've got to let it play out. The captain's a Delta boy. He's going to do things exactly the way people do them around here."

"I hear that," Desmond said. "Been trying to tell him."

Desmond and Tula looked at me like maybe I was the cause and source of all the upset and the carnage.

"I'm a straight-line kind of guy," I said. "No harm in going from here to there."

"Should have hit her a little harder" was all Tula could trouble herself to tell me. "Then Shambrough wouldn't have anybody to . . . uh . . . watch."

We needed a plan. Me and Desmond had a way of committing to make a plan. Occasionally we even sat down and attempted to devise one. We'd usually get a step or two in and then decide to improvise. Consequently, our plan was always *we'll do what feels right for us at the time.*

So when Tula asked us, "What now?" me and Desmond glanced at each other.

"We've got a base of operations in mind," I told Tula.

Desmond added, "Right."

"We'll get them safe." I pointed toward the Feast of Peking doorway. "Give Kendell some time to investigate. That was what he wanted from us. He might have evidence enough off that boy in Belzoni to get a warrant by now."

Tula shook her head and told me, "Nope."

"Maybe Skeeter, then," I said.

She shook her head. "Too soon."

"Izzy and that Sunflower woman?"

"Enough for a conversation," she said. "That's all we've got for now, and the captain's going to have it but, like I told you, in due time. He'll get Shambrough into the station house, probably with his Memphis lawyer."

"So me and Larry have got warrants out on us while everybody else is going clean?"

"Stop whining. You hit a cop," Tula said. "What the hell did you figure would happen? I'd take you both to jail for your own good, but that'd leave Desmond out here alone."

Just then Pearl and that Hoyt came out of the restaurant arguing about some TV lawyer. Not one on a show but the guy with the hair on the mesothelioma commercials. Pearl had decided he was a Christian sort, which our Hoyt was actively resisting.

"Not alone enough," Desmond told us.

Tula checked her watch. "Got to pick up CJ. Check in when you can."

"We'll be way out in—"

She raised a hand to stop me. "Don't want to know. I could still get the order to pick you up."

Then she was off to her cruiser, a Grand Marquis that was

slightly too dusty for Kendell. She whipped out onto the truck route, heading west toward Greenville and the river. Me and Desmond stood in the lot and watched her go.

We didn't see much point in making our Hoyt ride in the wayback anymore. Pearl sat between him and Larry on the backseat and chattered indiscriminately about all varieties of piffle. That Hoyt threw in every now and again while Larry just sat and sulked.

"Can we run by and see Skeeter?" Larry finally asked us.

"Where did they take him?" I asked Desmond.

"Greenville likely."

"Swing by and then down to Mayersville?" I suggested. "I'd kind of like to see him myself. Maybe that ninja schoolgirl said something to him while she was beating him half to death."

"Think Shambrough was in there watching?" Desmond asked me.

That was enough to raise a grunty groan.

We parked across the road from the Greenville hospital because there were cruisers in that lot as well. Me and Desmond prepped Pearl. The plan was to send her in to ask after Skeeter, but beyond "Heard a guy once call him Hank or Howard," Larry didn't know Skeeter's given name.

"I thought he was your friend," I said to Larry.

"Parchman friend," he told me.

Pearl had gotten it in her head that Skeeter had been injured in a tennis accident.

"Forget the racket," I told her, but she couldn't seem to do it and stayed confused about what Skeeter had been up to in the Walmart.

"I'll go with her," our Hoyt finally said.

"You'll just keep on going," Desmond told him.

"You got my gun," he said and tossed his head toward the disassembled 20-gauge in the wayback. "Used to be Daddy's. Ain't like I'm leaving it here."

Short of holding his hound or his mother hostage, we didn't guess we could do much better.

"Go on," I said. "See if you can get on his floor. Find out if they've got a cop on guard. I doubt it, but you never know around here."

"All right," our Hoyt said, and him and Pearl climbed out of the car together. They crossed the street and rounded the magnolia trees by the foyer.

"His name might have been Henry," Larry told us. "I think he's from Dyersburg or somewhere up there."

"Fine," I said. "Henry from Dyersburg."

"Or that might have been some other guy."

Desmond was troubled. I could tell. Anybody with ears could tell. He had a particular way of breathing when something was nagging at him. I wasn't sure I wanted to know what exactly was up, so I ignored him for a while. Then he got a little louder like a dog will when it's ready to be fed.

We'd been sitting about ten minutes before I finally asked him, "What?"

"I don't know," Desmond said, his usual preamble. "Seems a little off. That's all."

"Off how exactly?"

"Wasn't Dyersburg. It was Blytheville," Larry said.

Desmond just breathed some more.

"What seems off?" I asked him.

"That Hoyt was coming after you and him, right?" Desmond asked me and jabbed a thumb Larry's way.

I nodded.

"Skeeter probably, too."

"Probably," I told Desmond.

"And here we've sent him in there, just with Pearl, so he can check on Skeeter."

"Ironic."

"Is it?"

"We've got his shotgun."

"You even think it was his daddy's?"

Larry reached over the seat back and picked up our Hoyt's shotgun stock. It was all dinged and scarred like it had been tossed around for years and even recently battered about half to pieces.

"All tore up," Larry told us.

That was Desmond's method. I'd start out satisfied, and he'd steer me into doubts and sensible misgivings.

"Just wondering what he's up to," Desmond said.

"Why has he got to be up to something?" I asked him.

"Because he's a Hoyt," Desmond told me.

"I don't know from Hoyts."

"That's right. Didn't you scuff one up at the Walmart?"

I nodded.

"Cousin of his. Isn't that what he said?"

I nodded again.

"But he's put that completely out of his mind. Now you and him are buddies."

"We're going in, aren't we?" I finally said to Desmond.

Desmond unbuckled as he told me, "Yeah."

Me and Desmond climbed out of the Escalade, and Larry shifted up under the wheel.

"Stay right here," Desmond told him, "until you get run off."

Larry had gotten too busy adjusting the seat and sizing up the radio dials to pay proper attention to Desmond, who reached in and gave him a pop. "Right here."

Larry whined, "You always hitting." He rubbed his head. "The both of you, always hitting. Like that does anybody any good."

I followed Desmond into the main hospital reception area. There was a cop I'd never seen before back in a corridor behind the counter. He glanced at me and Desmond as we entered but then went straight back about his business. If the local PD was looking for me because of my dustup with Jasper in Greenwood, I didn't get the feeling they were looking for me hard. That was the virtue of the Delta. They all knew Jasper, too.

I didn't see Pearl at first, but I heard her soon enough. She was over in a corner of the waiting room, parked next to a woman on a couch. It turned out they were former garden club friends who'd fallen out of touch, and now here they'd run into each other at the hospital in Greenville out of the blue and all.

They had almost more catching up to do than Pearl could find the breath to manage.

"Pearl?" I said.

She introduced me to her friend, Minnie, and started in on an exhaustive explanation of who exactly Minnie was. I waited for a gap—it came right after news of Minnie's remarkable green thumb with Heritage Beauty roses—when I said, "Excuse me, but did you find out anything about Skeeter?"

Pearl nodded. "He's on eight."

"And your . . . friend?" I asked as I looked around for some sign of that Hoyt.

"Goodloe went to make a phone call," Pearl told me. She pointed in the direction of the combination gift shop and café.

"Goodloe," I muttered to Desmond as we headed for the shop.

Goodloe wasn't in the gift shop. He wasn't in the adjacent café either. I found the pay phone back down the slip of a hall that led to the public toilets. No Goodloe. I checked the men's room. Just an orderly on break. I described our Hoyt to him.

"Like he climbed out of a ditch. Teeth all sideways."

He shook his head. "Saw a guy with an eye patch out back smoking."

I thanked him anyway and went over to join Desmond by the elevators. "Skeeter's on eight," I told him.

A reception lady was saying to both of us, "Sir," by then. We ignored her. Me and Desmond were good at that, like we'd just popped in from Albania and didn't speak the English much.

"Sir."

The doors finally opened, and we entered the car with a candy striper pushing a cart freighted with flower arrangements. She was a bubbly teen volunteer who was having a blessed day. She told us all about it on her way up to seven.

"Cancer floor," she informed us in a whisper. "They'll be needing prayers from you and you." As she spoke she poked first me and then Desmond in the sternum. Then she winked and licked her pouty lips. She was probably all of fifteen.

"Bye now," she said as she rolled her cart off the elevator. She gave us a backwards wave.

Then we were at eight. Desmond stuck his head out of the car and looked up and down the hallway.

"Just a nurse down there," he told me.

He stepped into the corridor, and I followed him. We went off in the direction that would carry us away from the nurses' station, and we peeked into all the rooms as we passed. Most of the doors were standing half open, so there wasn't much of a challenge to it. We had to open a few. Desmond played the orderly, and he only walked in on one sponge bath. We finally found Skeeter at the far end of the hall.

He didn't have a roommate. The bed near the door was empty and crisply made. Skeeter was over by the window looking like a man who'd been little short of murdered outright with ground strokes. He was swollen and bandaged and wrapped and plastered. He had probes and drips and a tube down his throat. He was unconscious and breathing in a regular way, but he looked awful bad.

"She did that?" Desmond couldn't believe it. Skeeter looked like he'd been set upon by a quartet of longshoremen.

"With some kind of metal racket. Not even a pricey one."

"What sort of man could tug his junk to that?"

"That Shambrough bloodline must be getting awfully thin."

Then we heard a groan. Not from Skeeter but from behind the bathroom door. It was across the room, past the far bed. It was shut entirely. The toilet flushed, and when we didn't hear any wash-up water in the sink but instead saw that door straight swing open, I think we both knew who'd be coming out.

"Oh," our Hoyt said when he saw us. "Hey."

"Ribs go through you?" I asked him.

"I's just"—he held up a copy of the *Trading Post*—"kind of looking for a truck."

"Who'd you call?" Desmond wanted to know.

That Hoyt went profoundly perplexed. He tilted his head and squinted like he couldn't imagine what Desmond meant.

"Who," I said, "Goodloe?"

He shook his head a little like we had him confused with somebody else. Somebody who might have used a phone, while he most assuredly hadn't.

"Hit the fucker," I suggested to Desmond, who was already making a fist.

He sailed on over that way he does, just gliding across the floor, and put himself between our Hoyt and the hallway.

"All right now," that Hoyt told him mostly. "Might have dialed, but weren't nobody home."

"Dialed who?" I asked him.

He started a shrug, and that's when Desmond slugged him. If you let them, guys like that Hoyt could tell you nothing for days on end.

"Hey!" he snapped at Desmond, who, in a display of contrition, drew directly back and slugged that Hoyt again.

"Shit!" he told us and covered up. "Called a guy I know."

"And told him what?" I asked.

"Weren't nobody there."

Desmond caught him in the kidneys this time. It served to crumple that Hoyt and drop him. He piled up on the floor the way Larry likes to.

Desmond looked down at him with conspicuous disappointment. He shook his head and told me, "People any-more."

That's just when the hallway door eased open enough for a nurse to stick her head in. She looked over at me and Skeeter, took in Desmond and that Hoyt, and then appeared to decide we were more of a problem than she could manage.

She just said, "Well," and drew back out again.

"Let's go before she finds a cop," I told Desmond.

"And him?" He pointed at our piled-up Hoyt.

"I'll get him. You get Pearl."

I reached down and grabbed that Hoyt by the collar of his shirt. As I lifted, the collar gave way and left me with a handful of poplin and our Hoyt heaped up once more on the floor.

So we grabbed him each under an arm and hoisted him off the floor. He made out to be invertebrate there for a second.

"Walk," I told him and twisted a finger for emphatic effect.

He whimpered a little and told me, "All right."

There was an actual cop at the nurses' desk by the time we got into the hallway.

"Go on," Desmond told me and pointed at the stairwell door. "I've got this." He struck out down the hallway, gliding along and largely blocking me and that Hoyt from view.

That Hoyt complained all the way to the ground floor. He had hip troubles he told me about and a hernia that needed doctoring but he didn't have the scratch. He just prattled on and on and made me stop at every landing so he could catch his breath.

"Why don't you shut the hell up and see how that works?" I finally told him down on three.

"You're hard to like," that Hoyt informed me. Then he dredged and spat. It didn't seem to matter to him that he wasn't outdoors yet. I didn't hit him only because I didn't want him to pile up.

We came out on the backside of the building. We spilled out first into a hallway and then exited through a steel security door and set off an alarm. I was spending as much time looking back behind us as I was looking where we were going, just waiting for cops or troopers or something to come spilling out in pursuit.

So I wasn't paying quite the attention that I should have paid to just exactly where we were heading as we passed the assorted hospital Dumpsters and skirted around the ambulance bay. I was kind of following our Hoyt. He seemed to be heading for the road. He had pluck all of a sudden, and energy. He was scooting along pretty good. I was just happy I wasn't having to drag him.

We were out on the far edge of some kind of emergency room parking lot when I finally woke up to the fact our Hoyt was running me into trouble. I've got to hand it to him. He made it look random, and then I finally saw the car. It was a Biscayne with the finish gone. Dull blue with no shine at all to it, and a vinyl top that had rotted to tatters and was shedding its yellow stuffing.

It had more people in it than even a Biscayne ought to hold. Packed three across the front and four across the back. A couple of them looked a little to me like women. One of them stuck her head out a back side window.

She waved in that Hoyt's direction and told him, "Hey!"

Her hair was matted. She had no chin to speak of. The teeth I saw were all turned sideways.

It was a little like running headlong into a hornets' nest but for the fact that those Hoyts were far too chunky to come swarming out of that sedan. It turned out they didn't need to. They'd deployed a skirmisher.

I heard him behind me. He must have been hiding himself down between cars. He was adenoidal and a little wheezy, maybe sixteen years old. He delivered the first blow as I turned. He had a camp shovel like soldiers use. It must have been authentic surplus judging from how it hurt like hell. I nearly got an arm raised before he coiled and struck again.

He caught me right on the side of the head, and I collapsed just like Beluga. I kind of remember somebody airing the Hoyt variety of "Uh-huh."

TWENTY-THREE

I don't guess you've really lived until you've come to in the trunk of a car. Worse still, the trunk of a Biscayne owned and operated by Delta Hoyts. They seemed to store their excess wardrobe in it. Coveralls, I had to guess, from the zippers and the stink. There were quarts of motor oil as well because that Biscayne was a burner. I was getting the full treatment from the fumes seeping into the trunk.

Or rather, *we* were getting the full treatment. I found my companion with my foot, and I would have shot straight out onto the road but for the trunk lid keeping me in.

"Who's that!?"

Nothing. Not even a groan.

I probed with my foot. My feet really, since they were taped together. My wrists were taped behind me, but they hadn't bothered with my mouth. Their sedan was raising such a racket, any noise I might have raised could hardly have competed with it. If they had a muffler on the thing, it was bound to be mostly holes.

I shoved whoever was in there with me with my feet again.

"Hey," I said. Still nothing.

I decided it was a body. Not Desmond. I knew that for certain. He probably wouldn't fit in a Biscayne trunk, and I couldn't imagine Hoyts could muster the gumption to lift him.

I finally heard a groan that wasn't one of mine.

"Hey," I said.

More groaning. I shoved the guy some more.

"Quit it!" was what I finally heard.

"Larry?"

He told me, "Beluga."

"Great."

"What the hell's all this?" he asked me.

"Hoyts have got us," I told him. "They pull you out of the car?"

"Don't know," Larry said. "I was just listening to tunes. Some fucker hit me with something."

"A shovel," I said.

"I think I'm bleeding," Larry informed me. "This hasn't been much of a day."

On the contrary, it had been quite a day. It had started with a homicide and seemed about to end with two, and there'd been a solid quartet of assaults right there in the middle. It had been a signal day, all right, but I kind of knew what Larry meant.

"Smells like bears been living in here or something," Larry said. "Where are we going?"

"They didn't tell me."

"Shambrough'll be there. You can figure on that."

"Girl of his probably, too."

"Going to kill us, aren't they?"

"I would."

"Dying's bad enough without him jerking off."

I thought of our Hoyt's dumbshow, of his cracked tongue hanging out.

"I can't breathe," Larry told me.

That wasn't quite right, but I knew what he meant. There was plenty of air. The trouble was that all of it was tainted. The clothes stink was just unpleasant. The true problem we had was with the exhaust.

"We keep going," I told Larry, "that girl won't have to kill us."

"That'd be all right," Larry allowed. He was already slurring his words.

I kicked him. "Larry."

He mumbled a little.

"Larry. Stay awake."

I kicked him some more but just got the occasional grunt from Larry. Then I didn't get anything no matter how hard I hit him. I was fighting off drowsiness myself. I tried yelling at those Hoyts, but they probably couldn't hear me over the clatter. I don't imagine they would have done much but yelled back and hooted and hollered. Lucas Shambrough had deployed them after Larry, I had to figure, and they were bringing him in along with me for a bonus. There must have been a certain amount of triumph in that for those Hoyts.

I thought I heard them laughing. What with the racket,

I couldn't be sure. All I know is, I started dropping off and starting back awake. Then I was having a dream that I was sleeping in a baby cradle. It was big enough for me and my dappled pony, Frank. I was explaining to Frank how a barcode scanner worked but got distracted once I'd discovered that Frank was eating a carrot in bed. We had a rule against that. A firm rule, I told him. Frank kept chewing his carrot. Then he gave me a horsey look I didn't like. He kicked me twice.

When I woke up, I was out of the trunk and on the ground behind the car. I was lying on my back and looking up at Hoyts gathered all around me.

"Wake the fuck up," one of them told me. He looked a little like our Hoyt. A little like Frank my spotted pony as well.

He kicked me in the ribs and laughed.

I saw his teeth and thought, *Oh. Right.*

Some more of them kicked me but not hard enough to keep me from dozing off. I was aware of the clatter as they hauled Larry out of the trunk and tossed him down beside me.

Larry said, "Ow!"

I laughed and told him, "Yeah. Ow."

Then I slept some more, and I only woke up because my arms were hurting. I thought at first I was still lying down somewhere, but it turned out I was standing up. The light was low and gloomy. The air was dank. The place smelled like last year's laundry hamper. My wrists were cuffed at about shoulder height, and I was sagging so that my weight was about to tear my arms clean off.

That's quite enough to wake a guy up, even from CO_2 poisoning and the well-aimed boots of a pack of Hoyts.

I stood full upright as best I could, though I was a little

shaky still. As my eyes focused and adjusted, I could see I was in a basement. The view just confirmed everything my nose had already told me. It was a damp, seepy basement. A cellar really. Dug out for a furnace and a bunch of dusty bottles on shelves. Neglected preserves, they looked like to me. Miserly light came in from grimy transom windows. I counted four of them.

Larry spit up a little, and that harnessed my attention. He was three or four feet down the wall from me and shackled just like I was. It was hard at that point to imagine that this had all started because of some tires.

"Hey," I said.

Larry grunted. He vomited in earnest. All over his shirt. All over his shoes. All over the cement floor. It was hard to feel anything but pity for him, but I managed nonetheless.

"This is your mess," I told him, *"Beluga."* I said it with as much scathing contempt as I could muster, given my circumstances.

Larry looked around. Squinted and blinked. My eyes were adjusted to the gloom by then. I could see off in a corner a moth-eaten hunk of taxidermy. A beaver or a groundhog. I couldn't tell which, but I couldn't miss the fact that it was albino.

"Where are we?" Larry asked.

"Shambrough's," I told him. "Lair of the white worm."

"The what?" Larry was frantic now.

"We're fucked," I said, by way of clarification.

We were both locked up in two pairs of regular hand-cuffs with one bracelet attached to our wrists and the other U-bolted into the wall. It was an ancient brick wall, and the bolts had been sunk deep into the mortar joint. My left bolt wouldn't move a bit, but the right one had the merest hint of play.

"Try to move your arms," I told Larry.

"Can't," he said. "Locked up."

"Try," I told him. "See if you can move those bolts."

He made a halfhearted effort and then went pouty. "That damn Bugle," he said. "He didn't have no business under that truck and getting himself run over."

"I'm going to say this once," I told him. Then we both heard creaking from upstairs. All we could see overhead was floor joists and what looked like cypress plank sheathing. The house was stout and well built. We were probably hearing somebody walking, but there was so much wood between us and them, we couldn't be sure of that.

Silence followed, so I told Larry, "None of this is that boy's fault. You didn't start on time because *you* were late."

"I had . . . complications," Larry said.

"Right. We wouldn't be down here if you could do any damn thing like it ought to be done."

"Skeeter mostly," Larry told me.

Out of impulse I tried to hit him, but my handcuffs held me back. Larry grinned when he saw what I was up to.

"He was supposed to pay that boy off."

"With money you didn't give him."

"Well now, let's be clear. You and Desmond didn't get it to me in any hurry."

Now it was our fault. That was enough to prompt me to discover I could kick him. My legs were free to go where they wanted, so I caught Larry in the thigh.

"Hey!" he shouted and craned to get away as best he could since he wasn't able, like usual, to drop to the floor in a heap.

"Your doing," I told him. "If that girl doesn't take you out, I will."

"Now, boys."

I don't know where he came from. He might have been lurking in a corner all along. Over behind the stairs that led up into the house proper or just beyond the boiler, back behind his albino beaver. He might have come down while we were fighting. All I know is he was suddenly there.

Lucas Shambrough had on proper clothes. As it turned out, he was a chino and a sockless loafer guy, so I wouldn't have liked him even if I hadn't known reason to detest him already. He was wearing a button-down oxford shirt, freshly laundered and creased. He was shaved and coiffed. Presentable. He stood just out of kicking range.

"So," he said. He looked us over, Larry in particular. "Mr. Beluga LaMonte. So nice to finally see you."

Larry looked like he was hoping to find a way to pass through the solid brick wall behind him. Anything to get away from Lucas Shambrough, who had *creepy* about as down as a human could ever hope to get it.

"You, sir," Shambrough informed Larry, "have made a terrible mistake."

Larry pulled one of his victimized faces in a bid to let Lucas Shambrough know that mistakes were something that happened to him, not the sorts of things he got up to. Shambrough didn't appear to take his meaning or even try.

"Your friend told us what you did. Chapter. Verse. Whole damn thing."

"What friend?" I asked him.

Shambrough didn't even glance my way. "I'm not talking to you."

Since Larry couldn't find a way to seep into the wall, he asked Shambrough, "What friend?" as well.

"And my friend Bugle is going to have a limp. His doctor all but promised that."

When Larry started in on how that boy had no business under the trailer, Shambrough took a quick step his way and hit him once. It wasn't a punch. It was an open-handed slap. The sort of blow you might get if you'd offended a dowager at the opera. That didn't keep Larry from whimpering and informing Lucas Shambrough that he was a little goddamned tired of getting hit.

Naturally enough, that got him hit again. Another slap. It was either Shambrough's preference or he didn't know how to make a decent fist.

Larry looked around at the floor like he had designs to pile up on it, but given his restraints, he could only manage an ungainly squat.

"She's dressing for you," Shambrough told us. He looked my way. "Especially you."

I rattled my handcuffs. "Not very sporting."

"No," Lucas Shambrough allowed with a smile. "It's not."

Then he stepped backward into the gloom and climbed the steps up to the landing. We got a burst of light from upstairs as he opened the basement door. Then gloom again as he shut it.

"This ain't right," I heard Larry say.

It qualified as borderline sniveling, which made for helpful aggravation as I worked to further loosen my right-hand bolt, going at it like you'd go at a tooth. Back and forth. Back and forth. Larry just whined and pouted, and he was so accomplished at that sort of thing that I found I could draw off of Larry for fuel.

I even provoked him a little when I feared I might flag. "Think Skeeter spilled it?" I asked him.

Larry exhaled like a man who'd been asked to balance the federal budget. "Probably," he said. "He's like that. And it was all his idea."

That gave me a spark, and I went at that bolt until it was truly wiggling. An eighth of an inch to either side, enough to make me optimistic.

"That damn Skeeter," I said.

Larry was all over that in a second. He cataloged for me all the times that Skeeter had disappointed him by being unreliable and shiftless. "I don't know," Larry said. "Can't figure people sometimes."

He was like spinach for Popeye. The more pitiful Larry got, the harder I went at that bolt. Soon it was a quarter inch to either side, and I could hear the mortar going sandy.

"That guy in Belzoni," I said to Larry. "Probably told them all kinds of shit, too."

"Yeah." Larry exhaled. "Probably. I should have figured he might all along."

A half inch either side, and I could feel the cement going to rubble. I pulled at that bolt. It came a little. I worked it and jerked again. The threads were barely holding, and then the place lit up as the door upstairs swung open. I stopped what I was up to, pressed my back against the bricks, and made to look quite thoroughly restrained.

For his part, Larry swallowed hard and said just generally, "Shit."

She'd gotten dressed, all right. A tartan plaid wool skirt with knee socks and a crisp white blouse with a middy collar. A mixed metaphor as fashion goes, like Robert the Bruce at sea.

It sounded like her shoes—the shiny patent leather schoolgirl sort—had taps on them by the way she clicked on the stairs and then clicked on the concrete as well. She had clamps in her hair and was wearing horn-rimmed glasses with no lenses in them. She'd left in the eyebrow studs and the nose jewel. She couldn't do much about the tattoo.

She was an unsettling sight. I'll give her that, and you didn't have to be shackled in a cellar to recognize it, though the shackling and the cellar together probably didn't hurt.

Lucas Shambrough followed her into the basement carrying what looked like her luggage. It was one of those old-timey leather suitcases with straps. The thing appeared heavy by the way he was hauling it. Even he'd spiffed up some, had put on a blazer and could have been taken for her father, especially in that cellar where the light was gloomy and low enough for her to look a little like a child.

"Aw, hell," I heard Larry say. He was very nearly blubbering, and that girl hadn't even visited on him her sweet attention yet.

Shambrough set her suitcase down. The contents jangled when it hit the concrete as if the thing was loosely packed with railroad spikes. Larry warbled a little. I felt sure he was thinking of all the shiftless enterprises he wouldn't have the chance to fuck completely up now that he was about to get agonizingly dead.

Lucas Shambrough found sawhorses, stacked one on top of the other, back in an unlit corner. He dragged them out and set them up and hoisted that suitcase to rest upon them.

"Good?" he asked the ninja assassin.

She nodded. She removed her lensless glasses and handed them to him. He shoved them in his blazer pocket and backed up a step or two.

"You're not going to be back there pleasuring yourself, now are you, Mr. Shambrough?" Most wankers don't like you to know what they're up to. It drains the thrill out of it somehow. You had to hand it Lucas Shambrough, though. He was a different kind of fish.

"Not just yet," he told me. "I'm not so keen on the . . . preliminaries."

I heard Larry mutter, "Preliminaries." Then he warbled a little more.

"Gentlemen," Shambrough told us. "Lady."

With that he took his sockless self over to the stairway and climbed upstairs, threw open the door, and shut it loudly behind him.

"Mako, right?" I asked her. I doubted I could soften her up with chat, but you couldn't ever say for certain. It was worth a try.

She walked over to stand in front of me. She inspected me up and down. Then she delivered some kind of dire knuckle punch directly below my rib cage. It was surgically placed and had the odd effect of deadening both of my legs at once. If I could have fallen down, I would have. Instead I dangled by my wrists, scrambling all the while to get my feet back underneath me.

She watched me like you'd watch a cockroach struggle once you'd speared him with a pin. No outward sign of satisfaction. Just curiosity. Once I'd managed to get back on top of my legs, she turned toward her old-timey suitcase.

Larry glanced my way. He made a noise in his neck that sounded like a rusty hinge. She troubled herself to look at Larry but couldn't be bothered to punch him.

I heard her humming softly as she undid her suitcase straps and opened the thing. This sort of business must have been the delight of her existence. I guess it took her back to childhood somehow. That was about the only way I could explain the outfits. Now, instead of being the victim, she was the one delivering the blows.

She sorted through the contents of her suitcase just like a little girl might pick through her pocketbook. She seemed to favor blunt instruments from what I saw. She had assorted hammers. Claw and ball peen. A mason's rubber mallet. She had a length of what looked like an ax handle and a piece of rebar for hard cases, I had to guess. She must not have missed her Taser, since me and Larry were tame for her already.

Once she'd settled on the mallet, she turned and tapped it on her palm. It was the sort that was full of shot, probably about the size of BBs. I could hear the clatter of them as she closed on me and Larry.

Larry said, "Aw." It came out mostly spit.

For my part, I tensed and coiled as best I could and worked my ever loosening bolt. Back and forth. Back and forth. She couldn't hear me for all of the squirming. Larry's shifting feet on that gritty concrete floor, supplemented by his whining, was enough to cover any racket I might raise.

She stood before us looking from me to Larry and back to him, trying to decide who she ought to brutalize first. She was slow and deliberate about it. I imagine she enjoyed Larry's quivering, just judging from how she toyed with the mallet and didn't do anything else for a while.

"He's too easy," I finally told her. "Ready to be in a pile on the floor."

She took two quick steps over and hit me with that damn mallet in the armpit. I never would have thought to hit anybody there, but it hurt like hell. I clinched and grinned. I managed to tell her just, "Ouch."

She seemed intent on saving me for later. They knew Larry was the tire guy, and he must have been slated to get some special treatment. A long, slow round of pain, not that Larry needed any sort of lesson or instruction. He'd just been up to his usual shiftlessness, and no beating could alter that.

She moved over and stood in front of him, which left me to figure what kind of shitstorm I'd be into with Shawnica if I let Larry get all busted to pieces before I took the ninja assassin out. I knew if Larry got damaged while I just hung there and watched, Desmond's life going forward wouldn't remotely be worth living. Since me and Desmond shared nearly everything, I had to guess we'd share that, too.

I grabbed my bolt and yanked it. It nearly came entirely out.

"Sugar," I said.

She looked at me. All of her muscles tightened, and her neck vein bulged.

"I've got kind of an itch."

She turned back to Larry and held up her index finger so as to let him know, "One second."

She took a hard step toward me that way she was prone to. There was nothing girlish about it. I could tell me and her were from the same school. She went full out, just like me.

So it was a collision. Her coming hard to deliver another blow with her mason's mallet. Me closing my right hand around that bolt and jerking it from the wall. I just kept going, swept down, and caught her a punch square on the jaw. I'll always treasure the look she gave me, ripe with snarling anger but touched with wholesale surprise.

I hit her flush, bolt and all. Even still, she didn't go down. She staggered back toward Larry, though, and he wrapped his legs around her. He closed on her right at the midsection and squeezed with all he had.

"Push her this way," I told him.

He wrenched her around in my direction, and I hit her with my bolt hand again. It was a solid right to the chin, and she couldn't do much about it now. I grabbed the mallet from her before she could drop it out of reach.

"Let her go," I said.

Larry preferred squeezing.

"Let her go!"

He finally turned loose, and she piled up on the concrete just the way Larry would have. I heard her head hit the cement. She was sure to be out for a while.

I beat on my remaining bolt with that mason's hammer. The mortar went gritty and then crumbled, and I pulled the thing free in short order. Then I went over to work on Larry.

"Do her first," he told me.

"She's out."

"Best time for it."

"What? Just brain her with this?" I held up the mallet.

Larry nodded. "She was ready to do it to us."

"Well," I said as I knocked Larry's right-hand bolt loose, "that's the difference between her and us."

"I'll do her," he told me.

I knocked his left-hand bolt loose. The two of us stood there over her with our shackles and our hardware.

"Then we go up and get him," Larry told me, eyeing the basement stairway.

"Here." I gave him the mallet.

Larry even raised it with half-committed intent. He looked for a second there like he was meaning to crush her skull, but he couldn't bring himself to deliver the blow.

"Maybe you're right," he finally allowed.

"And we're not going up after him," I said. "Got no idea who might be up there with him."

Larry nodded. "So what, then?"

I pointed at one of the windows. We had to climb up to reach it. The sawhorses and the suitcase worked. I wriggled out first and then pulled Larry through. We were at the back of the house somewhere. It was full dark by then. There was moonlight shining down on the soybean field beyond the house. We were in a spot where the floodlights bathing the yard didn't quite reach.

"Try not to rattle," I whispered to Larry. I showed him how I'd caught my bolts and my handcuff chains up in my hands.

"Didn't we do this already?" Larry asked me.

Jasper and the Greenwood precinct house seemed like a week ago.

I pointed toward the soybean field. "Straight into a row, and just keep going."

"Right," he told me.

That's just when Shambrough's hound came wandering up. Instead of barking, he was wagging. He walked over to me squirming. I loved him up a little.

"Friend of mine," I explained to Larry.

"He coming with us?"

"If he wants."

He even did for a little ways. We crossed the yard running and keeping low and plunged into the field. The soybean plants were about thigh high and so didn't really hide us. I kept waiting for a rifle crack, but we didn't hear a thing. Just our breath and feet on that black, loamy soil.

Halfway across, I paused to look back. The house was all lit up, every window illuminated, and floodlights on what looked like a fleet of vehicles parked out front.

Even from halfway across that soybean field, I recognized a county cruiser.

TWENTY-FOUR

We came out on a blacktop hard by a silage bin. We could hear a semi downshift on the truck route to the west, so that's the direction me and Larry took. When cars came by—and only two did—we got clear of the road and hid since we didn't know if we'd been missed back at Shambrough's and he'd sent Hoyts to find us.

Otherwise we just walked, and Larry told me everything he would have done to that ninja schoolgirl assassin if he'd known the leisure for it.

"She'd have been hanging up there on that wall. Wouldn't have liked that much."

He described in detail the brand of slow agony Larry clearly was too decent to put anybody through. I let him talk. I knew how he felt. We'd been persuaded we were doomed and so had been obliged to face all our regrets in life, our missed opportunities, our considerable unfinished business. There's a lot of remorse attached to meeting with cause to think you're about to be dead. The actual being dead is probably the least of it.

So when Larry exhausted himself of plans for that girl, we didn't say much for a while. It took us nearly an hour to even reach the truck route. I could see to the west in the vapor light a couple of silos covered in vines.

"Wait a minute," I said. "I know where we are."

A scant half hour later, we were in front of Tula's house. Her car was in the driveway. Her new bay window was in the frame. It was still smudged around the edges where it had been wrangled into place. I saw the top of CJ's head as he dashed across the front room.

"Around back," I told Larry.

We went to the door off the kitchen, where I knocked.

I heard Tula tell CJ, "Go to your room."

I knocked again. "It's Nick," I said.

She still showed up with her service piece leveled in our direction. She flipped on the outside light. She threw the bolt and let us in.

I didn't know what I was going to say until it came out of my mouth. "Why aren't you out looking for me?"

She eyed our handcuffs. The bolts attached to them.

"Desmond and Kendell are on it," she told me. "I had other stuff."

"Other stuff? They were going to kill us."

"I didn't know that. Nobody knew where you went. Desmond said he came out of the hospital and the two of you were gone."

"That would have made me worry," I said. I was sounding, even to me, a little more put out than I'd intended. The camp shovel and the shackles and the mason's hammer all had something to do with that.

"Who says I wasn't worried?"

Tula opened the cabinet door over her refrigerator where she kept her pistol and her bullets.

"You didn't look it," I told her.

She laid her hand to my face. "You do it your way," Tula said. "I'll do it mine."

"Sorry," I told her. "Having kind of a day."

"Where were you?"

"Shambrough's," I said.

She pointed at the cuffs and bolts. "He did this?"

"And her," Larry chimed in.

"Ninja assassin," I said to Tula by way of elaboration.

"He got a dungeon or something?" she asked us.

Larry nodded vigorously.

"Cellar," I told her, "with bad mortar." I showed her the thread end of one of my bolts with the grit still clinging to it.

"What was going on down there?" Tula asked us.

"It was all about making us dead," Larry told her, "any damn way she might think of."

Tula was doubtful. Shambroughs didn't get up to such as that. She looked a little searchingly at me.

"That's about right," I said.

"I grew up with Shambroughs," Tula told us. "Even knew Mr. Lucas a little. He grew cotton. Flew a crop duster. Just a planter like everybody else."

"Yeah, well," I said, "he's kind of wandered off the farm."

"Got something to eat around here?" Larry asked her.

"You just had Chinese," I said.

Tula pointed at her wall clock. It was quarter after nine. "That was about five hours ago." She plucked up one of my dangling bolts and gave it a good once-over. "Guess we ought to do something about this."

She had kind of a ladies' tool collection in the cabinet beside the stove. A hammer. Two screwdrivers. A pair of cheap Chinese pliers. A hacksaw you couldn't have cut fishing line with.

"This is going to be a challenge," I said Larry's way. The hammer and the screwdriver seemed the best candidates. "Got a board somewhere?"

Tula fetched a foot-long piece of two-by-four she'd been using for a doorstop.

"Come on," I told Larry. I led him out on the back stoop.

"I'm hungry, man."

"In a minute."

I went at the hinge of Larry's left cuff with Tula's board for a backstop. I drove that screwdriver right through the fitting, and the pin came flying out.

"The stuff's crap," I informed Larry.

Tula had parked behind me, leaning against the jamb. "Didn't say Shambroughs weren't tight."

Once CJ had gotten liberated from his bedroom, I let him bust off Larry's other cuff that Larry tried to snivel about.

Tula made us omelets while I called Desmond, who in turn called Kendell. We heard cars out front soon enough. Shawnica didn't bother to knock, she just came charging right on in.

She saw me. She saw Larry. She told us both, "Uh-huh."

She was so happy her brother was safe and alive that she

didn't even hit him hard enough to make her stick-on nails
fall off.

"What did you bring her for?" I asked Desmond on the sly.

"Because," he explained to me, "she told me she was coming."

Shawnica was admiring Tula's decor by then. She was eyeing the front room, anyway, while telling Tula, "Well, all right."

CJ appeared to find Shawnica mesmerizing. What with
her sparkly nails and her clattering bracelets and her high-
volume approach to conversation, there was an awful lot (if
you didn't know her) to be mesmerized about.

"Hey, little man," she finally told CJ once she'd noticed him
gawking at her. "Come on here." She opened her arms to him,
picked him up, and held him on her bony hip as she passed into
the kitchen. It was the single most normal and motherly thing
I'd ever seen Shawnica do.

I must have glanced at Desmond with stark wonderment
on my face.

He grunty groaned my way and told me, "See."

Larry was busy informing Kendell what that Shambrough
and his ninja schoolgirl assassin had gotten up to along with
what they'd clearly hoped to be about, so all I had to do was
wait until he finished and tidy up the facts for Kendell a bit.

In the meantime, I asked Desmond, "How did you leave
it with Pearl?"

"She's out in the car," he told me. "Asleep."

"Why didn't you just drop her home?"

"I was driving all over looking for you. Come out and you
were gone."

"Hoyts," I told him. "Six or eight of them. The one with the shovel mattered."

"Was ours in the bunch?"

"Oh yeah."

"And they took you straight to Shambrough?"

I nodded and jabbed a thumb at Larry. He was in the middle of describing to Kendell all the basement trouble we'd been in.

"So there's some Hoyts we need to scuff up," I told Desmond, "a ninja assassin we need in jail, and a Shambrough I'd like to kick around the yard."

Larry was all for visiting vengeance on the bunch of them right then, but Kendell wanted to get the proper paperwork and arrange for suitable backup. Kendell was always a wait-until-daylight sort of guy.

I was too tired to care and even a little hungry by then. We all had eggs. We all had toast. We sat at Tula's kitchen table. Pearl finally wandered in around midnight and found us sitting at the dinette.

"I must look a fright," she told us. She was as right as she'd ever been. She looked like somebody had grabbed her by the ankle and dragged her through the yard.

"What happened to you?" I asked.

"I think I fell in the bushes a little."

"You okay?" Tula asked.

Pearl nodded. "That man startled me."

"What man?"

Pearl country pointed. "Had a whole bunch of teeth."

Desmond beat us all outside. He just went sailing across

the front room, down the steps, and into the yard with me
and Kendell and Tula behind him.

There wasn't anything to see, but Desmond held up his
hand to stop us all from talking. It turned out there was something to hear up the side road just west of Tula's house.

I know cars well enough to recognize a carbureted Chevy
V-6 grinding. Plenty of spark but not enough gas.

"It's that damn Biscayne," I said.

Kendell was the only one of us who had a gun, but we
were all pretty well armed (even Tula) with unchecked indignation. If these were the Hoyts who'd snatched me and Larry,
they'd need more than a camp shovel and a 20-gauge in seven
pieces to hope to hold us off.

We just followed the grinding. Up the road and around a
hedgerow. Hoyts were spilling out of the Chevy by then like
yellow jackets from a hole in the ground. The ones who could
run were bolting, including the boy who'd smacked me with
the shovel. Kendell played his flashlight on the pack of them.
I saw mine and tore out after him.

Goodloe was sitting behind the wheel pumping the accel-
erator.

"Hey, buddy," I told him as I ran past.

He looked flabbergasted to see me. I had to think people
they delivered to Lucas Shambrough rarely saw the light of
day again.

The boy I was chasing couldn't manage much running.
That pack and a half a day wouldn't let him draw the air he
needed, so soon enough he began to flag and I closed on him
and a cousin or something. They turned to meet me when they
heard me coming and got into the spirit of the thing. They

didn't have a folding shovel between them, but one of them had a pocketknife, and the other one, my shovel boy, went to pick up a stick in the road that turned out to be a copperhead.

"Shit!" he told us. He had it by the tail and threw the damn thing at me.

I think I screamed about like Pearl would have. I don't care for snakes.

That got them laughing. They seemed to believe a guy afraid of a reptile wasn't a proper candidate to beat them both the hell up.

So they got bold and came at me, with one knife between them and enough teeth for four adults.

First I kicked the snake aside. He was aggravated by then and gathered up in a coil at the edge of the road to strike at anything handy. When the Hoyt with the knife came jabbing it at me, I caught his arm under mine, wheeled around, and flipped him over. I wasn't aiming to drop him right onto that snake, but that's where he ended up. Then he screamed kind of like Pearl would have as it struck him a half-dozen times.

The other one told me, "Shit," again. That might have been all he had. He appeared uncertain if he should keep up the charge or turn around and run. That was all I needed to catch him. I lacked a shovel but had my fist, and I slugged him twice.

"Hit me with a damn shovel," I reminded him.

"Weren't personal!"

"Sure seemed it." I hit him again.

Pounding Hoyts and people like them isn't terribly satisfying. Though this boy didn't pile up like Larry would have, he wasn't about to become enlightened. He wasn't going to come around to the view that he shouldn't hit people with shovels.

He'd been charged to do it by a Shambrough and blood relatives together, so it wasn't like he could have kept from it even if he'd wanted to.

"Come on," I told him and grabbed his shirt collar.

"What about him?" he asked me of the envenomated Hoyt on the road.

"He can come, too."

"I'm bit," that one told me.

"Then you'd better come on before you start swelling."

He got to his knees. "Won't nobody help me?"

"Snake's coming back," I told him.

That sparked him some. We didn't gain on him until we were nearly to the car.

Desmond and Kendell and Tula had all of the rest of those Hoyts corralled by then. There were eight of them altogether, including my two. Three of them seemed to be women. Marginal females, anyway. They had higher voices and longer hair, but they were as rough and homely as the men. Even the one our Hoyt kept referring to as "my bride" looked like she had some Hoyt in the woodpile. She had bad Hoyt hair and a bad Hoyt nose and smelled just like a muskrat.

When she opened her mouth to yell at Tula and threaten her with a beating, she revealed a lot more snuff-stained gums than teeth.

"Honey," our Goodloe kept saying to her the whole time that she raged.

Once she'd barked out, "Fucker!" Tula popped her good. Just gave her one flush on the chin with a vigor I admired.

It didn't seem to faze that woman. She pointed at Goodloe as she informed Tula, "I was talking to him."

"This one's snakebit," I told Kendell.

He had his radio on his belt, so I thought he might order up a rescue squad truck straightaway, but Kendell was always his thorough self, no matter the circumstance.

"A snake, you say?"

"Copperhead," I told him.

The bit Hoyt had dropped to the road and was moaning. "I'm swelling up!"

"Where did it bite you?" Kendell wanted to know.

"Every damn where."

"He kind of landed on it," I said.

"You kind of made me." He groaned some more.

"Heat of battle, you know?" I said to Kendell.

"And that one?" he asked me of the Hoyt I had in hand.

"Hit me with a shovel. Knocked me cold. All of them here put me and Larry in the trunk of that damn car. Crime enough for you?"

Kendell guessed it was. He keyed his radio mic and raised the Greenville dispatcher.

"Captain still over at Shambrough's?" he asked, but the dispatcher couldn't say.

"Saw his cruiser," I told Kendell. "Some kind of diplomat?"

Kendell made his sour face, blew a breath, and nodded. "Thinks he can talk most anything smooth."

"So he was upstairs with Mr. Lucas while she was downstairs working on us."

"What can I tell you? They keep voting him in."

"He know anything about police work?"

"About twice as much as Pearl."

We walked those Hoyts over to Tula's yard and had them all sit in a row. There wasn't much to do while we waited for the cruisers and the ambulance other than listen to the snake-bit Hoyt raise a fuss and chat about this and that.

"Heard about something with Jasper," Kendell told me. "Some dustup over in Greenwood."

"He's always knocking into shit. You know how that goes."

"Tripped, did he?"

I didn't have to say yes. I didn't have to say no. I just had to look at Kendell and smile.

Pearl came out once she'd heard us. Shawnica followed her with CJ.

"Might want to stay up there," I told Pearl.

So she came straight down toward the road.

"He all right?" she asked of the bit Hoyt.

I nodded. "Bad clams or something."

The rest of the Hoyts were all sitting in a row. Pearl took her time looking them over.

She soon said with delight, like I'd figured she would, "Goodloe, is that you?"

TWENTY-FIVE

The captain came out with the cruisers and the rescue squad. He was all brass and martial finery and cologne. I'd never laid eyes on him before, but Desmond knew him well enough.

"Greer," he told me. "Went to school with him. Hasn't ever been worth a shit."

He was slick, though. I had to give him that. It didn't surprise me to learn that he came from a family of funeral home directors. He had that bittersweet eulogizing way about him like he knew where you hurt and precisely how much, and he was feeling that way as well.

Kendell introduced us. "This is Nick Reid, sir."

Captain Greer—his name was Riley—extended his hand while still looking at Kendell.

"Lucas Shambrough had him and that boy there"—Kendell

nodded in Larry's direction—"imprisoned in his basement when he was talking to you upstairs."

Captain Riley had a tight smile for news such as that. He nodded sharply, turned and finally looked at me.

"Imprisoned," he said. He still wasn't prepared to think such a thing of a Shambrough. His people had probably been paid in full for burying Shambroughs for years.

"Shackled to a wall," I told him. "You see a girl roaming around the house?"

"Brunette?" he asked me.

I nodded. "Plaid skirt."

"Might have passed through the foyer," he said.

"You know those beatings you're looking into?"

He knew just what I meant. He nodded.

"Her," I said.

Riley showed me his teeth. He turned and showed them to Kendell. "Just a child," he said to Kendell. Then he turned and said it to me.

"Naw." That was Desmond. He'd glided over.

"How you?" The captain said it like he couldn't begin to figure how Desmond hadn't been taken by heart failure or a stroke. He eyed Desmond up and down in a leisurely and disapproving sort of way.

"Wants folks to think she's not but a girl, but she beats people up, and your buddy, that Shambrough, he watches and jerks off."

You'd have thought Desmond had told the captain that Jesus was a cannibal.

"No!" Captain Greer told us all. "I'm knowing Shambroughs all my life."

"Ain't no count," Desmond assured him. "Been making a mess of this place for years."

The captain wasn't the sort inclined to take the word of a civilian, so he gave Kendell a chance to contradict Desmond, but Kendell let him down.

"Bad seed," Kendell said. "We've been looking the other way for too long."

Captain Greer sputtered a little. Hauling Lucas Shambrough in was bound to be socially unsavory.

Nobody said anything for about half a minute. It turned out the captain had a grunty groan, too, that he finally uncorked. "See what Lucas has to say for himself?" He laid it out as a suggestion.

"Right," Kendell told him, "but let's do it with a warrant."

The captain checked his watch. "First light," he said.

"What if they bug out?" I asked him.

Kendell and Desmond both chimed in on that. I got a decisive "Won't" and an emphatic "Uh-uh." They agreed that wasn't a thing a Shambrough would do.

"What about her?" I asked. "Ought to at least sit on the place."

The captain couldn't be immediately sure that was a bad idea, so I pressed the advantage and told him. "Me and him and Officer Raintree." I pointed at Desmond. "Out on the road just keeping track of who goes in and out. Nothing happens until Kendell shows up with the warrants."

"Where's your badge?" the captain asked me.

"Used to be a cop," Kendell told him.

That prompted some kind of aphorism about *used to be* and

shoulda coulda. As tough as it was, I think I even managed to smile through that.

It turned out the captain was one of those guys you just had to wait out. He didn't need everything done his way. He just had to seem in charge. So once we'd paid sufficient deference to his rank by saying nothing, Captain Riley Greer told Kendell, "All right." Then he shook hands all around, even with Desmond, who smiled while he compressed a bone or two.

Once the Hoyts were tidied up and hauled off, both the snakebit one and the rest, Shawnica and Pearl volunteered to stay behind at Tula's with CJ, and Larry proved keen to protect them, so we let him stay as well. Kendell went off to Greenville to catch a few winks at the station house and wait for a decent hour to call a judge.

For my part, I got to spend another night with Tula after a fashion. Tula and Desmond, anyway, in Desmond's Escalade.

We parked out past the commissary building on the Geneill Road where me and Desmond had first stopped when he'd showed me Shambrough's place. The floodlights were all still burning, and there were three or four vehicles in the drive.

I'd let Tula have shotgun with Desmond up front, so I was obliged to hang over the seat back like a kid.

"Who do you figure's down there?"

"Cronies," Desmond told me.

"Cronies?" Tula asked him before I could get it out.

Desmond looked at her. He looked at me. "Cronies," he told us again.

"Like who?" I asked him.

"Her, probably," he said. "How bad did you leave her?"

"Two hard rights. Larry wanted to brain her with her hammer."

"Wanted *you* to brain her." Desmond knew Larry.

"Uh-huh," I said. "Punching seemed enough."

Tula just listened, looking back and forth between us. She let the chat fall off to nothing before she jabbed her thumb my way and said to Desmond, "Is he any count?"

"I'm sitting right here."

Desmond eyed me in the mirror. "Mostly," he told her.

"Mostly?" I said.

"Dependable?" Tula asked.

Desmond thought about that one. "On time and all, if that's what you mean."

"Trust him with your life?" she asked him. She looked at me while she did it.

Desmond laughed. "About every third day."

"Tell her about that swamp rat," I suggested.

Desmond's hand went immediately toward the scar on his calf.

"Not the one with the gator," I said. "The other one. Guy down by Yazoo with the Thompson."

"That gun jammed," Desmond told me.

"I didn't know that."

"True enough," Desmond said. He turned to Tula. "He might have got all shot to pieces. Didn't."

"Just tell her I'm good in a fix and all right the rest of the time."

Desmond eyed me in the mirror again. "What he said. I guess."

The lights never went out down at Shambrough's, and nobody came or went. No cronies got dispatched or sent for. Only Shambrough's hound made a racket. About every half hour or so it would bark and bay for a minute or two but seemed to know enough to stop before the boot or the bullet came.

At around three, I switched places with Desmond so he could stretch out in the back. Or tumble over, anyway, and snore. Tula was dozing against her door by then, so it was just me sitting and looking. The moon was down. Even Shambrough's browbeaten hound was asleep.

Tula groaned and shifted my way. She grabbed my arm by the wrist and raised it, slipped in underneath, and laid her head against my chest.

"A Thompson, huh?"

"Full magazine. Guy didn't know from gun oil."

"Brave man."

"Fool sometimes. Don't want to keep that from you."

"You haven't," she told me.

She stayed where she was anyway and went back to sleep.

We were all awake and ready for Kendell by the time he showed up. Ready for coffee, anyway, and Kendell being a decent Christian had brought some. Being a cheap, decent Christian he'd brought it from home, where he and his wife drank flavor crystals. I dumped mine when I slipped off around the derelict commissary to relieve myself.

The captain was bringing the warrants.

"Thought he ought to," Kendell told us.

"He still think it's all a big misunderstanding?" Tula asked him.

Kendell nodded.

A couple of other cruisers rolled up to join us soon enough. The sergeant from the Alluvian men's room was driving one of them, and a beefy guy I'd never seen before but was happy to have along racked a round into his shotgun as he rolled out of his sedan.

"Bound to know we're up here," Tula said.

She hadn't bothered with her uniform. Just jeans still for her, but she'd carried her service piece along and dropped the clip to check it.

"This'll go quiet," Kendell told us. Told himself, I think, a little as well. You had to admire the way people cling to pedigree in the Delta. Lucas Shambrough would be polite and go easy because that's just what Shambroughs did. They were all so convinced of it I even let myself be convinced of it a little.

The captain finally showed up around eight. He had the paper, but he still lacked the conviction. He was wearing a different brassy uniform and a fresh dose of his piney cologne.

"Let me try this," he said mostly to Kendell.

"Try what?"

"Go down. Have a private word."

"Just you?"

He tugged at his uniform jacket and gave a curt nod.

"Don't like it," Kendell told him.

"Mind's made up. I'm going down."

"They've got a body on them already," Kendell said.

"We don't know that."

"We sort of do," Desmond told the captain.

He wasn't the type to tolerate counsel from some blubbery Delta local who wasn't remotely a Shambrough or anything close.

"I'm going down," the captain said. He added just generally, "As you were."

So we stood around like we had been and watched him ease down the drive in his cruiser.

"Might go all right," the sergeant said, the one from the Alluvian men's room.

Kendell looked like he thought differently. I know me and Desmond did. Desmond went fishing in his Escalade and brought his rifle out. It was a .30-06 that Desmond could hit any damn thing he pleased with. Desmond only raised it when he wanted something dead.

"Who all's down there?" That from the beefy officer with the shotgun.

Tula told him, "Don't know. Haven't seen anything but the dog."

There'd been nobody in the yard. Nobody on the drive. I couldn't even remember a car passing by, and we were kind of on the way to the truck route. It felt like anybody who could steer clear of us already was.

We saw Captain Greer get out of his cruiser. We watched the hound close on him and cower. Only Kendell had proper binoculars, so he told us what was going on once the captain had slipped under the canopy of Lucas Shambrough's massive live oak trees.

"Knocking," he said.

Then nothing for a bit.

"Knocking," he told us again. "Here we go."

"Little black woman?" I asked him.

Kendell shook his head. "The man himself. Looking up here." Nothing for a quarter minute from Kendell. Then he lowered his binoculars and told us all, "Inside."

"How long?" Tula asked.

"I'll give him ten minutes. Maybe fifteen," Kendell told her.

It turned out we didn't have to wait nearly that long. Kendell was explaining to his officers just how he wanted them deployed when me and Desmond heard a *pop* from down around Shambrough's house.

The cops all missed it, huddled and talking cop strategy and all.

I glanced at Desmond, who nodded the way he does.

"Gunshot," I said.

Kendell clammed up and wheeled. "Where?"

I pointed toward Lucas Shambrough's pile of a house.

"You sure?"

We all heard the second one.

I told Kendell, "Yeah."

They went scurrying to their cruisers. Kendell told me and Desmond, "Stay here."

They were hardly into the driveway before we heard a flurry of shots. Pistol fire, it sounded like, in lethal concentration.

I pulled two .45s from my duffel.

"I'll go down and around," I told Desmond.

"I'm going to plug up the drive," he said.

So I found myself on the near end of the bean field I'd run through with Larry just the night before. There wasn't any cover to speak of out there, but everybody sounded a bit too occupied already to trouble with the likes of me. I ran down and around and came out at the bottom of the Shambrough lot, not twenty yards from where me and Larry had crossed the yard and escaped.

The gunfire had flagged a little by then. I still heard the odd shot. Definitely pistol rounds. Ground floor, as best I could tell. Not the cellar at least.

Then I heard Kendell barking out, "Police!"

I crawled across the yard, leery of crossfire, and got joined by Lucas Shambrough's hound, who wriggled when he saw me. "You again!" he might as well have said for all the prancing and licking he did.

"Come here, boy," I told him and shifted him behind me. About the last thing I wanted to do was get revved up and shoot a dog.

I heard the squeal of what proved to be a sash in a jamb. A second-floor window slid open, and the ninja schoolgirl assassin—in a denim shift—came crawling out over the sill. She tossed some kind of machine pistol down onto the lawn, hung for just a moment, and then dropped straight to the ground. She didn't even roll when she hit but just crouched and staggered a little. Then she went scrambling for her gun as Tula came out over the sill.

I had a fistful of hound scruff in my left hand and my .45 HK in my right. Just as that girl reached for her gun, I squeezed off three quick rounds. They kicked up dirt all around the thing and caused the creature to raise up.

When she saw me, she seethed about like a child might. I half expected her to stomp her feet.

"Hey, sugar," I said.

She bent. I fired. Another dirt explosion.

By then Tula had done her hanging from the sill, had found a spot she liked, and had dropped her lanky self onto the ground. I thought maybe she'd just pull her piece on the ninja and corral her the conventional way, but Tula wasn't in the mood for anything as civilized as that. I couldn't be sure what had gone on inside, but I could see that Tula hadn't liked it by the way she dove at that schoolgirl assassin just like a cornerback might. She was laid full out when she hit the girl, rammed into her torso with her shoulder. The force served to pile the both of them up on the ground.

It seemed an even battle at first. They rolled and tussled and grunted. Then Tula caught that ninja with the heel of her hand square on the bridge of her nose. The blood fairly squirted from both her nostrils, which made everything slicker and a hell of a lot more grisly. The sight of her own blood made that ninja madder than she'd been. She loosed a shriek of rage and went at Tula with every kung fu thing she had.

She worked free and got up. Tula got up, too. They'd forgotten about firearms by then and were just going at each other. The ninja schoolgirl was bleeding all over her shift. She went stalking toward Tula and then whipped around and tried to fell her with a kick, the sort of kick Dale would have visited on Desmond if Dale had even a scrap of talent. The ninja assassin knew just what she was about. The trouble was that Tula did, too.

Tula dodged and ducked. She caught the ninja with a punishing blow to the throat. The ninja came back with an elbow. Tula blocked it with her forearm and then shoved down the ninja schoolgirl's head and delivered a knee to her brow. The creature stumbled back, but Tula kept right on her. She delivered a sweeping kick of her own to the ninja schoolgirl's knee. It staggered her further, and then Tula came through with a sweeping roundhouse right that was such a thing of glorious leverage and intent that I was wishing I'd thrown it before it even connected.

The dull thud of Tula's fist on that ninja schoolgirl's jaw was so powerful and concussive I think I felt it in my feet.

Mako/Isis—whoever she was—piled up like Larry might have. Tula dropped on top of her like a good warrior should and rained down a few more blows.

"Hey!" I said.

She kept on punching.

"Enough!" I told her with volume.

When she didn't stop, I finally fired a shot into the air. That snared her notice. Tula glared my way like I just might be next. I had a nose she could flatten, a throat she could punch, a jaw she could slug and shatter.

"Dead or in jail?" I asked her.

Ninja schoolgirl looked lifeless by then. Tula was straddling her with her fists clinched still. She studied the creature's battered face. She stood up and told me, "Done."

I walked over to where she was standing. I did it slowly and in stages because I know from experience it can take a few minutes to get unprimed from a fight.

"You okay?" I asked from just out of arm's reach.

Tula nodded.

"What happened in there?"

"She shot up the place."

"The captain?"

"Ducked behind a couch or something. Hit in the arm. Foot, I think."

"Kendell and them?"

"Fine. She mowed down a bunch of . . . cronies," Tula told me. "Went crazy with this damn thing." Her foot found what turned out to be the ninja assassin's TEC-9. Tula kicked it halfway across the yard.

Shambrough's hound wanted to chase it, but I still had him by the scruff. He whimpered some on general principles.

"Who's that?" Tula asked me, looking at the hound.

"Friend of mine," I told her.

We both heard the engine turning over and the roar of it starting up.

"Where's Shambrough?" I asked.

Tula had her cuffs out. She shook her head. "Never saw him."

I'd been in the Delta long enough to know an Air Tractor when I heard one. That big Pratt and Whitney engine was singing as the plane headed off away from us, down some kind of airstrip, I had to guess.

I hustled across the yard with Shambrough's hound giving chase. There was the usual Delta dirt strip at the edge of the soybean field. Just as I got to where I could see the full length of the runway, a canary yellow crop duster pivoted around, and the pilot goosed the throttle.

Kendell and the beefy officer jogged into view. They got as close to the strip as they dared. They both had their sidearms drawn, but neither one of them raised and aimed.

"Shambrough?" I shouted.

Kendell nodded. He holstered his pistol and watched as that bright yellow Air Tractor came bumping along the dirt strip and lifted into the air. Shambrough tipped his wings at us as he nosed up over the live oaks. He had the big plane. Even I could tell that. If his tank was full, he could fly probably six or seven hundred miles before he had to set down.

He made a tight circle around the house, not a hundred feet off the ground. I walked out toward the front of the lot.

I saw Desmond standing in the driveway with his rifle raised and level. He was drawing a bead.

Lucas Shambrough kept circling and grinning at us from under his canopy. Desmond exhaled and squeezed slowly like he'd been taught. He wasn't the sort to miss.

That Air Tractor kept on for a bit, went up the road about a mile. It was flying slightly south of level and so finally clipped a power pole. It didn't explode or anything gaudy. It just plunged straight into the ground with a *thump* and raised a cloud of loamy Delta dust.

"Wasn't counting on that," I said to Desmond once I'd reached him in the drive.

"Never had much use for a show-off," Desmond told me.

TWENTY-SIX

Ninja schoolgirl assassin's given name was Alice Marie Fennick, and she was a public school product from Zanesville, Ohio. According to the records Kendell dug up, she'd stolen a LeBaron once in greater Cincinnati, but that was the only crime she'd ever been convicted for.

It turned out she was forty-eight years old and had a son named Luther. He was a chiropractor in Phoenix. Kendell talked to him on the phone. He still didn't know who his father was and hadn't spoken to his mother in years.

"Kind of a hothead," Luther told Kendell.

I think Kendell just told him back, "Right."

Captain Riley Greer got written up in the *Memphis Commercial Appeal*, mostly for having been shot twice in the line of duty. He had an upper-right-arm through-and-through and got a slug dug out of his ankle, which meant he went around for a while with both a sling and a walking stick. It turned out the gunplay had started when one of Lucas Shambrough's cronies had dropped his sidearm on the hardwood floor and it went off. Apparently, that was the sort of thing to bring out the worst in a ninja schoolgirl assassin.

She wasn't much of a delight to interrogate. She never said anything useful, and when she got bored or put out with a question, she'd dredge up something choice and spit. She wouldn't talk about Lucas Shambrough. She wasn't interested in a deal, and she didn't seem to care if she got locked up for the rest of her natural life. Fortunately, they didn't need her to build a case since they had Izzy and Skeeter and the Sunflower lady along with Kendell and Tula. The thinking was they'd put her away for assault and wait for the Hoyts to start barking. The odds seemed high they'd add on the murder of that catfish boy after a while.

Lucas Shambrough, naturally enough, didn't survive his crop duster crash, and he didn't survive it in about a half-dozen pieces. The rescue squad boys had to haul him off in a sack. His relations—sisters mostly—tried to get Desmond indicted for murder, but the county attorney declined. The state's attorney as well. Word was they even petitioned the governor, who just told them, "Hell of a shot."

Me and Larry got off with a letter of apology to Jasper and the Greenwood PD, and when I rode with Desmond to K-Lo's to see what help we could offer, Kalil informed us that Dale was plaguing all of his shiftless deadbeats just fine.

"You don't need us," Desmond said.

K-Lo didn't have to think about it. "Nope."

"Got nothing?" I asked him.

"He's a goddamn terror."

Me and Desmond couldn't complain. It was almost rewarding to see Dale make a little something of himself.

The money we'd given to Larry more or less evaporated. Not just actually but also in Larry's head. Not that we pressed him for it, since he would have needed to rob a casino to get it, but he might have pretended like he owed it and apologized a little. Instead he tried a new scheme on us until Desmond shut him up.

I ended up with Lucas Shambrough's hound, fairly commandeered him, in fact. His given name was Octavius, to judge by the brass plate on his collar. He wouldn't answer to it, and I decided I'd rather him not answer to Buddy instead. He kept Fergus up in the Nuttall oak. He liked to sprawl in Pearl's impatiens. He could hardly believe I'd let him sleep in the bed or eat Pearl's freezer-burned casseroles. He rode in my Ranchero like a champ, with his head out the window and his ears blown back. Mostly Buddy delighted in just going around not getting kicked anymore.

The dinner we had was Pearl's idea. Skeeter and Izzy were both up and around by then. We dressed up Pearl's screen porch, threw good linen on Pearl's picnic table, and then proceeded to get tamale and cole slaw juice all over the place. Kendell brought his wife, Myrna, who was too Baptist for most parties but seemed to start enjoying herself once Pearl had nattered at her for a while. Pearl was like a prattle jackhammer. She'd loosen anybody up in time.

Tula parked right next to me on the bench, and I was grateful for that. I hadn't seen much of her, what with her shifts and her depositions. I'd taken CJ fishing a couple of times, and

I guess I'd won points for that, but dinner out on Pearl's porch was the most time we'd had together since Tula had jumped out of Shambrough's window and taken that ninja assassin on.

It was only two days later as I was whipping past Herndon in my Ranchero when a cruiser lit me up. It was crowding dusk, and all of the pivot irrigators were going. I pulled over by a wheat field and could hear the rhythmic slap of the spray hitting the plants. I fished out my expired Virginia license—hadn't yet made time for the DMV—and I went fishing for my registration in my cluttered glove box.

"Step out of the car, sir."

It was Tula. I exhaled with relief and kind of laughed.

Not a dent from her. "Step out of the car."

I climbed out of my Ranchero.

She closed one bracelet on my right wrist, cranked my arm down, and cuffed my left one as well.

"Watch your head," she told me as she shoved me into the back of her cruiser.

She went back and got Buddy and let him up front with her. Without another word, she eased onto the road.

"Nice evening," I tried. Nothing. "What's CJ up to?" Not a thing.

She cut north across the truck route and then back west on a road I knew by now. She reached back to unclamp her hair and let it fall as we pulled in her drive.

"Step out of the car, sir," she told me again.

And that's precisely what I did.